Her mout... against ...into his ...ing crotch clung to the bulge of his loins. He bent her backwards, and held her tight, putting into his kiss more brutality than tenderness. She remembered a previous occasion when his roughness had frightened her, but she smiled voluptuously. His ferocity no longer terrified her. It excited her. Suddenly he broke from her, and huskily demanded, "Get stripped!"

Humbly she hastened to do her imperious lover's bidding. She made a show of it, taking her time with the removal of each item of her finery. Under her pastel-green linen dress she wore a slip of white nylon and matching panties whose brevity was mitigated by the fact that, together with a very short, frilly skirt, they formed one garment. Her firm breasts neither required nor enjoyed the benefit of a bra....

PROFESSIONAL CHARMER

ROBERT DESMOND

MASQUERADE BOOKS, INC.
801 SECOND AVENUE
NEW YORK, N.Y. 10017

First Masquerade Edition 1992

First printing January 1992

ISBN 1-56333-98-X

Cover Photograph © 1992 Robert Chouraqui
Cover Design by Eduardo Andino

Manufactured in the United States of America
Published by Masquerade Books, Inc.
801 Second Avenue
New York, N.Y. 10017

I.

Jorge's ejaculation of sperm lacked enthusiasm. The fact that he had to catch a plane within the hour was not the sole reason for the instant withdrawal of his deflated penis from Rick's posterior. During the week they had spent together in Paris, entirely at Jorge's expense, Rick had been more demanding than previously. Not content with sharing his handsome Spanish friend's bed, feasting at the best restaurants, occupying the most expensive seats at theaters and drinking throughout the nights in cabarets, the pale, blond English boy had allowed no day to pass without his whining self-pity. This caused Jorge to feel obligated to make him presents of such things as shirts of excellent quality, costly shoes, a beautiful pair of cuff-links, a leather wallet, a Shaeffer fountain-pen and several popular records.

Jorge could afford to be generous, being the only son of the proprietor of the Hôtel des Vents Parfumés at Menton. He was in the habit of lavishing money on youths of a certain sort, just as it had once been his custom to shower gifts on girls whose bodies were appetizing and at his disposal. He was, however, too proud a man to wittingly patronize prostitutes, male or female. Physically nature had been so kind to him that it was difficult to imagine a man less likely to need to buy a woman's favors. The truth was that, from an early age, his success with women had been so great that each new conquest had meant less to him than the previous one, with the result that he had turned to boys for a relief from heterosexual boredom; and Rick Haylett was the latest of a series of young men who had pretended to love Jorge, while being more interested in his money than in his jet-black curls, his bronzed, gauntly handsome visage, his broad shoulders, slim hips and subtly muscled limbs.

As usual, however, it had taken the trusting Iberian a long time to realize that a gold-digging boy can feign affection as convincingly as any mink-hungry woman. After more than a year during which Jorge, blinded by love, had regularly visited his lover in Peterborough, a week in Paris had convinced him that he had been living in the proverbial fool's paradise. The experience was not new to him, which did not reduce his chagrin; but he hoped to avoid parting from Rick in obvious anger. He knew too well how vile these male whores can be when they are unmasked, and he attached great importance to the avoidance of cheap brawls. His only reason for indulging in a final copulation had been that Rick had dutifully offered him his rump, acceptance of which had seemed preferable to a quarrel; but Rick was a shrewd operator, while Jorge was an unconvincing liar. The former knew that it was the end of the line, and he was worried. He had profitable contacts back home, but nothing financially in the same class as the Spaniard. Hitherto each of his gilt-edged victims (male and female) had withdrawn his or her patronage only after having introduced Rick to moneyed friends amongst whom there had always been at least one willing to contribute to the poor, but charming, male slut's maintenance. There was, however, no doubt about the fact that Jorge was abdicating without providing a successor, which was most remiss of him.

Rick hoped this one, last good fuck would somehow help get him to the next stage—finding a new sugar daddy or mama. He kneeled before Jorge, his butt up in the air, and spread open the cheeks of his ass with his hands, exposing the still-tight and puckered opening that Jorge had come to know so well. Jorge grabbed a tube of lubricant, and rubbed some of the gel around the rim of Rick's opening, pressing his thumb slightly inward as he did so. Once his finger entered the familiar canal Jorge's cock once again hardened with desire for the male whore's tight bumhole; he finger-fucked him for a while, as he applied some of the cool gel to his own growing machine. Then he bent forward, cock in hand, and brought the swollen purple head to the well-greased asshole. He pressed the head to the hole and pushed in. Rick flinched for just a moment at the invasion, and then spread his ass-cheeks even further apart.

"Oh Jorge," he moaned, like a good whore. "Oh Jorge, that big cock is so wonderful. Fuck me real good, and go in deep, deep as you can. I want you all the way inside me, man."

Jorge obliged, and could feel his groin swept into the pleasure of the sweet pressure of Rick's tight hole closing in around his hard cock. He began to fuck more vigorously, allowing the younger man's canal to devour his cock.

"That's right, Jorge, fuck your sweetheart's bum like the animal you really are. Hurt me if you want, just fill me up with that cock, give it all to me."

Rick's sphincter muscle tightened as he spoke the words and with each clenching twitch, Jorge came closer to climax. Rick, shrewd whore that he was, knew his clenching asshole trick would suck the jism right out of Jorge's engorged cock—and fast. This would give the "client" a memorable good time, while lessening the wear and tear on Rick's well-used behind.

Jorge's movement picked up speed as he began pummeling Rick's asshole, pressing himself as deeply as he could fit into the cock-loving canal. And he soon grabbed hold of Rick's also erected rod and rubbed it deliciously as he filled his asshole with his generously sized, about-to-explode cock.

Jorge rubbed the swelling cock head, and then began to masturbate the younger man's pole. "You come for me and I'll come for you," Jorge whispered into Rick's ear. "Give daddy some jism, and I'll fill your asshole to the brim with mine."

Rick, now fully enrolled in the delicious combination of having his cock masturbated while having his bum filled with a big prick, was breathing heavy—but not as heavily as Jorge, who was suddenly quite swept away in the moment of lust. He was lunging forward and fucking Rick hard, and he was squeezing Rick's cock with equal ferocity.

"Let's have that juice, now," Jorge demanded of Rick. "Let's have it, all over my hand. And then you can lick it off my hand as I squirt my own load into your bowels."

He began jerking harder on Rick's cock, and fucking deeper, in aggressive, animal-like moves, until Rick finally began rocking back and forth violently, to force the final stage of copulation to occur. Both men were panting wildly, and moving frantically, when finally Jorge felt the warm drizzle of Rick's love juice squirt all over his hand.

Jorge caught some of the escaping semen in the cup of his palm, and as promised, brought it up to Rick's mouth. "Drink your own come," he demanded, "and lick my hand clean."

Rick's obedient tongue immediately lapped at his own jism, and removed most of the sticky stuff from Jorge's palm and fingers. To make sure, he drew each finger into his warm mouth and sucked it clean. Feeling the warm wetness of Rick's mouth was the final step to bringing Jorge off. He removed his hand from the younger man's mouth, brought them to Rick's hips and hoisted Rick's butt closer to his sex-flesh as he pounded every last drop of his juice into the now gaping, dripping asshole.

They lay their for a moment, Jorge's still hard cock embedded in Rick's ass. Then Jorge said quietly, "You know what I want now."

Rick knew because he'd been obliging Jorge for days, and now would one last time bow between Jorge's loins and suck and lick his spent cock until it was free of jism and soil. Jorge held Rick's head closely to his cock as he sucked up the juice of their final fuck. In fact, he pressed Rick's head down hard, so that every inch would fill the mouth that was tongue-bathing him. He seemed forceful and mean, as he commanded that Rick "remove every trace of this last encounter with your tongue." Jorge wanted to degrade Rick, only because Jorge felt so degraded by sleeping with him—yet he also felt a strange powerlessness, as if Rick had cast him under a spell and Jorge could not refuse the sweet, tight feel of the asshole that fit like a glove around his pole.

When he felt a sufficient tongue bath had been administered, Jorge demanded that Rick stop.

"Ring the desk," Jorge commanded, "while I freshen up my loins and get dressed! I must pay the bill and be out of here inside ten minutes."

From the bathroom Jorge heard Rick say, in his ridiculous imitation of the Oxford twang, "Oh hello! Room sixty-nine here! Would you sort of get our bill ready? O, jolly good show, what! We shall be down there in about a quarter of an hour or so. What? Oh, yes! Add on the next three days for one, will you? O, bang on! Of course! All on the one note, what! Jolly good show!"

Had he felt less bitter Jorge would have laughed at his vulgar male mistress' confident use of a silly English which had ceased to be fashionable ten years previous. To avoid unpleasantness he was willing to cover Rick's expenses for the following three days; but he resented the harlot's taking it upon himself to claim as a right what was, in fact, a privilege granted by a man of means to his less fortunate friend. He resisted the strong temptation to reprimand Rick, whom he had no intention of seeing again.

The telephone rang. Rick, the wealthy man's cur, hastened to answer. The woman at the other end of the line refused to identify herself, but asked to be put in touch with Jorge, who snatched the instrument from his doxy's hands.

"Bella darling! Here? In Paris? You just got here? Caramba! I'm sorry, dish, but it's out of the question. The old man's got this big Costa Brava deal on, and he insists I be home this evening to take the reins from him. What about Harry? No! So he's going in with Traubmann? Frisco opens her golden gates to Partham and Traubmann. They'll make a million each on the greenslade project, and neither of 'em needs it. Listen! Can't you make Menton? Balls! Tell Balmain to...what? The airport? Cream-cake, you do still love me! *Moi aussi! Tu l' sais bien*. In forty-five minutes! Bye-bye."

He rang off, turned to Rick, who had not missed a word, snapped his fingers imperiously, and said, "Right! Help me dress, finish my packing, call me a cab! Take enough cash from my wallet, and pay the bill when I'm gone! I must be out of here in ten minutes."

Jorge hoped to leave the hotel alone, but Rick knew that, at the airport, there would be the wife or mistress of a man who did business with the world-renowned financier Karl Traubmann. Harry Partham and Karl Traubmann were in San Francisco, and Bella was the sort of woman who wore exclusive designer dresses, which means that she was the sort of person Rick would find interesting. If Jorge thought he was going to spend a tender minute alone with Bella, he underestimated Rick, who found time to help his benefactor to dress without neglecting to put the finishing touches to the latter's packing; yet, by the time Jorge had finished dressing, Rick was ready to leave. He had pulled on a pair of beige slacks, a blue sweat-shirt and blazer and black shoes, and Jorge had to admit that he looked delicious.

In the taxi Jorge and Rick kissed and cuddled as though it were the beginning, instead of the end. At the airport Jorge took a back seat from the moment Bella and Rick met. Bella and Jorge were friends from way back. She regularly visited his father's hotel, with or without Harry; and, with or without Harry, she invariably found time for love sessions with the handsome young Latin. Harry was nobody's fool, but he was a discreet man of the world and complaisant husband, whose idiosyncrasies were tolerated by his spouse. Bella expected no gallantry from her southern lover, who had viewed her from all angles and had her in every possible way; but his taking her for granted was too flagrant in comparison with Rick's grossly exaggerated attentions. The street-corner boy did not actually fall to his knees and lick her shoes, but he conveyed the impression that he would do just that. Bella made the mistake of preferring such base conduct to Jorge's just claim to be her equal and her admirer.

Bella and Rick scarcely noticed Jorge's negotiation of the steps leading from the tarmac to the entrance of the plane; and their waving as the vessel took the air was so perfunctory as to be rude.

Jorge was superior to Rick physically, intellectually, culturally, ethically, financially and socially; but he lost out against a man with the soul of a whore.

While the better man flew unhappily to Nice his illiterate friend magnanimously treated Bella to a taxi ride back to the center of Paris; but, during the drive, he painted for her so grim a picture of his finances that she insisted on paying for the taxi herself. The boy's modesty and unpretentious frankness enslaved her. Instead of claiming to have achieved great things, he humbly admitted to being a simple clerk who earned twelve pounds per week. He was not brash and too sure of himself, like most of the boys of his age; and, far from exploiting their proximity in the back of the cab for making amorous advances to her, he seemed to her to be a trifle too deferential. She was flattered by the fact that he obviously liked her as much as she liked him; and she hoped he was not going to allow a poor man's pride to deter him from suggesting they meet again. Bella was either too vain or too naive to have suspected that, while her feelings for him were sudden and genuine, his were premeditated and simulated. He had learned from Jorge's telephone conversation with her that she was the wife of the sort of man who did business with Karl Traubmann, whose name was almost daily in the news as a result of his fantastic property deals on both sides of the Atlantic; and, if there was one thing that interested Rick more than prosperous men, it was the maturely attractive wives of such men. Bella was a mackerel, a fat juicy one, to catch; Rick was prepared to cast a skinny sprat on the waters. So, Bella insisted on paying for the taxi, but her persistence was that of an amateur, while his was professional. He paid the taxi, using money Jorge had given him to cover his incidental expense during his three lonely days in Paris; and Bella was almost moved to tears by the fact that a boy to whom life was a constant struggle to make ends meet should pay taxi fares for a woman who often spent as much on an evening out as he earned in a week. The urge to kiss him was scarcely resistible.

Supposing Rick was too modest to suggest another meet, Bella sought to encourage him by saying:

"I must find time before leaving this lovely city to prove to you how much appreciate your kindness. I haven't much time now, because I always take it easy for a couple of hours before dressing for dinner, and I've got to be at the Elysées Matignon at eight; but I'd like to drink a cup of tea some place and arrange for you to be my guest for lunch or dinner tomorrow."

Bella spoke the sort of language Rick understood. Rubbing his metaphoric hands, he replied:

"Here we are! *Le Café de la Paix, et c'est moi qui vous offre le goûter.*"

What a man! she thought. So modest, and he speaks French like a native! He spoke French like a native of Rochdale, but in Bella's ears his every word was sweet music.

The waiter arrived to take their order, and Rick asked, "Tea?" Her smile was warm and affirmative, so Rick ordered:

"Un thé à l'anglaise, un café noir et une fine…s'il vous plaît!"

The waited answered, "Yes, sir! One strong tea, with milk, one coffee and a little brandy, no?"

"Oh, bang on! Bang on, old boy!"

The waiter left their table, and Rick asked Bella, "Wouldn't you like a cognac or a whisky?"

"Just tea!" she answered. "Most evenings I'm under a social obligation to drink more than is good for me, so I never touch the hard stuff before sundown. Do you really need brandy at this time of the day? Really I hate interfering, but your parents ought to tell you it's silly to start drinking in the middle of the afternoon. Doesn't your mother tell you that spirits do you no good?"

The pathetic orphan replied, "Well, I've sort of lost contact with mother and father since I got married."

"Are you married?"

"Afraid so."

"Well, no man ought to lose contact with his parents…least of all with his mother. How'd it happen?"

"Oh, you mustn't think I'm not very fond of my parents, especially my mother; but, you see, they never really forgave me for marrying Liz, because they didn't think a girl who'd spent several years at sea could ever be a good wife."

"At sea?"

Taking care to tell Bella only what was to his advantage, Rick explained, "When I first knew Liz she was stewardess on board a Norwegian tanker.

14

She'd never done anything else; so, when we discovered, a few months after we'd got married, that we couldn't live on what I earned, she tried other things, like working in a lingerie shop, in a laundry and in a café, but she couldn't get used to it, and she went back to sea. Well, when my folks told me, right at the beginning, that people who have the sea in their blood can never get rid of it, I didn't believe them; and they did all they could to stop us getting married; so, you see, I never really broke with them...I mean they still send me a card at Christmas and on my birthday, and I do the same...but they won't accept Liz; and I sort of feel that she's my wife for better or for worse, and if they don't want her they don't want me, if you see what I mean."

Bella felt she did not know Rick sufficiently to give him advice, but he seemed so much in need of a wise friend that she ventured to ask him to explain his remark to the effect that he and Liz been unable to live on his wages. Momentarily confused, Rick averted his gaze, and allowed half a minute to elapse before replying, "Well, Liz had always been used to the best of everything; and we were both too young to realize that my money wouldn't buy all the lovely clothes she was used to. I was in love with her, and I'm like that...I never think about myself...only about those I love...I mean, as long as I've got money none of my pals go short; and, well, Liz was my wife, and I was fond of her, so I gave up everything...drinking, smoking, movies, my football match on Saturdays; and I stopped bothering about clothes for myself. That's how I am...but I'd come home after a hard day at the office, and Liz would take off her dressing-gown, and there she'd be in a new set of undies that had cost the same amount as a dinner for two. Usually I'd be so thrilled at the sight of her I

15

wouldn't even think of the cost. I'd just get hold of her, and it'd be hours before I got my tea, but I didn't mind. Other times she'd see I was upset, and she'd go through the old routine, gyrating her hips against me, and telling me she bought nice things only because she knew I liked her to be sexy. It was true, I did like her to be sexy, it turned me on to see her dressed like that. She'd tell me that I was the only man who'd ever take her fine undies off her, so I'd do just that...I'd take off her fine panties and I would spread her legs wide apart. With my hands, I'd part the sweet pink lips of her pussy and I would look into her lovely snatch, admiring the fine thin lines, the succulent, wet hole and the protruding clitoris. I would feast on the sight of her, the smell of her, the feel of her flesh.

"She was a tease. Sometimes she'd keep her legs open just long enough for me to love her with my tongue and fingers—but would close them when I wanted to slip my hard cock inside. But I could never resist her, not with her cunt laid bare before me, not with those sweet lips beckoning my tongue to wash them with passionate kisses. So I would kneel before her shrine of love and pleasure her with my mouth, for hours. I'd hold the lips very far apart, so her opening was fully exposed, and I would fuck her with my tongue, pressing it into her hole, deeper and deeper, until my teeth were nearly gnawing at the opening. She would moan and groan and tell me I was the only one. And this would make me work harder to please her.

"Sometimes, I would ever-so-lightly caress her clit-bud with my tongue, while slipping one or two, sometimes three, fingers into her wet pussy. As I finger-fucked her, and licked her love bud, her legs would tremble wildly and passionately, and the lips of her cunt would swell up three times the size and before I knew it, my fingers were filled with her creamy love dew and her cunt muscles were twitching around my fingers. But right after she would come, she'd sometimes pull her still pulsating clit from my mouth and nudge my fingers from her cunt-hole and would say she had to get some rest. She would often roll over and sleep.

"But then there were other times, when she would let me inside her. She would tantalize me and seduce me and then open her wet cunt wide for my aching cock. I'd poise at the opening and rut my cock head against her swelling lips as long as I could and then, finally, I would have to plunge into her and go deeply into the warm, wet opening between my wife's legs. Ah, I can remember the velvet feel of her sweet cunt lips wrapped around my hard pole. And how she'd hoist her hips to meet my thrusts and groan over and over how I was the only one.

"Sometimes she'd grab hold of my butt, and pull me down further to her pussy. She would come, and her clenching cunt muscles would bring me off too. I'd pour my seed deep inside her, unless it was her fertile period, in which case I'd cream all over her belly. These were the best times, when she would let me have it all.

"By the time I'd finished making love to her, my anger would vanish. The trouble was that I was going without everything, and we still weren't making ends meet; so we had a few tiffs, and then, like my parents had always warned, she went back to sea as stewardess on Norwegian ships. I think she really couldn't live without travelling. When I first met her, she'd just about been all over the place, and she speaks I don't know how many Scandinavian languages."

How was it possible that this Liz woman had gotten herself so charming a husband, and she could leave the poor boy alone for weeks on end? Bella had never experienced life on twelve pounds per week for two people, but she was convinced that, given so attentive and loving a man as Rick, she would have been happy to wear no undies at all rather than either leave him or oblige him to sacrifice all the little luxuries to which he had been accustomed as a bachelor. This boy must love his unworthy wife terribly. Bella asked him, "Was there no other work so intelligent a boy could do? Something more remunerative?"

Rick ingratiated himself still further with her by answering, "Well, you see, I never had much of an education. My parents brought me up nice and all that. They taught me to be honest, generous, polite and all that; but Liz and I got married before I'd really had time to realize that there was more to life than slogging away eight hours a day for twelve quid a week; and then I was too busy earning that much and trying to be a loving husband to have time to study and improve myself. It all happened so suddenly. One day she asked me for two or three quid to buy a skirt or a blouse she'd seen in a shop. I hardly had any money in my pocket, and she was so upset. She sat down, and wrote to the shipping company she'd worked for before we were married, and a week later she was off to Rotterdam to join one of their ships that was going to South America."

Bella was tempted to tell Rick what a "bitch" she thought his wife was, but, convinced he loved the woman in spite of everything, she contented herself with asking:

"But how long does she stay away?"

"Five, six, seven months sometimes! You see, the only way she can come home is either when they dock somewhere in England for a week or two or by getting paid off. Then she comes home with the few pounds she's saved. That goes in no time, because she always says she's ashamed to go out in the shabby clothes she's got, so she goes on a spending spree. Then we manage on my wages until she sees a frock or a bikini I can't buy her, and then she's off to sea again."

"To let her go, when she's used up all your money, and then to take her back, when she wants a rest from roaming, you must love her very much."

If Bella had been elderly, Rick would have sought to impress her by assuring her that he did love his wife. Here, however, he was dealing with a woman who, although she was his senior by fifteen or twenty years, retained a high measure of sex-appeal. He was not yet sure she was amorously interested in him, but he hoped she either was or would eventually be. He found her so desirable that he entertained the idea of seducing her, although he was too intent on impressing her favorably to be prepared to run the risks involved in trying to hasten her into sexual intimacy with him. Quite apart, however, from his lust after her, he counted on making himself so attractive to her, in every way, that she would be disposed to treat him generously. He believed her to be the type of woman who, being no longer in the bloom of youth, would be flattered by the thought that she was the only woman of importance in the life of a younger man. Therefore he told her that he had ceased to love Liz and, to explain his continuing to welcome her on the rare occasions when she came home, he expressed a sentiment which he had once heard one of his colleagues at the office setting forth in complete sincerity. He said:

"No, I'm no longer bound to her by love, but by

pity and a sense of duty. What annoys my parents most of all is that I stick by Liz even though she's proved they were right when they said she'd never settle down to being the wife of a humble clerk like me; and that's why I don't see much of them. You see, they can't seem to understand that Liz and I made this mistake together, so we've got to suffer the consequences together. As long as Liz doesn't want our marriage to break up, it wouldn't be fair for me to lock the door on her. I ought not to have married a girl I couldn't keep in the luxury she was used to, and that's all there is to it. Her solution to the problem is really the only one; so, however disappointed and lonely I may be, I can't blame her for leaving me for such long periods."

"But surely," asked Bella, "you don't believe that a woman of normal sexual appetite can go without it for months on end, especially in the unsettled atmosphere of a seafaring life?"

Bella was getting too close to the aspect of the truth which Rick was particularly eager to hide from her and indeed from everyone: He used his long separations from his wife as a means of cadging hospitality from his prosperous friends and acquaintances. He would win their sympathy by posing as a home-loving boy whose home life was in ruins as a result of Liz's wanderlust; but the facts were that her long absences from home resulted from an agreement between them both. It was an agreement, furthermore, into which he entered willingly, since it left him free to have a good time at the expense of others, while increasing his bank balance with the gifts his grateful friends and acquaintances bestowed upon him. He lied when he said that Liz came home almost empty-handed. It was not true that she battened on him until his money ran out, and that she would then leave him to solve the financial problems she had created for him. On the contrary, instead of being the victim of an extravagant woman, he was the ponce who enriched himself by means of her immoral earnings; for, if she appeared on the books of Norwegian International Shipping as a stewardess, it was because the Norwegian fiscal authorities would not tolerate her being paid double what is normally paid to a seaman performing the duties she officially discharged, if it were known that she was, in fact, one of the perks which N.I.S. grants to its skippers. Not only was she extremely well paid for a type of work requiring no skill whatsoever, but the various captains under whom she had served (in more ways than one) demonstrated their appreciation of her amorous aptitude with the generosity for which sea-going men are noted.

At the time of Rick's meeting with Bella, Liz was on her way to Venezuela on board the tanker *Margomer*, whose master was a hard-drinking seadog renowned in half the ports of the world as a sadistic sexual pervert. At sea he was not content with using Liz mercilessly both as boy and girl, and with submitting her privately to every obscene humiliation imaginable, but he also took pleasure in making her erotic submission to him known to all his officers and men and to all those whom he brought her into contact with ashore. When he was too drunk to copulate with her himself, he invited his officers to bid against one another for temporary possession of her body. Since his officers had often been at sea and womanless for long enough to permit of their pockets being well-lined, they offered fantastic sums for the privilege of burying their sexual organs briefly in Liz's vagina, and everyone concerned was happy. The captain had the satisfaction of having obliged his doxy to auction herself off, the highest bidder was usually too drunk and too sex-starved to realize that, at the next port of call, he would get an equally sexy tart for a quarter of the price he was paying Liz, and the latter was thrilled at the prospect of increasing by twenty or thirty dollars the amount of money she would be able to hand to Rick the next time she managed to get home. With friends and contacts in all the ports at which the *Margomer* called, the master was pleased to get his teeth into meat other than that which formed his daily diet at sea; but he usually put Liz in contact with some local lady-killer or bar proprietor, so that she incurred no expense during her few days of freedom; in fact, she'd be earning herself a further contribution to the cost of the villa she and Rick had built. Few of Rick's colleagues at the office (where he was the most popular employee) could figure out how a twelve-pound-per-week clerk could have a house built on his salary. To the victims and prospective victims of his mendicant campaigns, he of course made no mention of his villa, preferring to draw attention to the inadequacy of the tiny apartment in which he was obliged to receive his wife whenever she deigned to return to him.

Determined to put Bella off the scent of the truth, Rick assured her that Liz was not highly sexed, and that she was very narrow-minded.

"Of course," he admitted, "no man in his right mind denies the possibility that his wife is unfaithful to him; but in Liz's case, I'd almost put my fist in the fire to prove my trust in her. I don't know whether or not she loves me. In her own way, perhaps she does; but, when you say you think I love her very much, what you really mean is that I pity her. I've talked about leaving her, but the effect of such talk on her convinces me that she'd probably do herself an

22

injury. To her, marriage is sacred. She and I went to church together, and swore eternal fidelity; and her church rejects divorce, so that's that. She needs me, or at least, she knows the day will come when she'll need me. She's young, healthy and adventurous; but the day will come when she'll be glad to come home to her husband, and I feel it's my duty to be there, waiting for her. If it's not too late, we shall have the children I want; two or three lovely children I can knit for and make frocks for. And we can start making a nice home for them and for ourselves, doing everything ourselves, painting, papering, making curtains and that."

Bella thought she had never met so nearly perfect a man. Like herself, he wanted children, for whom he could knit and sew. She was tempted to laugh at the thought of a man knitting and sewing, while his wife went out buying frilly undies for herself, but he was too nice and sensitive a boy to be ridiculed. His attitude about marriage was more feminine than masculine. The fact that he was willing to keep the nest warm for his hen until such times as she felt inclined to fly back to it endeared him to her. Such selflessness was scarcely credible, and yet there was no doubting the sincerity of this dear boy. She felt the urge to do something for him, but what?

She wished she did not have to leave him so soon, but she was sure she had shown in him such interest as would give him the courage to suggest they meet again. She summoned the waiter, and endeavored to settle the bill; but Rick never minded paying the small bills for someone who would reciprocate by settling the large ones, so he paid, and they stepped out into the Place de l'Opéra. He walked with her to the entrance of her hotel, just round the corner on Boulevard des Capucines. He offered her his hand at the moment of parting, and she was thrilled by his gallantry.

"We didn't g round to discussing our next meeting," he whined. His obvious desire to see her again brought a ravishing smile to Bella's dark eyes and tiny, sensitive mouth.

"Tomorrow is the only day I've left absolutely free," she answered, "for just wandering around, shopping, and filling my ears, eyes and nostrils with the sounds, sights and aromas of this lovely, romantic city. I'm in Room 109. Collect me at ten, and don't dare to be minute late!"

"Ten o'clock sharp! It's been nice making your acquaintance. Until tomorrow then!"

Happy and rejuvenated, Bella went up to her room to rest and put on her "war-paint" before meeting friends for dinner. Rick wandered along in the direction of his hotel with mixed feelings. He was looking forward to the morrow with wealthy Bella, together with whom he foresaw many lucrative tomorrows, but he was peevishly disappointed that she had not suggested he join her party for dinner the same evening. He would have liked to put on the midnight-blue tuxedo Jorge had given him, and escort her into the star-studded cocktail bar of the Elysées Matignon.

II.

Blissfully unaware of the fact that he was undersized, Rick admired and stroked his pale nudity before the mirror of his hotel room. His bejeweled hands patted his blond curls, and he was pleased with himself. He had enjoyed four or five years of remunerative success with men and women of various ages, so it is not surprising that he was ignorant of the fact that he had the face of a vulgar woman. He fancied himself an Adonis, and his self-confidence gave him a measure of success denied to worthier but more modest men.

He dressed, without putting on a single garment which he had bought himself; and he appraised himself afresh. Pleased with what he beheld, he rang for breakfast; and ten minutes later, he warmed himself in the approving glances of the pretty girl who brought him his coffee, roll and butter. He slapped her fleshy bottom playfully, and she, failing to recognize him as one who is a payee rather than a payer, chuckled invitingly and thrust her posterior out provocatively. After breakfast he brushed his teeth,

applied drops of perfume here, there and everywhere, and left the hotel.

Clad in pointed suede shoes, cavalry-twill pants, a
navy-blue blazer, white open-necked shirt and a blue
cravat, he walked along the boulevard, nonchalantly
tapping his right knee with his pigskin gloves. Even
though he was in no hurry, he minced along with the
short, quick steps which were his trademark. His bum
twitched to left and to right like that of a sexy hooker
on high heels; he was on top of the world.

In Room 109 of her hotel Bella would be waiting
for him. He would take her in his young arms, and
she would be flattered by the ardor of a man fifteen
years her junior. He was not feeling particularly lustful that lovely October morning, but, his eye on her
checkbook, he would simulate such desire for her as
would not be gainsaid. Once she had tasted his loins,
she would lose no time in convincing herself that it
was her love rather than her lust which had betrayed
her; and, loving him, she would shower him with
bounty, since, to those who love, giving comes more
easily than taking. Having given him her body once,
she would insist on his taking it regularly, even if he
had to be tempted with little gifts such as suits bearing rich designer labels, the occasional five-pound
note and invitations to oyster-and-champagne week-
ends at her home.

Whistling a popular American song in praise of
Paris in the fall, Rick entered the lobby of Bella's
palatial hotel, where he was disagreeably surprised to
find his new friend waiting for him. Small and slim,
she looked delicious in a bust-flattering blouse of
white linen, so low-cut that it imparted to her throat
a swan-like grace, and a skirt of soft, black velvet,
which clung lovingly to her loins and thighs. Her
stockings were of sheerest black nylon, and her

shoulder-length black hair shone like dark blue water in the light of silver stars. The brightness of her eyes and the friendly warmth of her smile conveyed to Rick the impression that he was going to spend the day with an expectant young virgin. She dazzled him, and there was in the lobby not one man whose eyes were not turned in her brilliant direction. She looked so healthy that the sight of her was gloriously painful. It made Rick's task so much easier. He just did not have to pretend she knocked him sideways. He was speechless with admiration, and she loved him for his inability to hide his feelings.

"I waited down here," she explained, "because the girl wanted to tidy my room; and she's very sweet, so I didn't want to get in her way. Say, you look like a million dollars. Did you go to bed early, have a good night's rest, a relaxing bath and a healthy breakfast?"

"All that, and heaven too! I mean, you talk about me looking fit, but you shine like an angel. What's the program?"

"Well, it's the sort of day for dreaming up there in Montmartre. I want to see la Place du Tertre, l'Eglise du Sacré Coeur, le Lapin Agile and all that stuff. I'd like to find for Harry the sort of painting that'll make his hair stand up on end, some saucy frillies for my maid, an Alpine beret for the chauffeur and for poor little me several months' supply of Carven's 'Ma Griffe'; and I hope you're going to find time to make love to me."

Rick was in luck, and he could scarcely believe his ears. Resisting the impulse to utter an exclamation of astonishment was a "tour de force," but Rick was a professional. While regretting that the presence of the chambermaid in Bella's suite rendered immediate love-making impossible, he managed to convey to Bella the impression that, impatient as he was to fuse his young body with her ripe flesh, his love and respect for her were such that he would willingly wait a decade for the privilege of "loving" her.

She took his arm, and they strolled along to the Madeleine, turned right into the rue du Tronchet, and entered the Magasin du Printemps, where she made Rick accompany her from department to department. She asked him for his advice on undies for her maid, and she made him try on every sort of male headwear imaginable. Together they fought against the Parisian hordes of bargain-seekers; and Bella, fastidious Bella, enjoyed it, while Rick (the poor little poor boy) valiantly sought to hide from her his nausea at this contact with "the people," his own "people."

When she had made her purchases, they took the Metro to Place Pigalle, whence they wandered up to Place du Tertre. On the way they brought hunks of Dutch cheese, which they munched peripatetically. He would have liked to sit down under a brightly-colored umbrella for a copious lunch with wine, but she insisted that cheese was healthier than a heavy meal, and that it was unwise to drink during the heat of the day.

In a tiny art gallery Bella bought from a large, rotund artist (for three quarters of the price he quoted) a painting of a bald, pimply monk licking the valley between the almost naked breasts of a lovely young girl, her face contorted with the agony of her open-mouthed ecstasy. She gave the painter her name and her hotel address, and instructed him to have the picture delivered. As she and Rick left the shop, Bella assured the artist that the mere fact that his work would hang in her home would result in his acquiring a British market for the fruits of his genius.

They went into other galleries. Bella was enthusiastic over all she saw; Rick just wished she would suggest returning to her hotel for an hour or two of fornication. He did not dare propose such a thing himself, the secret of his success being that he had no real pride or personality, preferring to flatter his victims by making himself no more than their shadow. Bella knew when her body and its shadow would merge, and she knew how she wanted to fill the intervening hours; so, like a cur, Rick followed her upwards in the direction of Sacré Coeur.

But as they walked, Rick couldn't help but daydream about how he would seal his relationship with Bella by plugging her cunt with his cock in such a way that she would never let him go. She was very physically attractive, so it wouldn't be at all difficult for Rick to part her creamy thighs and first visit her precious, rich pussy with his attentive tongue. He could nearly hear her moan and groan and beg for more as he rolled his wet tongue around her excited clit bud and simultaneously dipped a spit-wet finger into her juice drenched cunt. He'd slip the finger in and out, in and out, creating delicious friction, all the while licking and teasing her love bud with the tip of his tongue.

Or maybe she'd like her asshole devoured first. This way, he could please and tease her, he could make her cunt lips swell and ache for him, but without yet touching the hungry pussy lips. He could enjoyably put her on her belly, hoist her butt up by placing a couple of fat hotel pillows beneath her hips and then gingerly open the assuredly sweet-smelling bum-hole by pressing the smooth ass-cheeks apart with two thumbs. Ah, how she'd squirm as he spread the tight opening far apart as he could while pressing his probing tongue to the rim, licking around it and then finally—as she begged and pleaded to be fully tongue-fucked—plunging his tongue into the deepest depths of her anal canal. He would fill her with the warmth of anal excitement until her cunt was so hot, she could burst. Perhaps then, and only then, would he bring her to the point of begging for his cock. At that juncture, she'd pay hard cash for his hard cock, Rick was confident of this. He would simply turn her over on her back, leave the pillows under her butt and bring his nice, youthful, hard cock to the very opening of her sweet pussy lips and he would fuck her. He'd fuck her nice and tenderly, and then, good and hard. And he would manipulate her clitoris in such a way that she would soon reach a blissful, explosive climax and she would know that she could never let his cock stray far from her hungry cunt.

Rick realized, in the process of his daydream, his cock had risen in his pants. He had the urge to grab Bella's hand and place it on his aching groin, to tempt her back to the hotel. But he was too smart to rush things. He just kept walking, following her lead.

The Place du Tertre behind them, they were about to enter one of the steep narrow streets leading to the startlingly white church, when Bella's attention was attracted to a painter standing at the corner, working feverishly at a somber canvas. She said to Rick, "Now there's an artist with an individual view of sun-drenched Montmartre!"

To her surprise, the man turned to her, and in an unmistakably Australian voice complimented her on recognizing greatness when she met it. He made the remark in all modesty and with more banter than conviction; but Bella insisted, "I really mean what I said, but I'm sorry you understand English, because I think too generous praise can rob a truly talented artist like you of the will to do better. You see, one of the uses I make of my wealth consists of helping and encouraging young, struggling artists; so I know what I'm talking about. I'd like to see more of your work. If we can find time, may we visit your studio sometime?"

Smiling, the handsome, athletic-looking Australian produced a wallet from the back pocket of his corduroy pants, and handed Bella a card bearing the name Dane Mollison and an address in the region of Montparnasse. His smile betrayed his conviction that, like so many wealthy Anglo-Saxon women, she met a struggling genius on every street corner in Montmartre, but that she never got round to helping one of them.

Bella and Rick continued their stroll, neither making any further mention of Dane, although he filled Bella's thoughts. There was about this tall, rugged man a shy, unassuming air of physical and spiritual strength. She had spoken to him for only a couple of minutes, but she was sure he was not the sort of man who would allow even the wealthiest of women to make a lap-dog of him. A woman would have to win a man like him. Such beings are not bought.

Rick was fifteen years younger than Bella, but the climb to the summit of the Butte left him breathless, while she, swinging along at his side like a slender girl of twenty, reached the top with a healthy smile in her eyes. Together they admired the panorama, leaning on the white stone parapet surrounding the icing-sugar temple. All around them other couples feasted their eyes on the beauties of the roofs of late afternoon Paris, allowing themselves to fall under the romantic spell of the city of love. Here and there two mouths were fused in a promising kiss. A man's hand caressed the back of his female companion until his fingers squeezed her bottom through the stuff of her skirt. Another man had his girl pinned against the

low wall, her thighs parted and holding his legs tight
so that his bulging front was pressed against her lightly clothed mound of Venus. A few yards from Bella
and Rick was a girl who was obviously enjoying a
bearded youth's massaging of her young breasts
through her corsage. Rick would have liked to feel
Bella's body in contact with his; but he did not wish
to offend her by presuming to take the initiative. It
seemed to him that she reserved for herself the right
to take all the initiative she deemed necessary, and
her attitude was so platonic that he wondered
whether he had heard and understood her correctly
when she had spoken in the lobby of her hotel about
making love. He could scarcely believe that a woman
could invite an almost total stranger to make love to
her at some unspecified later hour without feeling, in
the meantime, the urge at least to rub her front
against his. They had been together about six hours,
during which time he could not recall her hands
touching his, her lips grazing his; and up there, taking
it easy for a few minutes, she stood about a foot away
from him, near enough to leave no one in doubt that
they were friends, but sufficiently distant to permit of
no perspicacious individual's mistaking them as a
couple who were on the way to a shared bed.

After a long, dreamy silence Bella pointed out
over the city, and pronounced, "Down there are your
hotel and mine; and down there somewhere we're
going to dine. You're my guest, so you can say exactly where, but it must be down there; and we're going
to walk."

For an instant Rick forgot that a whore must
never even appear to contradict the keeper of the
purse. He allowed the ghost of a grimace to cloud his
features, inciting Bella to snap, "It'll give us an
appetite, make us feel we've earned dinner. Where

32

would you like to go? Where would you take a girl, if
you were paying?"

The question was a shrewd one. Bella was not a
moron. She would gladly have treated her charming
new friend to the most expensive dinner Paris had to
offer; but she wanted to go to some relaxing restaurant, where they would run no risk of being tucked
away in an inconspicuous corner on account of their
informal dress. Furthermore, she was offering him
dinner with all the trimmings, as much food and wine
as he could absorb; but she saw no point in beginning
what she hoped would be a long and exciting association at a level they would later be unable to excel.
Maxim's and the Savoy would come in good time, he
being a wise host who keeps the best wine until the
end of the feast.

If, however, Bella Partham was no half-wit, Rick
was an astute boy. He had two reasons for suggesting
Les Noces de Jeannette. First, impatient as he was to
acquaint a certain small portion of his anatomy with
the corresponding part of hers, he felt the need of a
good feed, which was precisely what one gets there in
the shadow of the Opéra-Comique. Second, he wanted to convince her of the simplicity of his desires,
when another than he was footing the bill. At the
Noces, Bella would not pay dearly for the privilege of
playing hostess to the gigolo and she would so appreciate the modesty of his demands that she would
insist on subsidizing the remainder of his sojourn in
Paris.

After their walk to the corner of the rue Favard,
Rick was more than ready for the apéritif with which
Bella reluctantly permitted him to begin his meal. He
enjoyed studying the bill of fare, while Bella made
herself miserable wondering what health-imperiling
fats and spices went to the preparation of all those

tantalizing dishes. Rick ordered what he fancied, and gorged himself, swilling the *vin à discrétion* as though it were water. Bella set the waiter's nerves on edge by demanding a detailed description of everything on the menu, and then ordering simplified versions of whatever came nearest to her conception of healthy food. In fact she ate little, and used a glass of white wine and a glass of red for the mere moistening of her lips. Rick's gluttony revolted her, yet she would not really have wished him other than he was. He was perceptibly having fun, and she rejoiced in his pleasure. It pleased her to paint terrible pictures of what the food and wine he was consuming were doing to his constitution; but she consoled herself with the fact that, if she was dining with a pig, she would shortly be in bed with a swine.

She recognized the vintage Burgogne served a wide choice of cheeses as a wine to be treasured; and she insisted on Rick's drinking wine with his Roquefort, so that she could drink both her and his glass of mellow red with her chèvre. A man would have reminded her that a docile woman merits gallantry, while a domineering harridan deserves a sound thrashing; but Rick knew that the successful prostitute is the obedient one with neither pride nor opinions. He meekly surrendered his solitary glass of smooth Moulin à Vent, contenting himself with a further glass of the heady table-wine of which he had already drunk more than half a liter.

They took their time over coffee, she being determined that they adjourn to her hotel suite at the moment of her choice, while he drunkenly wondered whether she had not changed her mind about their becoming lovers. Certainly, for a woman who wanted a man so badly that she bluntly told him she hoped he would find time to make love to her, she had

seemed sexually cool all day, and Rick detected in
her none of a nymphomaniac's pathological impatience to get her clothes off. It was a pity. Relieving
her of money or presents in kind was of greater
importance than lying down with her, and he had
confidence that she was going to prove to be a lucrative victim of his genius for begging, but work need
not always be divorced from pleasure, and he would
have liked to soak his penis in the vaginal liquor of
the first woman who had ever flatly asked him to.

Bella paid the bill, deriving from so openly playing
the hostess to a young man a satisfaction which was
at least equaled by Rick's delight in observing how
enviously the waiter looked at him. Rick differed
from a man in that, whereas a man is ashamed of
being the object of a woman's exaggerated generosity
(or even of another man's), the individual who is neither wholly masculine nor feminine tends to interpret
other people's liberality towards him as his right and
as a deserved compliment to his beauty and his pleasing ways. It was, therefore, a happy British couple
who left Les Noces de Jeannette shortly after ten
o'clock.

Rick had drunk so much that he made a mistake
for which he might have paid dearly, had not two
glasses of wine mellowed his companion somewhat.
Walking along the side of the Opéra-Comique, in the
direction of Boulevard des Italiens, he put his arm
around her slender waist. Whispering, "Not in public,
please!," she swayed out of his grasp; but she swayed
back again, so that they sauntered along closer
together than at any time during the day. Her wide
skirt of black velvet flapped intimately against his
trousered legs, and their flanks touched lightly at
each slow step they took. She said nothing about
returning to her hotel, but there she led him. As she

collected her key from the desk, and they crossed the hall together, Rick hoped those who observed them knew that she found him so desirable that she was willing to pay him for a night of copulation. Had he dared, he would have made to her in the elevator such remarks as would have betrayed their relationship to their neighbors; but he feared that she, an older woman reduced to buying boys' favors, would take a poor view of such indiscretions; and he had no wish to offend Mrs. Bank-balance. Bella, however, had not the least objection to the world knowing that her youthful escort was about to plunder her loins. She was as proud of him as he was of her; and she was convinced he was going up to her room with her for no other reason than that he found her irresistible. In her joy at being the chosen mistress of the most seductive man in Paris, she was quite willing to be admired and envied of all. What she (but not Rick) realized was that few of those around them would have guessed either that she was more than forty years of age or that it was at her instigation that this boy was going to do to her what nine out of ten virile men would have gone to limitless trouble for the opportunity of doing.

Bella handed Rick the key to Room 109, and he drunkenly stabbed the door until the key found its niche. He would have stumbled into the room ahead of her, but she eased him out of the way, switched on the lights, and preceded him into her love-nest, a pretty suite consisting of a small hall, a spacious, shining bathroom whose predominant color was the pink of warm, female skin, and a boudoir caparisoned as a Sybarites retreat from the realities of life. It was an exquisite collection of pastel tones, and the warm air was heavy with perfume which seemed to owe nothing to manufacturers' formulae, but everything to Mediterranean gardens in the heat of still, vibrantly expectant sunsets. Although Bella had not created this bedroom, it breathed her name and it bore the impression of a decorator who (although he had never met her) knew her as profoundly as she knew herself. It was precisely the room she could have devised for herself or for some friend whom she wished to hear sighing in the throes of a torrid love affair. It was a room for love, a fitting place for such a woman as Bella to receive a friend of the opposite sex, a tender trap whose prisoner would die rather than think of escape.

For Rick, however, it was a workroom, an agreeable one, but still an apartment in which money could be earned. It was also a measure of wealth of the lady whose body he was going to possess. He knew how much Jorge had paid for their room at the Edward VII, nor did he doubt that Bella was being charged as much for hers; and he said to himself, "If she can afford so much for the nest, the bird is worthy of his hire."

"Like it?" she asked, as though inviting him to admire her baby.

"Nicest room and nicest occupant I ever saw!" he replied, swaying so that she figured she would have to use him soon unless she were willing to have him lose consciousness without having done his duty.

"Am I really your cup of tea?" she asked adolescently.

"The snazziest bod...figure..."

"You mustn't be shy about calling my body 'my body,'" she broke in, "because I'm very proud of my lovely body. Not only because it's naturally beautiful, but also because I intelligently keep it youthful, supple, pleasing to the eye and to the touch. I'm very much aware of my woman's body. I love it, and I associate with the sort of people who share my devotion to my body. I demand of my friends, men and women, respect for my flesh; and I respect it by feeding it properly, cleansing it with care, exercising it enough, but not too much."

She paused, hoping her words would inflame his blood, and give him the courage to try (in vain) to take the initiative from her. She was accustomed to being seduced, but not to being the huntress. Rick, however, was playing safe. If she was platonically exploitable, he was prepared to take her money, while leaving her skirts undisturbed; but he was even more ready to take both her riches and her genitals. What he intended avoiding was taking a single step before she gave the word or signal.

"I'm going to show you my perfect body," she announced, "and I'm going to see what too much food and wine have done to yours. Take your clothes off!"

Removing his jacket, he said archly, "Bell, you say the cutest things."

"My name's Bella. The first thing to learn is to go to a helluva lot of trouble to give folks their right name. Okay, Ricardo? Blond dago strips for society beauty! Strip, honey! Strip for Bella means strip fast. Just watch my fine, civilized fingers unbuttoning my crisp, snow-white shirt. Tell me, sonny boy, did ever proletarian eyes behold such creamy globes? Nice school-boy torso you got there. How d'you like this torso, boy?"

She had taken off her skirt. Her breasts were supported, but not concealed, by a black, lace-fronted garment which stopped just short of a pair of arrogant, dark brown teats. Against the brilliant black of her skirt and the misty black of her glorified girdle her shoulders, her arms and the upper reaches of her bosom were of such a whiteness as Rick had never seen on a human body. Her right hand held above her head, while her left hand raised one side of her skirt until one thigh was half-exposed, she posed so provocatively that Rick just stood there, appraising her black-and-white beauty instead of continuing to undress. He was bare from the waist up. She dropped her pose, moved across to him, unzipped his pants, and let them fall to his ankles.

"I never before stripped a man or stripped for a man who hadn't even bothered to kiss me," she complained.

He took her in his arms, fingered the cool smoothness of her shoulders and bare back, and glued his mouth on hers. His lips were good on hers, and she liked the way his expert tongue delved into her face. She was held tight, but with tenderness. She clung to him, her heat and her flesh longing for his love. He was not steady on his feet, so she opened her thighs, allowing him to lean on her, the bulge of his underpants a living thing in her velvet lap. Her fine, white hands were fresh on the back of his neck, as she held her questing tongue in the closest possible contact with his. She purred like a hot cat, and rubbed her clothed pussy against his concealed tom. She was so warm that his "professionalism" melted into the fluid of genuine desire. He was too drunk to resist the primeval call of her honest femininity. He broke the skin of her lips with his teeth, and the taste of her own blood intoxicated her. Like one demented, she broke from his embrace. On her knees, she seized the waistband of his underpants in her quivering fingers, and tugged until the sight of his incandescent manhood tore from her throat a cry of wonder.

Each of her hands grabbed one of his buttocks, and she dug her teeth into the top of his left thigh, feeling the heat of his sex against her left cheek.

"Make it a stand," she mumbled against the sweaty fumes of his loins.

She fell backwards, with her shoulders against the pink silk of the cover of her bed. His hands were like petrified claws approaching her breasts, the undersides of which were veiled in black lace. As though afraid of his touch, she pressed her back against the mattress; but she threw back her lovely head, and pushed forward her desire-filled mounds; her taut, dark nipples pointed toward him. The tips of his thumbs touched each other in the small hollow at the base of her proud, white throat, and his fluttering fingers were like gossamer wings tapping her shoulders and descending until each of her tits was squeezed between the index and second fingers of one of his hands. His thumbs climbed from the depth of the valley between her breasts, and joined his fingers in a merciless nipping of the brown-mauve extremities of her udders. A short groan escaped from her mouth, to which the quivering of her thin, parted lips imparted a quality redolent of a hungry beak. Rick leaned over her, touched her lips with his, and stuck his tongue crudely into her mouth. She held him tight for a minute, their mouths constantly changing shape against one another as saliva passed from one to the other. At the end of their lewd kiss his tongue wandered all over her face, moistening her chin, her cheeks, her ears, temples and nostrils. Her fingers were buried beseechingly in his long, blond curls, while inside her velvet skirt fires raged. Her knees jerked open and closed, her crotch twitching backwards and forwards as though she were reaching the end of an orgasm.

"My skirt," she panted, "I want it off." Her hands flew to the button at her waist, and he heard the whir of a descending zipper. He raised her to her feet. At first her skirt accompanied her, but a flick of her haunch enabled her to appear before her new friend clad in nothing but diaphanous black nylon stockings (which reached only halfway up her marble-white thighs) and a black full-body bustier consisting of a bra which contented itself with giving the bosom a little uplift without concealing more than was absolutely necessary. She wore a skimpy, snuggly pair of undies, too. Rick had seen such things on naughty calendars and in "pin-up" magazines, but he had never believed women actually wore garments of that nature. She was certainly the loveliest thing, animate or otherwise, he had ever set eyes on; and she could tell. Her tapered, immaculately manicured finger invited him to admire her; and that is precisely what he did. He noticed that, while the back and sides of the garment were of some substantial elastic material, the front was a panel of limpid lace through which her exquisite body shone like an illuminated white rose behind a dewy cobweb. Only at her sex was the lace a little less flimsy, which served to rivet Rick's attention on that particular part of her person.

Bella rotated slowly, in imitation of an Arabian dancing girl, giving him an opportunity to feast his eyes on the nudity of her back down to her waist and on her delicately molded rump, to which her panties clung so lovingly that it was like two glistening, juice-filled plums. She stood still, and asked, "Well?"

He was too drunk with wine and her beauty to answer, but his erection betrayed the intensity of his feelings.

"If you think it's worth taking," she cooed, "it's all yours."

He took her in his arms, kissed her lasciviously, and lowered her gently to the bed. At her stocking-tops his hands tried to unfasten her garters, but she had to do it herself because in his eagerness his movements became clumsy. All he managed to do was to unzip her from under her left arm down to her haunch. She peeled off her stockings, and then kneeled to allow him to divest her of the remainder of her attire. Naked she lay on the bed, so slim, so pale, so like a little oriental doll waiting to be debauched by a vicious potentate. Rick's hands wandered deferentially over her smooth, drily warm shoulders, breasts, belly and thighs. He drew her upwards into his arms, and stroked her back and buttocks. The second finger of his right hand lingered for a few seconds deep in the crack of her posterior, touching her rear aperture. He turned her over onto her flat belly, the better to see the perfection of her back. She thought he intended playing his homosexual tricks on her, and she said to herself, "Oh, no, my boy! The first time you have me, I'm going to feel your weight on my belly, and your cock in my cunt. Time enough for perversity, when straightforward loving begins to pall on us!" Rick, however, knew his business too well to make so gross an error. Furthermore, he saw no point in using her as though she were a boy when she had delicacies which no man could offer him. He rolled her over again onto her back, and devoured her firm little breasts with his eyes. Bella was not skinny, nor was there a superfluous ounce of flesh anywhere on her body. She was like a faultlessly proportioned statuette in a porcelain so dainty that it seemed to glow transparent. She was so soothing to the eye and the touch that even Rick was temporarily aware of her more as a desirable girl than as a wealthy client. The nails of the fingers of his

42

right hand combed the hairs of her crotch, and her slightly parted legs opened wider, begging him to acquaint his digits with the nectar of her loins. He responded by laying his hand flat on her mound of Venus, so that the palm pressed heavily on her belly, while his fingers hid the hirsute triangle. Rubbing her hard, his hand advanced until it was the palm which covered the curly mat. By keeping his fingers briefly out of contact with her he teased her. He looked her full in the face. His excitement was such that he would have liked to possess her profoundly at once; but he wanted her to plead with him, so that his granting of her requests would place her in his debt; and, because she was an amateur, she did not realize that they were engaged in a trial of will-power. She gave in. Her mouth wide open, the tip of her tongue agitatedly licking first one lip, then the other, she threw her head backwards and from side to side, murmuring, "Be nice to me, darling!"

"Nice!" he exclaimed, as his right hand abruptly bent at the knuckles, so that four fingers formed a wall guarding the entrance to her love-tunnel. With his fingers he exerted pressure on her secret flesh, which was humid and warm. She sighed softly, and he found the sensitive clit button, which vibrated at his aggressive touch.

"You're playing with my clitoris," she whispered, "and you haven't washed your hands."

Astonished and pained, he made a sulky move to rise, intending to do his lady's bidding; but she grabbed his penis. "It doesn't matter now. Stay! I want you."

He did not need two invitations to stay with her. His fingers went into her again, and he masturbated her until she writhed, moaned and gasped, "Love me, Rick!"

Her thighs were open to the limit, so that he could see the rosy lips of the mouth which was eager to eat his manhood. Kneeling between her legs, he stuck into her the forefinger of both of his hands, as deep as they would go. Then he moved his fists outward, pressing the tips of his index fingers closer together. Thus the two digits formed a V which opened her wider than even the thickest phallus could. He did this to her so coldly that she was humiliated as never before in her life. It was as though she were not a woman who had begged to be loved, but a thing which excited his curiosity. His fingers inside her were like a spear holding her helpless while he inspected her hole to decide whether or not it was worth going into. Paradoxically, however, and perversely, the mere impertinence of this boy thrilled her to such an extent that, whereas her initial anger had advised her to throw him out of her room, she found her longing for him increasing until, for a taste of his sex, she would have been willing to offer him a Jaguar.

"Rick!" she cried, "I beg you. Love me, darling."

Despite her pleas, he continued his juicy finger fucking, spreading her deliciously wet quim even wider with every withdrawal and return of his fingers. With an adept thumb, he began to massage her aching clitoris, which affected Bella so delightfully that she was suddenly writhing wildly beneath his touch.

"Oh, love my clit," she cried. "Love my clit with your tongue. Lick my cunt, please darling."

He continued to finger fuck her wet pussyhole with his finger forming a V, while dropping his head to the very top of her cunt to find her swelling, engorged clitoris with his mouth. He placed his lips just above the bud and kissed it, very lightly, until Bella was weak with wild, untamed desire.

"Oh, baby, that's so good, the way you kiss me there," she cooed. "Now suck me, please, I beg you, suck me."

Rick took the bulging bud into his warm wet mouth and sucked softly first and then more fiercely, until he could feel Bella wiggling so wildly that his fingers nearly slipped from her cunt. He shoved them in harder, and faster, as he sucked her with all his strength, until he could tell by her uncontrollably wobbling thighs and gyrating bottom that his fingers would soon be filled with her creamy love dew. He decided he wanted her to have her first cunt explosion with his cock buried deep inside her.

He advanced his phallus until its tip was within the V of his fingers, and, as his hands retreated, his genitals gained ground. His hands went up to her face, and she smelled her own vaginal oil. Holding her head tight, he kissed her passionately. Her response to his kiss was so ardent that his penis lost contact with her sleeve of iniquity; but the kiss continued until they were both breathless, at which moment the helmet of his scarlet knight found again the portal of her cunt castle. He rode into her, and she rose to meet him. His invasion of her was utter, taking him so deep that the upward crotch ground its hairs fiercely into the beard of his descending fork. He went into her and he came out of her with the ruthless strength of a man who was too drunk to estimate how rough such aggression could be to a woman. Fortunately for him, however, Bella's great need of him at that moment so lubricated her that she was immune to any roughness. Consequently, far from inconveniencing her, it delighted her. The flames within her rose higher and higher. She felt her first orgasm coming when suddenly Rick, too excited and inebriated to discipline the rise of seminal fluid in his pipe, hurled into her jet after jet, the first of which sprang forth just as he was reaching the end of a powerful thrust. He was given no notice. All seemed to be going well, and he was rejoicing in his total possession of this fine, fastidious lady, who would not forget hurriedly that she had not been seduced. It was delicious; she was delicious; and delicious too was the fact that she was the easiest lay he had ever had. She had never had it so good, and that was going to cost her money. He was riding her; he was riding a winner; and he was a jockey who had never had cause to question his own skill until that terrible moment when his mount had taken the bit between her teeth, and run away with him. If any blame attached to Bella, it lay in the fact that the heat of her lust caused Rick to boil over too quickly. He had drunk too much, for a great factor in the fiasco of their first copulation was that she had made herself excessively easy to get, with the result that an inordinate sense of his own seductive powers had temporarily robbed him of his professional skill as a lover. Overexcited, he had battered her sex with an enthusiasm which not only brought him prematurely to a climax which was a disappointment to him; but it also left him so weak that, for the moment the first globules of cream shot out of him, he simply lay on her, all further jerkings of his softened sex being involuntary, like the postmortem spasms of a pig in a slaughterhouse. He had not the energy or the will to help his mistress to attain her moment of ecstasy, nor had his phallus the rigidity which would have permitted of her using it as an object against which to bring herself off. She was left in mid-air, her body and her heart aching and full of frustrated yearning.

She was tempted to put her own hand between her hungry legs and massage her aching clitoris until it exploded under her own touch. She could pretend it was Rick's mouth, sucking her until the jism squirted out. Or she could pretend it was Rick's finger rubbing her engorged button so as to finish her pleasure. Or she could fantasize that his cock was big and strong and hard enough again to invade her insides with as much passion as before and bring her off into sexual oblivion. Thoughts of coming again gave her a thrilling feeling in the pit of her stomach.

She spread her silky thighs and touched the sweet bud for a moment, rubbing the hardened gland very lightly. She brought a finger to her lips and wet it, then brought the same finger down upon her cunt and proceeded to masturbate while her new lover still lay upon her. Her cunt was ablaze with an even more intense fire. She needed more!

She rolled him off and lay him on the bed, and straddled his thigh, pressing her spread open cunt lips upon his flesh. There, she rubbed and maneuvered herself until a small shriek escaped from her throat and the warm jism fell onto Rick's leg. She had made herself come without the benefit of his cock.

She rolled off him, lay beside him and let his limp cock rest against her leg.

Afterwards, Rick did not sleep. He was too wretched for that; but he rested, using Bella as a cushion. Her anger and frustration about his not fucking her into that last orgasm slowly subsided. In repose he was so pretty and defenseless. Neglected by his wicked wife, he had wanted and needed Bella so urgently that he had fallen into brief disgrace; but she would give him another chance, provided he took manfully whatever punishment she was able to devise for him.

Against her thigh his manhood stirred, stiffened and grew. The moment was approaching when he would be able to give himself to her again. His grip on her tightened, and he kissed her. Thrilled by his tongue's invasion of her mouth and by the renewed strength in his hands, she was ready to open her legs to him; but she was even more determined to teach him a lesson. She waited until he was indisputably awake before saying, "You must go now, darling."

"Go?"

"Yes, dear! Go."

The wine fumes were still in his head. He was being required to use his reasoning powers too much. Go?

"But...the night is young, and you're so...so...desirable. I sort of made a bit of an ass of myself; but, you'll see...it'll be different this time."

His hands sought to convince her, but she drew back from him, pushing him away from her.

"Be a good boy, darling!" she suggested.

Unable to hide his pique, he scowled at her.

"Listen, honey! I asked you to make love to me; and you did just that...and quite nicely too; so you'll have to love me again; but you must understand that I can't tolerate messiness, disorder and that sort of thing. I order my life intelligently, and I expect my friends to do likewise...to organize their lives properly and to respect my love of a planned way of civilized living."

"I only want to spend the whole night having a ball with you."

She kissed him tenderly and whispered, "I would like nothing better than a night with you that was all balls, my darling; but tomorrow is my last day in Paris; and I must buy a new dress from Pierre, and have my hair done by René. From now on, honey, my

pussy hairs are your business, but nobody arranges
the hair on my head like René, and in London you
have to go on your hands and knees for the privilege
of joining the queue of titled ladies and film actresses
who hope he'll be able to spare them an hour. All in
all, lover-boy, I've a heavy day ahead of me; and I'm
not the slovenly sort who lives for tonight, and then
goes out tomorrow looking like an overworked
whore. We've been on the go all day, and we've dined
not wisely, but too well. You've proved your love for
me, and now we're going to have eight hours sleep."

"Why can't we have eight hours sleep together? I
promise I'll leave you in peace."

"If you promise to do that, my sweet boy, I know
you'll do your best to let me sleep tranquilly; but I've
just tasted you, and I like it. Now, knowing me better
than you do, I don't trust me as much as I trust you.
You stay here, and you'll love me a little bit more,
then a lot, tonight; and I shall go to my very good
friends Pierre and René looking like what I suppose I
really am...a tramp, honey. Anyway, tomorrow
evening, after going our separate ways all day, I'd
like you to take me to the Monseigneur...getting into
the mood for a night of love by dancing to the
Hungarian orchestra...thirty fiddles tearing at your
heartstrings, and whipping us both into an erotic
madness! I want to dance...with you...until dawn
breaks, the working-people leave their homes and
the air around Les Halles is heavy with the aroma of
onion soup; and I'll pay for the rest, if you'll treat me
to a bowl of early-morning soup. After that we'll
sleep and make love until long after midday. We'll
have late lunch either here or à la Quetsche, rue des
Capucines. It's fun there...either sitting at a sort of
counter on the ground floor...all glass and erotic
things to eat and drink...or upstairs, in the restaurant

proper, surrounded by people of every imaginable nationality...*spécialités de la cuisine alsacienne.* Then, darling, a stroll along the quais, another hour of loving either here or at your place; Orly North and the night-flight to London, another wicked night in the Regent Palace Hotel, and then we shall have our next meeting to look forward to...perhaps in Ladbury the next time you have a few days or weeks to spare."

She made it all sound so attractive that Rick decided against expressing even the slightest objection to her program. Before him were three exciting days which were going to cost him two plates of onion soup; and beyond that he had just received what sounded like a standing invitation to Bella's home. It would be time enough to figure out how he could exploit Bella and her prosperous husband once he had infiltrated their home, but he did not doubt for one moment that they would be of value to him in one way or another, even though they might do for him no more than to bring him into contact with other people belonging to their own financial and social class.

He kissed Bella tenderly, and left her room quietly, after agreeing to call for her at eight o'clock the following evening.

III.

Throughout the following day Rick thought of the evening, when he intended being so punctual that he and Bella would have time for a session of fornication before she put the final touches to her preparations for going out. After wandering happily around Saint Germain des Prés during the afternoon, he returned to his hotel at about six o'clock. He bathed, dressed with care, perfumed himself, and set off at a leisurely pace for Place de l'Opéra. He arrived at her hotel too early; and, fearing he would anger her if he arrived before she wished him to, he sat on the terrace of the Café de la Paix. Determined to remain sober and to conduct himself with the acumen of a professional, he ordered coffee, which he made last until a quarter to eight. Then he went up to Room 109, knocked on the door, and went in.

"Darling!" she cried, running into his arms, "like a true gentleman you're really on time; and just in time to zip me up the back. No, darling! Don't kiss me now! You'll muss up my face, and I worked hard to make it young and beautiful for you."

If kissing his paramour was going to spoil her makeup, there was, thought Rick, little chance that she would let him pour sperm into the chasm between her loins; and he had been counting on beginning their evening with half an hour of the sort of loving which would wash out of her vagina and out of her mind the memory of his premature ejaculation of the previous evening. He hoped to excite her by holding her tight, allowing his hands to wander impertinently all over her; but, the moment he tried to enter her bodice, for the purpose of touching her breasts, she said, "Darling, I want you to be a good boy, and not to ruin the good impression you made by arriving on time just when I want to get away from here early. Zip me up the back, and we'll have a whole lot of fun and games when we come back in the wee hours of the morning. You see, honey, I phoned our new artist friend, Dane, this afternoon and he's going to be at the Dôme in Montparnasse at eight-thirty, to have dinner with us before you and I go to the Monseigneur. Zip, lover-man!"

Too peeved to play his professional role to the hilt, Rick turned greenly pale, perspired profusely, and stammered, "If that digger's taking you out, you won't need me."

Bella turned to face him, placed a hand on each of his cheeks, and touched his lips very gently with hers. Her tongue was like a naughty little serpent, inviting his to play the love game. When he tried to convert their sweetly obscene kiss into a more aggressive one, she withdrew her mouth from his, and whispered, "My darling Rick, your anger is the nicest compliment any boy ever gave me. Your jealousy proves that you really love me after only two days. Thank you, darling! I'll ring the Dôme, and have them tell Dane we can't make it."

Her words having convinced him that she imagined herself in love with him, Rick decided to win an even greater share of her affection by showing her how magnanimous he could be. He would not only take her to dinner with Mollison, but he would offer her the Australian artist on a silver platter. A painter with all Paris to choose from might make an almost middle-aged provincial English lady an exciting partner for an hour of carnal love in an attic studio, but he would have better things to do with his talents than to waste them on Ladbury. He would sell her a painting, vouchsafe her two or three orgasms, throw her back into Rick's servile arms, and invite them both to call again whenever they wanted to enrich their collection of works of art. Bella would enjoy the little adventure, and she would be eternally grateful to the man who had acted as her guardian-angel while she was engaging in bohemian debauch. She and Dane were on the verge of submitting Rick to a humiliation which the wily Englishman would know how to turn to his financial advantage. If there is no other way of buttering one's bread, there is nevertheless blackmail.

He placed a restraining hand on her bare shoulder, and said gaily, "Let me zip your zipper, princess. You're not going to tinkle the jolly old Dôme, because you're looking like a million dollars, and I'm just a-rarin' to show you off to this paintin' hombre."

As excited as a child with a new toy which had initially been denied her, she exclaimed, "Rickie, you're the best! There's not another man on this lousy earth who understand a woman the way you do. You'll never regret humoring this silly girl. Zip me!"

He zipped her, and they went down to take a cab

at the junction of Boulevard des Capucines and Avenue de l'Opéra. Over a simple, bosom-revealing, backless black cocktail-dress she wore a short coat of dark fur. René had done her proud, for her long hair was a cascade of highly-polished jet against which her skillfully creamed, powdered, painted and lipsticked face shone with the pale transparency of a seductive Madonna. In the cab they held hands, and he knew she expected much of the evening and night ahead. He would give her all she wanted, and the bill would be heavy on her purse.

Dane was drinking an apéritif on the terrace of the Dôme. The mere fact of his remaining seated until Bella and Rick actually reached his table (although Bella knew he had seen them step out of the taxi) testified to his refusal or inability to prostitute himself. There was not so much as a trace of impoliteness or arrogance in his rising nonchalantly only at the very last moment. On the contrary, Bella was thrilled by the worldly self-confidence of this incorruptible artist, who was willing modestly to sell a painting, provided no attempt were made to buy his body, his soul or his pride in his work.

Rick so enjoyed the céleri remoulade with Burgogne, rognons flambés with a couple of glasses of Pontet Canet, a little bleu de Bresse with a further glass of the same red wine, black coffee and a mouthful of Grand Marnier that, if he noticed that his companions were warming each other, he did not object. Dane ate copiously, nor was he unduly sparing with the wine; and Bella attacked her food almost like a normal person. She also drank three glasses of wine. Consequently it was a gay dinner-party, after which Dane surprised Rick (but not Bella) by suggesting a visit to his studio. Rick tried (unconvincingly) to pay the bill, but Bella was not the sort of girl who would allow one man to buy her the right to lie on another man's bed. She settled it herself.

Within five minutes the three of them entered Dane's second floor studio—a square room of unplastered bricks, painted a dark blue-grey color. Dane took Bella's coat and Rick's into a adjoining room, his workroom being so crowded with new canvases, half-finished and finished pictures and all the tools of the artist's trade that it really was not a fit place into which to bring respectably dressed people. When he returned, Bella was already pointing out to Rick the virtues and shortcomings of the visible pictures. Dane poured three generous glasses of calvados, which they sipped while he showed them the forty or fifty paintings from which a choice would be made for his forthcoming exhibition. That Rick was the wallflower at the dance was due partly to his abysmal ignorance in matters cultural, but more to the fact that his companions were unwilling to allow his presence to interfere with the rapid development of their relationship. Scarcely a moment passed without one of them touching the other in some way or other, and neither addressed a remark directly to the gigolo.

There remained at least a dozen paintings to be seen, when Dane asked Bella, "Have you see enough? The rest are all treatments of subjects I've already shown you, but in different light and seen from varying angles."

Bella answered, "I'd like to stop there, if you won't think it indicates a lack of interest. I'm afraid that, if I see much more, I shall get all confused. What I suggest is that you invite Rick to help himself to another glass of your exciting apple brandy, while you take me through to your bedroom."

If her bluntness surprised him, Dane played it real

cool. As though such propositions were everyday events, he said, "Yeah, Rick, you hit the bottle, boy, and wait for us here."

Bella placed a hand on each of Rick's shoulders, murmuring, "You don't mind, darling? You won't run away?"

Peevishly Rick replied to the effect that he saw no point in his hanging around, in view of the fact that they obviously wanted to spend a few undisturbed hours together. Bella, however, insisted that she would not be away a few hours, that he had brought her to Montparnasse, and he would be the one who took her home and spent the night with her.

"...and to be quite sure you don't run away," she added, "your coat is in there, and it stays there until I come out."

She kissed him with tender warmth, prior to hastening to join Dane in his bedroom. He had put on the light, which she turned out as she passed the switch. Dane flooded the room with light again, and Rick heard him say, "I like to see what I'm buying. No pig in a poke for this man!"

Bella retorted gaily, "You're not buying me, and I'm no pig...just a hot bitch...hot for you at this moment."

There was a brief silence, which was agony for Rick, who noticed that all Bella's endeavors to close the door had failed, age having so warped the wood that the door swung a hand's breath open the moment one released the handle. Full glass of liquor in hand, Rick approached the door stealthily, grateful to Dane for having insisted on the bedroom being ablaze with light. The door was open just enough to permit of the peeping Tom's seeing about half the bed and the room's occupants, who were standing close to it. Dane had taken off the jacket of his Bond

Street suit, and Rick noticed how sturdy his rival was under a shirt of brilliant whiteness. The powerful arms of the Australian held Bella in such a way as to suggest that he intended tolerating no nonsense from her. As long as she realized who was the boss, she would have a good time; and there was no doubting the fact that Bella knew she was dealing with a real man, to whom she had given the right to play the dominant role in their relationship. Rick had been forbidden to smudge her make-up or crush her dress, but Dane was greedily sucking the lipstick from her crazy, savage mouth, while his usually gentle hands clutched at the material of her dress as though he intended to reduce it to shreds.

Bella was bent backwards, almost lying in his arms; and one of his thighs was so well ensconced between hers that her narrow skirt was bunched up above her hips. He was not kissing her. He was devouring her, and she was enjoying it, twisting and turning ecstatically, grinding the important part of her anatomy against the corresponding portion of his. Rick heard the dry sound of the opening of the zipper of her dress, and he saw Dane release his grip on her waist and head. Bella stood waiting, submissive. Dane's hands went behind her back, and tugged the bodice of her dress forward and downward, revealing a vermilion bra and a pale midriff. He stepped back a pace, to allow her to ease her outer garment down her slim shanks. She loved that little black dress, which she had bought that very day from Pierre, but, as one in a trance, she left it on the floor. Stepping out of the dress she toed it disdainfully to one side, and stood before her master like a red and white flame. In addition to her bra she was wearing nothing but a tiny triangle of red silk, masquerading as a pair of panties, a garter belt of the same hue, flesh-tinted stockings and black spiked heels. She was seduction personified and as close an approach to bodily perfection as either of the two men had ever seen. She was looking her best at that moment; and, even on an off-day, Bella resembled a thirty-year-old woman with the body of a girl of twenty.

Her slim arms disappeared behind her back, her bra fell, and Dane beheld the breathtaking loveliness of her naked breasts...firm, proud, provocative, like two snowy doves. She observed the effect of her beauty on her host, and her green eyes shone victoriously. He hurled himself at her, and she fell back on the bed, cradling him in her hands and between her parted thighs. His kiss toothed, tongued and lipped her mouth, descended to her bosom, and gnawed her hard buds. Her groans were like the coughing of a mare in a smoke-filled stable. She held his head close, closer and closer than close to her anguished breasts, and uttered his name several times. "You're a great Dane," she groaned. She knew he was, and she longed for him to be; and she longed for him. There was neither hiding nor gainsaying her yearning. She desired a lust-racked man, and sparks flew in all directions. Breathless, she broke from his sweltering embrace. Her febrile hands yanked his tie from the collar of his shirt, whose buttons melted in the erotic heat of her fingers. Excited as she was, Bella was so conversant with the grab of men that the negotiation of the zipper fly of his pants represented no problem for her. The urgency of her need of his loins enabled her to bare them in double-quick time. He slipped off one shoe with the other, so that her passing his trousers over his stockinged feet presented no difficulties. Her stripping of the fruit she was eager to get her fangs into was a prodigious feat; and what fruit! Bella had been had by men and boys of every conceivable shape and size, but even Jorge (being too prettily beautiful) faded into insignificance alongside the tall, slenderly muscular, masculine, hard Dane Mollison, whose walnut-brown rod had both length and breadth. He was as handsome a man as she was a dainty morsel of femininity; but there was a fly in the ointment. Dane was undraped, while Bella's intrinsic garments still clung to her, scorching her loins and injuring her feminine pride.

"Un-pant me!" she cried. "Tongue my stockingless feet! Worship me as I worship you, with heart, soul and aching body! Adore my flesh; explore my secret flesh! Worship my woman! Dog me, like an animal in heat."

Deftly she freed her stocking-tops from the rubber jaws of her garters, and rolled her nylon hose down to her heels, under the soles of her feet and away. His hands went to the waist of her panties, and then descended with the silken triangle and her garter belt. He beheld her naked, and she was proud of the wild flashing of his eyes, as they concentrated their gaze on the hair-covered place where the inner side of the top of her slim, white thighs ran into the lower portion of her trunk. Lying on her back, waiting, she touched the mouth of her vagina with the index fingers of both her hands and she spread open the sweet pink meat between her legs, ever so slightly. She was ready. He could enter her, whenever he so wished, without any preparations. Opening herself wider and invitingly, she bestowed upon him a smile which was distorted by her impatience. Her cunt glistened with excitement, with wetness, as she held it open to his view. One of her wet hands reached for his weapon, upon which she took so firm a grip that, when she tried to draw him nearer to her loins, he did not resist, for fear that she would tear his penis off. His right hand went to her sex, and two fingers went into her, casually feeling her, fingering her, to be sure that she was greasy and warm enough not to graze the skin off his precious tool. Then he seized a pillow and a bolster, which he thrust under her rear, raising her crotch until her genitals were a sitting duck waiting to be speared. The lips of her nether mouth shone rosily through the dark beard of her mound of Venus. A sweet musky cunt scent rose from between her milky thighs. His phallus had grown to such a length and breadth as would fill any normal woman with high hopes. Certainly Bella expected great things of him; and he did not want to disappoint her.

He raised her legs unceremoniously, tied them in an ankle-knot behind his powerful rump, and plowed into her softest meat with his relentless prick. A loud cry broke from her throat, but it was not so much a cry of pain as of incredulous joy. She had observed that her nakedness, her wanton openness and the imminence of her becoming his thing had inflated his sex to admirable proportions; but the size of it within her surprised her nonetheless. He filled her cavity, in depth as well as in breath. His first thrust took him so deep into her that he had nothing more to offer her. He was packed into her as tight and as far as could be, and the yearning caress of her muscled pit so thrilled him that, inside her, he continued to swell, to harden and to get hotter. He pulled back, almost out of her, and her over-oiled tube registered its protest by uttering a rude sound. His sinking into her again was effortless, but, buried in her intimate flesh until his scrotum fondled her arse, he moved forward and upward slowly and strongly, increasing the contact between their respective sex organs until she thought their bodies were one creature. He pulled out again, completely this time. She groaned, and reached for him, to draw him onto and into her again; but her gesture was superfluous, for he was already poised for a new incision of her weeping wound. He flashed into her, and out, and in, and out. Ten, twenty, thirty times he flew into her, jerked quickly back, and plunged in again, the speed of his movements never robbing his thrust of depth. Every jab went to the depth of her, jolting her defenseless body upward and backward. Her legs hugged his posterior, holding him lovingly, and her arms held his torso with a similar ardor.

Her loins quivering added to her excitement and his. She felt that she was really being done, had, possessed, used. Never before had she felt herself so utterly the property of a man. She had given herself to him without ceremony or finesse; and he was doing no more than she had given him the right to do. He was laying her, dominating her, taming her, having his selfish, masculine fun with her, with all the lights brightly burning, and her lover on the other side of the open door, witnessing her humiliation with his ears and almost certainly with his eyes too. The temperature rose, as did also the volume of Dane's savage grunts and Bella's sighs of ecstatic shame as his pole thrashed her. Large as his phallus was, her pleasure had so widened her erotic passage that his rapid probings scarcely did more than to flick her flesh as he whipped in and out; and that roused her passions even more than had the tightly packed copulation of the first minute or two. What really broke her down, however, was an involuntary change of tempo on his part. He had been giving it to her more vigorously than any normal man could for more than a few seconds, and suddenly he had to slow down; and it was the unexpected languor in his movements which brought her to a second of ecstasy filled pain, followed by the bursting of the dam at the heart of her guts. Open-mouthed, she uttered a series of high-pitched squeals, each accompanied by a shivering twitch of her nether parts. The music was too sweet for Dane, who had been holding on to his muck for some time. It flew out of him, and he was as one paralyzed for a second or two, after which his reduced member continued its tender stroking of her grateful pipe. He lay on her, kissed her mouth, fondled her face, her shoulders, breasts, buttocks and thighs. He leaned backward, and held her upright, so that she could see how total was his possession of her. He was as gentle with her as any adolescent boy who does not yet know that his little sweetheart is going to let him put his hand inside her pants.

His lips, his tongue, arms and hands loved her, while his manhood delicately moved in and out of her lady. He grew within her, stiffening and regaining his former cockiness; and her belly, enjoying his weight, undulated gently to get nearer to his essence. His pubic mound pressed against her clitoris as they fucked; he rocked back and forth and rubbed against her to stimulate the tiny joy bud. Thus they went up and up until Dane's cream went out to her a second time as he rubbed his erupting engine against her swelling cunt lips and clit; it triggered off another delicious orgasm for her. Neither his climax nor hers was as searing as the first, but their coming off almost together was sweet and friendly. They kissed at great length until Bella whispered sleepily, "Take that dirty little devil out of my pocket! Rick'll be cursing like mad."

Making no move to obey her, Dane said, "If he were the cursing type, he wouldn't have let us do this. Stay the night with me. He can sleep in the studio next door. Belongs to one of my buddies, and he left me with the key."

Professional Charmer

Rick grew to be ten feet tall as he heard Bella answer, "He's spending the night in no lonely studio, but in my arms and in my lap, reaping the harvest from the fertile seed you've just sown in me. It was great, Dane. If Rick approves, you must come over to Ladbury, and give me some more. You certainly can fuck."

"I dig you. Bella, you can't just go off like this, leaving me to sleep alone. We just had us a ball, but there's firecrackers to come."

"Rick's going to come, Dane, and he's going to come in my belly from the time we get home to tomorrow lunchtime; and, if it's tough on you, having to sleep alone, at least I leave behind me the smell of our sweat and our come. Rick's got it coming to him. You're a loving lover, lover; but I shall never again find a lover like Rick. Greater love hath no man than he who gives his own doxy to a perfect stranger. He'll never regret what he's done for me this evening. I really mean it when I say I'd like you to go over and meet Harry, and give me some more of your loving loving, lover; but Rick'll have to approve or it's no go. Now, take your nice worm out of my body, and I'll mouth the muck off him!"

It was Dane's turn to sulk. He rose to his feet, dried his dripping genitals on Bella's scarlet panties, and started to dress before she grasped that he did not want to be sucked. She got up, put on her garter belt, stockings, shoes, dress and fur jacket, tucked her bra in the pocket of Rick's coat and left the bedroom together with Dane. Rick was innocently pouring himself a glass of liquor. She took the glass, poured some into her mouth, kissed him, and squirted the liquid down his throat. She stayed in his arms, kissing him passionately, and tacitly begging his forgiveness for her infidelity. He held her close, rejoicing in the knowledge that his caviar would be served with champagne for some time to come. She freed herself from his embrace after a tender minute, and placed her head on Dane's breasts, murmuring, "If I pay you now, with a sterling cheque, will you have 'le Lapin Agile' delivered to Orly before nine-o'clock tomorrow evening?"

He hugged her, in a brotherly way, smiled sincerely at Rick, and answered, "Of course I will. Can you convert the price into pounds?"

"I want twenty percent."

"No sale!"

Slowly, deliberately and menacingly, she repeated, "Dane, I want twenty percent."

Dane made a present of her to Rick.

"Take her away," he joked, "before I twenty percent her!"

"Dane, you're a parsimonious bastard."

"And you're an over-rich, spoiled, money-worshipping bastard, who strips like a porcelain goddess and gives more generously than the Salvation Army. I love you, and I shall be over at Ladbury the first chance I get. Do you want this picture or not?"

"I just let you have it cheap, on the bed. What more do you want? You know the price. Pay it or it's no sale."

"You know I do; but I shall never be happy with it, unless you let me have it cheap."

"Bah!" she snapped, genuinely upset. She signed a check for one hundred and thirty-nine pounds, and handed it to him.

"Why not a hundred and forty?" he asked, handing the slip of paper back to her.

"I'm charging you a pound for the ride I just gave you."

"No takers at that price!" replied Dane, laughing.

He put his arms about her, kneaded her breasts through the stuff of her frock, and kissed her lasciviously. She broke from his grasp, and turned to look at Rick, who was obviously impatient to separate her from her newest lover. She moved across to him, and took his hand in his. With her back to Dane, she called, "You will make sure the painting is well packed when you have it delivered to Orly before nine tomorrow evening, Dane?"

He moved closer to her, fondled her bottom, and said, "Unless you give me either a pound or fifteen francs, there'll be no painting at Orly tomorrow evening."

"You cheap, fornicating crook! Just you try to cash that check! I'll have you behind bars so quickly that your feet won't have time to touch the courtroom floor."

She winked at Rick, who drew her close, and kissed her warmly. Dane stood behind her, his front so close to her back that she could feel the bulge of his desire against her bum. His hands held her waist, caressed her strongly up to her armpits, and then moved to her breasts. She broke the contact between her torso and Rick's, to allow Dane to get his fingers around her breasts, and then she pressed herself as close as possible to the English boy, pinning the Australian's hands between her body and Rick's. She had a male hand on each of her shoulders, an excited penis nudging her rear, and another trembling against the lower reach of her belly.

"I love you both," she sighed, "Just like this...my favorite up my front, and my number two up my back. Hold me tight, my darlings! Hold me here! No! Take me back in there, and love me until lunchtime!"

She seized Rick's head in her hot, trembling

hands, stuck her tongue crudely in his mouth, and jerked her loins against his. The same movement caused her little posterior to rap Dane's ready sex. After a long kiss, she said to Rick, "You'll take me real, eh, honey? While Dane uses the tradesmen's entrance? If you'd rather go back to my hotel, and have me all to yourself, we'll take a taxi right away."

Before Rick had time to answer, Dane unzipped her dress, pulled her out of her favorite's arms, picked her up, nodded imperiously to Rick, and carried her into the bedroom. She cried out for Rick to rescue her from the rapist; but she made no attempts to deny Dane the passionate kiss he stole from her eager mouth; and it was he who stripped her, handing her pretty garments one by one to Rick; but he relinquished her, naked, to the gigolo, who crushed his lips against those which Dane had so recently kissed. Seeing that the manlier man was almost undressed, Bella advised Rick to follow the other's example; she made such a fuss of Dane that the effeminate blond was bare before his rival had removed his pants. Returning to the arms of her most treasured one, she eased him down onto the bed. He lay on his back, his pole reaching for the ceiling. She straddled his hips, and lowered herself onto him until their respective sexes formed an erotic unit, and he felt the moisture of her vaginal lips in the hairs of his crotch. He moved his shaft up and down, by contracting the muscles of his buttocks, as her loins swayed to him and away from him. She possessed him deliciously, every fiber in his body and hers tingling with the joy of the usual roles being reversed. He was hard within her, and she was soft, warm and wet about him, her juices flowing so liberally that they both had the sensation of copulating in a bath of warm milk. The light in her eyes was paradoxically both affectionate and demoniacal. Her tight breasts were cradled in his hands, while she crouched over him like a bitch on all fours.

Dane was unclothed, and ready for the fray, but he was momentarily content to watch this amazing woman laying her girlish lover. When he eventually decided to intervene, he began by rummaging in a bedside drawer until he found a tube of sex gel, from which he squirted a one-inch worm into her anus. As the nozzle of the tube entered her rear aperture, she exclaimed, "Dane!" but she was too far gone in passion to wonder what he was sticking into her. He squeezed out another inch of lubricant against her asshole, threw down the tube, and spread the golden grease immediately around her orifice prior, rimming her tight, pink orifice before easing his lubricated index finger into her.

"Dane!" she repeated, but more languorously this time. The circle of forbidden flesh opened and closed about his finger as it moved more smoothly in and out of her.

"Dane!" she begged, and her prayer was answered. He kneeled behind her, his knees outside hers, and he pulled her buttocks apart with his thumbs. Then inching his thumbs inward, he continued to spread open the tight hole, spreading it open enough to gain access and penetrate her from behind. Then he moved closer to the kill, his hard cock anxious to visit her sweet back door entrance. The knob of his staff touched the jewel deep in the crevice between the pale globes of her tail, and she cried impatiently, "Dane! Dane!"

The following "Dane!" which exploded from her throat was a cry of agony, as a hot poker burned way several inches into her flesh. He whispe her ear, "Just let me in and it will feel so goo she began to relax her tensing sphincter muscles to let him ride inside her slightly aching, but lusty and desirous asshole. Dane pulled back, and then went into her again. He went a little further, retreated, and then pressed into her with all his strength. She almost fainted, and would certainly have collapsed on top of Rick, if Dane had not held her close to him, with his hands under her belly. He moved back and forth, deep and strong within her. The pain subsided, and Bella began to activate her rump in such a way as to heighten the contact between her and the naughty man behind her. Her excitement was such that she and Rick lost each other for an instant. He crawled out from under her, and she protested until she saw what his intentions were. He raised her to a kneeling position, and rammed his buck into her doe. As a few minutes previously, in the other room, each of the men had his head on one of her shoulders.

"That's right, my lovely boys! Now I want to be really loved."

They both went at her with fervor, and it seemed to her that two knights crossed enormous swords at the very center of her boiling body. Every particle of her being was involved in this thrilling copulation. She turned her head, to kiss Rick, and she felt Dane's teeth biting the lobe of her left ear, as his hands tortured her swollen, desire-heavy breasts. Rick's hands were at her buttocks, holding them apart so that Dane could probe her more effectively. The temperature rose until her vagina and her anus melted and flowed into each other. Rick and Dane became one incredibly large and hard phallus, which was battering her into the surrender of an orgasm. She sighed, and she called them, "My darling boys!" Hoarsely she begged them, "Make me, boys. Make me come. Let's all come together!"

She writhed against Rick's front, and Dane moved closer to her squirming back. Both men lunged into her, ground themselves against her, withdrew almost entirely, and then rhythmically sank into her again. Instinctively they timed their motions so that Bella never felt she had to waste one in order to get the full value of the other.

Suddenly Rick clung to her. "Bella!" he howled, and his joy was so intense that he sobbed as his semen shot into her, whipping her into an orgasm which broke towards the final, feeble spasms of his. When the trembling of her moment of supreme pleasure subsided, she held him gently and lovingly against her front, and whispered, "I love you, Rick. I love you, because you're good to me. Hold me, so that Dane can do my bottom proud. Love me again, Rick!"

Rick obeyed. He held her close, tonguing her mouth, and moving his reduced sexual organ lazily in and out of her drooling gash.

Dane was still strong, but the distortion of his features and the clumsy speed of his jabbing at her backside announced that the moment was imminent when his cream would fly into her, and he would cling to her limply and gratefully. At that juncture he gathered Bella to him, his left arm around her belly, and his right about her throat. His mouth was close to her left ear. He gasped, "Take it," and she did. She had no choice. He stiffened, deep within her, his belly tight against her buttocks, and he jerked into her load after load of his sweet jism. She threw her head back onto his shoulders, trying to get at his mouth without tearing him from her rear. It was not a comfortable kiss, but it was a long one, in which each expressed appreciation of the other's ardor. Dane's orgasm had been so wild that he had wrenched her from Rick's grasp, but, even while she and her sodomite lover swapped saliva, her arms reached out for the boy who had just pleasured her the natural way. Her mouth left Dane's, and went to Rick's.

Bella would gladly have started again, each man taking the other's place; but she was not the sort of woman who contents herself with anything less than the best; and she knew that both men would be of greater use to her after an hour or two of kissing and cuddling in bed, with the occasional falling off into the sleep she and they merited. She lay in the middle of the bed, with Rick on her right, and Dane on her left. As long as possible, she remained on her back, a hand on each male organ; but the longing for closer contact with one or another of them became too great. She turned to Dane, kissed him briefly and sweetly, and then snuggled up close to Rick, her mouth on his, her breasts squashed against his torso, and the moist lips of her sex couched on the front of his right thigh. Her other bed-partner moved closer, and they slept as one pile of flesh.

Toward dawn, the three awoke to a glorious morning of fucking and sucking, but this time, the men switched positions. Dane was the first to take action, gingerly parting Bella's thighs and probing her pussy with two fingers until all the stirring juices let him know she was ready for his hard cock. He lifted her onto his body and hoisted her hips over his standing penis, lowering her wet pussy onto his pole in a deliciously erotic manner, until all of him was buried deep inside her wetness. She lay her body down on his, her titties crushed to his chest as prick and pussy pushed and pressed against each other in a delicious fuck.

Before long, Rick, not permitting Dane to out-do him, was in the picture, tantalizing Bella's bumhole with the delightful tortures of his probing finger which, wet with his spit, was slipping into the rim of her asshole, then boldly swooping down to her pussy, pressing in between her and Dane's cock, and collecting more moisture for its adventures in her anal canal.

She was wild with pleasure, her cunt filled up by one man and her asshole being teased into submission by the other man. Rick was soon enough pressing his finger in deeper, fucking her asshole rather wildly, just to make sure it was nice and lubricated for his cock. Finally, he rose, maneuvered his body over Dane's stretched-out legs, while bringing his hardened cock close to Bella's asshole, and readied himself for the kill.

He used two fingers to guide his rocket to her rear opening and when the head bit its way into the path, Bella was jolted enough to jump hard onto Dane's cock. But it was not meant for her to escape the second penis, for it was soon tunneling its way toward her bowel, spreading her narrow canal in a deliciously fulfilling way. Soon, Rick had taken full possession of her ass and Dane was buried in her bush to the hilt. The two penises could feel one another against the thin sheath that separated the orifices and the combination of cock against cock, with each being sucked deeply into its respective hole, was overwhelming. The cocks were each about to burst.

Dane, sensing the nearness of the inevitable, maneuvered Bella's tits into his mouth and sucked them hard, and he pumped his cock into her pussy with great gusto, to bring along her orgasm. Within moments, Rick was panting as Bella's clenching ass began squeezing the come out of him, Dane was writhing beneath Bella as his cock began to spurt into her hole, and Bella was humping like a wild woman, gleefully taking in all of each cock as she rocked her way to a thrilling long-lasting cunt explosion.

The whole event lasted for an ecstasy-filled half hour, which seemed like forever. And when the three detached, both Bella's holes dripped with semen, so Dane and Rick both went to work on licking clean the hole each had respectively invaded; thus, the lovely and rich Bella was getting the come licked out of her cunt and her anus, by the two men who had deposited there.

Rick generously left the room to make some breakfast for the three of them. While he prepared lightly cooked omelets, coffee and toast for the threesome, Dane enjoyed Bella's full attention on his cock. She licked her own juices from the delicious rod and then went on to give him a delightful blow job, one which started by making him good and hard again, and which climaxed with yet another delicious load of Dane's jism being deposited in Bella's body—this time, her mouth. She drank it all, swallowing his seed with great delight. She sealed the moment with a kiss, slipping her sperm-tasting tongue into his warm, wet mouth. Finally, Rick brought the food in and they all enjoyed a naked breakfast together.

After the meal, Dane wanted to take Bella to bed again; but she insisted that she and Rick were going to return to their respective hotels, to bathe, change and pack, while the artist busied himself with making an easy-to-carry and open (for the customs officers) parcel of the painting she had bought from him. Dane said, "Until you pay me the pound you owe me, the painting is mine." Bella smiled at him seductively, and answered, "If you'll forgo your right to the pound, you can join Rick and me in his hotel room at about six for a farewell session of mad, passionate love, and then you can accompany us to Orly, and have dinner with us before we take off. How's that?"

Dane placed his arms about her, and kissed her tenderly, but lewdly. "If I accepted your offer," he argued, "I'd be paying you a quid for a little of what I fancy, and I hope to die without ever stooping that low. Never mix business with pleasure! That's my motto, honey; so, I accept your invitation to the bon voyage party in Rick's room and to dinner at Orly; but I shan't have the painting with me unless you give me now either a pound or fifteen francs."

She pulled his face down to hers, and placed her mouth on his. His attitude won her admiration. She knew he attached no importance to the small sum of money involved, caring only for the principle of the matter. He would neither sell himself nor buy the favors of others. It would have given her some personal satisfaction to obtain possession of the painting without paying him the twenty shillings, but she knew she had to admit defeat. Still in Dane's embrace, with her arms about his neck, she ordered Rick to give the miser fifteen francs. The English boy obeyed, but he was not happy about it.

The cab stopped at the Café de la Paix, and Bella got out, surrendering to her escort both the vehicle and the right to pay, at the door of his hotel, the whole of the fare from Montparnasse. He did not like that either, but he would get the cash back in one way or another. As the taxi moved away, Bella called, "I shall be at your place within minutes of taking a bath and packing my cases, so don't take too long about your bath and packing, sweetheart!"

When she entered his room, an hour later, all he still had to do was to dress, the clothes he intended wearing for the journey home having been left out of his suitcase. He was naked. She threw her arms around him, and asked, "Did you stay bare for me or have I come too early?"

"You could never be too early for me," he flattered her. "I've been ready ten or fifteen minutes, but I saw no reason for putting my clothes on and taking 'em off again when you arrived."

After bestowing a lascivious kiss on his open mouth, she fell to her knees, slipped the ring of her lips over the knob of his genitals, and gently sucked him for a few seconds. Then she threw back her head, looked up at him at him provocatively, and asked, "Does he want me?"

"What do you think?"

"He can have me...how and whenever he wants me. I love him, Rick, and I fear I'm falling in love with you too. Could I ever compete with Liz for a little of your love?"

He joined her on the rug, fondled her thighs under her skirts, and answered with all the conviction of a great actor, "I love you, Bella, more than I ever loved anyone in my whole life. I love you more than I love myself, more than life itself."

They kissed. His hands went to the top of her legs.

"Why, you saucy bitch!" he exclaimed. "You're not wearing panties."

An impish sparkle in her eyes, she whispered, "I thought the same as you...why put on a garment that'll soon be coming off anyway. At least, I hoped you'd soon want me to be panty-less. I'd like you to come into me now—very gently. I want to be tenderly rocked into a long orgasm, and I want you to be in me when that money-grabbing artist comes bursting in on us."

Her referring to Dane in such offensive terms was sweet music to Rick's ears, but he burrowed a little deeper into her affections by pretending such was not the case.

"You like him," he said, "I'm sure of that; and I admire your taste; but you mustn't think you have to call him names to please me. I love you, like I said, with all my heart…enough to want your happiness, even when it's bought at my expense."

She interrupted him to beg him to believe that she had not meant to humiliate him or make him jealous. "You gave him to me, darling, and I was temporarily too weak to refuse your gift. I took it without stopping to think what your noble, loving gesture was costing you; but, as I told Dane, you've proved your unselfish love for me, and I swear you'll never regret it. If you'll have me, I'll be your slave. You can do with me and with all I have whatever you wish."

Her words were a signed check which he was at a liberty to make out for the figure of his choice. He could not recall ever having registered so great a success in so short a time. She was as desirable, as erotically exciting and as sexually apt a woman as he had ever laid hands on, and he was going to be paid for plundering her lovely body. Well, he would ensure that she never had cause to complain that she handed out money and gifts in exchange for services inadequately rendered by him. He removed her dress, under which she was wearing nothing but her garter belt, which he unfastened, while she peeled off her stockings. They copulated deliciously on the rug, and had each enjoyed a series of orgasms when Dane entered without knocking. The newcomer took over from Rick, whose limp penis had shot Bella's cunt full of hot jism. Dane bent between her legs, parted her sweet pussy lips, and lavished her cunt with delightful licks and kisses while lapping the other man's come from her hole. She moaned as the artist's tongue snaked her inner sanctum. He added the excitement of pressing his thumb to her clit bud, rubbing the hard, pink pleasure spot as he licked deep inside her opening. Soon, she came in his mouth, her hips gyrating with spasm after spasm of pleasure. He dove even deeper into her drenched cunt, collecting the fresh juice of her explosion on his tongue. As the artist gamahuched her more, she pleaded with Rick to help get Dane's pants off his body, so she could suck his cock one more time. Little did she know that Rick was well versed in the matter of removing a man's pants. Rick gladly obliged, unzipping the artist's slacks, slipping them down the hips and finally removing them over his ankles. Dane did not resist, in fact, he aided the process by moving with the motion of Rick's hands. Next, Rick returned to Dane's groin for his underwear, and, carefully stretching the band enough to get them over Dane's distended cock, Rick also slipped off the underwear. Dane's bulging manhood and strong thighs were now exposed and would in moments be closer to Bella's face, but what Bella did not see was that Rick grabbed hold of the other man's cock and erotically patted and rubbed it, making it even harder, stiffer, bigger. Dane, at first startled by the sexual aggression, decided to go with the flow and relaxed as Rick leisurely played with his cock, rubbed the purple head until the first drops of jism began to escape and played with the balls.

Initially, Rick commenced this activity to startle Dane and yet suddenly found himself drawn to his rival; he found himself desiring Dane. Bella, who was busy having her pussy gamahuched by Dane, did not know that Rick's fondling had become more intense and that the reason for Dane's heavy breathing was not just due to having his mouth filled with her lovely cunt—it was from having his cock massaged by Rick. But because he so expertly licked her depraved pussy, her eyes were sealed as her moans echoed into the room, and Rick was able to briefly bend toward Dane's cock and take it in his mouth, giving him the first taste of the cock he had been intimate with in other ways during their threesome adventures.

When Bella began to stir, Rick raised his mouth from Dane's cock and Dane watched as Rick moved his body closer to Bella's. At that moment, Bella rose, and pushed Dane onto his back so he would lie flat, while she lifted her pussy over his face. She planted it firmly on his mouth while grabbing hold of his hugely excited cock. And she sucked him like there was no tomorrow.

Bella felt Dane's groans of pleasure increase, as his muffled noise vibrated through her pussy, and she smashed her hot cunt onto his flicking tongue so that he could tongue her deeper and faster. Rick, realizing the climax was near, pressed his tongue into her asshole and gave her a nice tongue fucking through the backdoor while Dane worked her over up front. Her number one lover plunged his tongue into the depth of her bowel while Dane sucked her clit with loud, slurpy motions, until come began to fly, from Dane's cock and then, her cunt.

She rolled off of Dane and lay back, with knees apart. And Rick, ever the thoughtful slut, poised between his lady's legs and licked her cunt clean of come, giving her the pleasure of more stimulation—and of knowing he cared!

Afterward, Dane rose to get some wet washcloths and towels from the bathroom. He handed one to Rick, who immediately washed Bella's loins with it. And he handed one to Bella, who reached up to clean up Dane's cock. Then Dane took hold of Rick's penis and very casually cleaned it head to balls. Bella thought nothing much of it, but Rick and Dane both smiled at one another with the knowledge of their secret touches. Soon the hot, soapy washcloths had removed all traces of the sticky encounter!

At Orly Dane insisted that they be his guests for their "au revoir" dinner. He was in high spirits. He had sold a painting to a woman who genuinely appreciated its artistic worth, he had experienced twenty-four hours of highly satisfactory sexual intercourse with the same woman and her lover, and he had a standing invitation to visit her home whenever the fancy took him. Bella was a radiantly happy woman in the company of two men who had devoted much time and energy to pandering to her erotic cravings; and Rick had the world on a string. He had spent in Paris (first with Jorge and then with Bella) a fortnight which had cost him less than five pounds. He was going home with his suitcase heavier and of greater value than when he had arrived in France; his travelling companion was so infatuated by him that he was sure he would soon be living at her expense; and he was feeling sexually replete. Is it, therefore, any wonder that their dinner party was a gay one? They ate and drank of the best the restaurant at Orly had to offer, and they chatted gaily about their shared joys of the past twenty-fours hours and the night of love which Rick and Bella had ahead of them in London.

Dane took a cab to town as soon as the other two answered the call to embark; and he fell almost into oblivion the moment he was out of sight. Bella had her lover, and Rick had his wealthy client. In the plane they kissed and cuddled like a couple of love-sick adolescents, and they continued thus in the bus which took them to West London Air Terminal and in the taxi in which they accomplished the remainder of their journey to the Regent Palace Hotel just off Piccadilly Circus.

Wishing to be fresh and alert when she was with Harry the following day, Bella insisted on limiting their love-making to two sessions, one before going to sleep and another immediately prior to leaving the hotel.

As they parted, at Victoria Station, Bella, with tears in her eyes, said, "May I count on you, darling? Give your boss notice first thing in the morning! Come to us, ostensibly for a long weekend, and make it clear that you happened to be in London, attending an interview for a job, which you've refused because the salary was scarcely higher than what you were getting in the job you've just left. I shall already have spoken to Harry about you, how nice, generous, considerate and sensitive you are, and about your talents being thrown away on a job which pays you little more than six hundred a year. I know he'll take to you at once. I doubt whether anyone could resist your simple, honest charm; and he'll find something for you. We know everybody of any interest in and around Ladbury, so Harry will soon fix you up with something."

Rick kissed her gratefully, told her she was too good for and to him, and promised to be at her home two Saturdays later. Her train chugged lazily into motion, and the two lovers waved to each other long after either was visible to the other.

In the train from King's Cross to Hull, Rick had lunch as the guest of a middle-aged schoolmaster and his sister, to whom he had recounted his tale of woe after helping them with their very light luggage.

A week after he gave a fortnight's notice to his employers, Rick was entrusted with the task of train-

ing his successor, the pretty, self-confident daughter
of one of the manager's closest friends. The girl was
so impressed by her tutor's eagerness to help her in
every possible way that she repeated to her parents
the heart-rending account Rick had given her of his
wife's inability to cooperate with him in the founding
of a real home and a family. Moved to compassion,
the girl's mother suggested that they express their
appreciation of Rick's kindness to Brenda by inviting
him to dinner that evening. The result was that, during his final four days in Hull, Rick almost lived with
Brenda and her parents. His success was such that he
almost regretted having to leave Hull. Before the end
of the week he reached the kiss-and-cuddle stage
with the chaste Brenda, who extracted from him the
promise that he would write often and return to her
whenever circumstances permitted.

Eventually Rick travelled from Hull to London,
not by train and at his own expense, but by a sleek,
black Daimler driven by Brenda's father, with Mama
at his side. In the back of the car Brenda and Rick
necked as though her parents were at the other end
of the world.

Brenda and her parents spent the weekend in the
big city, while poor old Rick, after a free meal at La
Casa Pepe in Soho, bravely ventured into the wilds of
Ladbury.

IV..

Bella's lips were motionless against Rick's. Only her tongue moved, its tip flicking the extremity of his. They were both bare, lying on her sun-drenched bed after a half-hour of fornication.

"Ricky!" she gasped, "you really loved me there. It was delicious. Why don't you do me more often? Sometimes you have me wondering whom you came here for...Harry or me."

"But, darling," he replied, "I've got to be nice to Hank. What else does he pay me twenty a week for? After all, it was your idea that he should take me on as his secretary, instead of getting me a job with one of his pals."

"Rick," she moaned, "I need what you just gave me. I need it all the time. That's why I wheedled Harry into keeping you in the house; but what do you and he do all the time? What do you find to keep you busy for hours on end, while poor little Bella lies here, frigging her clit? You and he may be making fortunes together; but who wants to be a millionaire?

I don't if it means spending lonely hours while you rugged males coin money."

With a look of sadness on his pale face, Rick answered, "I'm not coining money, and it's not me who decides when, where and how I shall work. Hank's the boss, so I'm free when he tells me I am. He's a good boss, and I like him as a person."

"A good job for your too! I'm a bitch...I know that...a high-class tramp...but I wouldn't allow even you to spend another night under this roof, if you didn't get on well with Harry. Without ever having known anything definite about my conduct in his absence, he's always allowed me to go my own way, and I've cuckolded him almost from the day we married. I don't know how he behaves when we're separated; and, although I'd like to know more, I'm not so stupid that I'd be offended to learn that he's as unfaithful as I am; but of one thing you may be sure: I shall never allow any of my fancy-boys to sneer at Harry; and I shall never expect Harry to entertain a lover of mine whom he doesn't like."

Rick ran a sweaty hand over her cool belly, and lisped, "Well, what are you worrying about then? Harry and I get along together like a house on fire. I admire him tremendously. I mean, he's sort of got everything, don't you think? Looks, personality, dress sense, poise, culture, intelligence—and what a businessman!"

"He took to you, like I did, the moment he set eyes on you. What puzzles me though, dick-boy, is this: Harry often said he needed help with the management of his estate and that sort of thing; but we used to laugh at him, and he was as amused as any of us. I thought I could exploit this little joke to sell you to Harry; but I never thought you and he would find work to do together. Before you came he phoned

New York, Geneva and London once or twice a day, and he occasionally toddled off to the States or the Continent for a few days or a couple of weeks; but, now that he has my Rick to help him, he seems to be frantically busy from morn till night, and poor little Bella hardly sees either of you. The way I saw things, he'd keep dashing away to London, Stockholm and Buenos Aires, leaving you to hold the fort here; and then we'd have a few nights together. Do you realize you haven't slept with me since London? Darling, don't think I don't like sleeping with Harry! He's the greatest; but I don't eat pheasant three-sixty-five days a year. I wake up in your arms once in a while. I want you to love me into a coma, and I want to drift you on the gentle ripples of a tropic stream of spent passions. I love you, Rick. God knows I want you. Love me some more; make me!"

"But...er...Bella...he told me to be at Levine's by three, and it's half past two now."

"All right! I'm not going to kneel to you. Take the Mercedes, and you'll be on time! Harry will give you full marks. My feelings don't count."

He kissed her with feigned passion, and said, "You and your feelings count with me for more than all the Harrys, Levines and Ricks in the whole wide world."

"Love me then!"

He loved her briefly but competently; and then hastened into his clothing .

Bella subsided into a troubled sleep, while her sleek, black Mercedes-Benz hurtled along in the direction of the home of Mendel and Ida Levine.

Rick drove with the brio of one who is too canny to buy an automobile. He braked at the entrance of the Levines' palace in the sort of sandy cloud which set Ida's pulse racing. Mendel worked hard to earn the money with which to purchase the latest Jaguar.

Consequently he treated his car with respect. His lovely sister, however, would have gladly traded all the industrious, shrewd, cautious brothers in the world for one gay moron who treated other people's cars and other men's wives or sisters as expendable objects. She relished the idea of being an occasional sex object! She almost floated into Rick's lady-like arms; but Mendel was there to restrain her, while Harry took charge of Rick.

Harry and Mendel bade each other a friendly "Till we meet again!" Rick and Ida exchanged distant, quasi-poetic farewells. Mendel led his sister into the house. And Harry took the wheel of Bella's Mercedes-Benz. At his side, Rick simpered girlishly as the car sped towards Ladbury. A mile and a half short of the outskirts of town, Harry turned the car to the left. They climbed the hill, and veered into the lane leading to the hut which had once been the gamekeeper's sanctum. Harry brought the car to a halt, and drew Rick to him. Their open mouths fused in a moist, tonguey kiss, during which Harry's left hand held the younger man's head while with the other he kneaded the gigolo's buttocks. A few minutes later they were in the hut, where Harry lost no time in divesting himself of all his clothes. At his behest, Rick followed suit prior to kneeling before his benefactor, whose already erect penis he sucked until it attained enormous proportions within his servile mouth. Harry sighed contentedly, and gasped, "Good boy, Rickie! Turn round now, and let me give it you where you like it best!"

Rick obeyed with his customary alacrity, and his lover went into his anus with a powerful thrust. Each jab of Harry's sex took him deeper into the bottom of his favorite boy, whom he then went on to ride vigorously. Reaching round Rick's slim, pale body, Harry seized the whore's phallus, and masturbated the boy as delicately as Bella might have done. After a few minutes, feeling that his own orgasm was new, Harry cried, "Come, boy! Come, you boyish little bitchy boy!" and Rick did his master's bidding at almost the very moment when the other's seminal fluid began to gush forth. Harry held his sweetheart male slut close to him, nibbling the lobe of his left ear. With his sperm-befouled right hand he caressed the flat young belly, smearing it with the boy's own come-slime. After a while they drew apart, and Rick's mouth went to work, cleaning the loins of his employer, who moaned words of encouragement and gratitude.

They dressed, and went off into the woods that form part of the Partham estate. Harry was tall, heavily built, but light on his feet, strong and brimming with health and vitality. Tiredness was but a word to him. He strode along the narrow winding paths of his woodlands, enthusiastically filling his lungs with the scented air. Rick trotted at his heels like a cringing cur. He had difficulty in keeping up with the older man, and he was soon breathless. Harry did not immediately notice his paramour's condition; but, the moment he did, he suggested a few minutes of repose as though it were he who needed it. While stationery, they kissed and cuddled in a patch of sunshine until Harry's genitals threatened to split the seams of his pants. He zipped open his fly, and allowed his cock to crow rosily in the fresh air. Desire again filled his loins and his hands went to the waist of Rick's slacks, which were soon pulled down to the young man's knees. Rick obediently got down on all fours, without having to be asked, and awaited Harry's next move, which was to place his large hands on the younger man's bottom globes and part them slowly so as to gain sweet access to his ass. He looked tenderly at the inviting, delicious sex glove that was before him and then he oiled Rick's entranceway with the small tube of sex gel he had carried in his shirt pocket (knowing it might come in handy on this walk). Harry rimmed his lover's anus with the gel, rubbing it around the puckered opening and teasingly dipping it inward. Rick responded to the glorious stimulation by pressing his ass up to meet Harry's probing fingers, which was a sign that Rick was ready for the real thing—Harry's big, manly cock, shoved deep inside his boy-girl hole! Before penetrating the younger man, Harry pressed three fingers into the awaiting anus, to ensure Rick was stretched enough for comfort, but all the touching and finger probing had gotten Harry to a state where he could barely contain his desire.

"I've got to go in now, Rick," Harry said, panting slightly. "I'm going to put my big cock in your little hole, and fuck you hard, boy. You want that?"

"Oh yes, Harry," Rick moaned, "bust me open with your big prick. I love the way you fill me up."

"This time, I'm going to fuck you without feeling your cock in my hand. I'm going to pump cock into your ass, but I won't rub your cock until I'm ready to come. I want you to come with me, you understand."

Rick, who generally wasn't wild about getting his ass pummeled without return, was so filled with desire that he liked the idea of Harry's postponing his orgasm, just to tease him into coming at the same time.

"Harry," Rick uttered, "I love whatever you do to me. Even if you wanted to fuck me hard, come, and leave me stiff and lonely, that would be all right by me."

Rick's passionate surrender flamed Harry's already enflamed cock and it wasn't long before he was grabbing hold of the younger man's penis and massaging the hardened weapon until Rick too was near to exploding. Once again, Harry felt his own jism boil within his belly and then ejaculate in wild spurts into Rick's asshole. And he cried out for Rick's own outpouring. "Come again, for Daddy," he pleaded, jerking Rick off in his hand, "give it all to me."

Within moments, Harry's hand was wet with Rick's explosion. He brought the hand to Rick's mouth and told him to lick it. Rick obliged, sucking his own come from the hand that literally fed him, and then falling into the older man's arms.

After a decent rest in the beautiful country air, Harry was once again roused to lovemaking with his young "assistant." But this time, it was Harry who wanted it square in the ass, and it was Rick who gingerly licked the older man's asshole, then oiled it with lubricant and inserted himself deeply while fondling Harry's cock and balls. When Harry's ejaculation squirted wildly on Rick's hand, it was Rick who licked the jism from his own hand in front of Harry, impressing upon the older man his willingness to please at any cost. He then bent between Harry's strong thighs, took his cock into his mouth, and licked and sucked him until the last traces of come and of ass-fucking were removed from his lovely cock. He slipped Harry's clothes back on like a slave girl tending to her master. As he rose to pull up his own pants, he gently touched Harry's cheek with his well-worked cock. Harry kissed the penis, and rose. They headed back to the house.

They did not rejoin Bella until almost dinner time. While Harry's back was turned, his wife made various gestures and grimaces at Rick to express her disapproval of his being away again so long with Harry; but Rick just shrugged his shoulders, feigning unhappy inability to do anything about the situation. Secretly, however, he rejoiced at the thought that Bella's jealousy would bring him expensive presents in the near future.

For the promise of such gifts Rick did not have to wait long. They were drinking coffee and cognac when Sir Ivan Franson arrived unexpectedly to discuss a property deal with Harry. Sir Ivan, however ruthless in business, was a considerate gentleman. He addressed himself to Bella. "I'm awfully sorry to come here unannounced and monopolize your husband for the remainder of the evening; but I have a lot of things to talk over with him before I fly to Napoli tomorrow morning. Can you find it in your heart to forgive me?"

Bella assured Sir Ivan that her charming young guest would save her from boredom while Harry fatigued himself with the details of the deal he had come to discuss. She was so frank about the importance she attached to Rick's presence in the house that Harry took Sir Ivan into his study, his mind free of the slightest suspicion of the real relationship between Bella and his assistant.

No sooner had Harry and Sir Ivan left the drawing-room than Bella threw herself into Rick's unwilling arms. He kissed her briefly before calling her attention to the possibility that Harry would come back for this or that.

"You frightened little silly!" she replied. "Apart from the fact that there's nothing Harry needs that isn't there, in his study, why are you so afraid of being found out? You don't think he'd beat me, do you? All right, darling! I know you're thinking about your job; but there are two things you mustn't forget. One...I'm not entirely in the palm of Harry's hand. A large part of the money he plays with, both on the stock markets and in real estate, is mine. He and I are partners. I'm no poor girl who married a financier for his money. I contribute as much to our common purse as he does. He multiplies our joint fortune, but I get my share of the loot by right, not as the privilege of a tart who opens her legs wider than others do; so he can't dismiss you without my approval, and I won't give that until you fail us professionally. You're now enjoying an employee's normal hours of leisure. What you do now may entitle him to refuse to house you, because you live here as our friend, but he has no right to allow your cuckolding him in your spare time to influence him in his professional appraisal of you, nor will I let him get away with such an injustice. The other thing, darling, is that it'd flatter Bella just a little to think you were ready to sacrifice everything for love of her—your nice home and your good job. I'm not suggesting we strip, darling, as long as Harry's on the premises; but, if you just pulled my frivolous panties down, and dug it into me for a few minutes, would the risk be so great? We'd hear them leaving the study, in the unlikely event of their doing so, and it'd take only a second for me to pull up my undies while you zipped up your pants. Let's go outside. It's a lovely evening; so what's more natural than that we should take a bit of air after a good dinner? You could dog my bitch in the moonlight?"

Rick asked for nothing better than to copulate with Bella, who was resplendent that evening, in a dress of dark green tulle, but he was not willing to put pleasure before his profession. He was on the horns of a dilemma. He could afford to offend neither Bella nor Harry, and he did not doubt that the former would be angered by his refusal to prove his love by "loving" her. However, he hesitated long enough to allow her the time to think of a means of winning him over to her way of thinking.

"Do you really love me?" she asked.

"Do you need to ask such a question?"

"Do you love me enough to tell Harry tomorrow that you're going to town in the afternoon, to help me with some shopping?"

Convinced that she would not take him shopping without buying him something, Rick was so eager to go with her that he decided to curry favor with her by asking Harry to allow him to take Bella to London, even at the slight risk of inciting his master to jealousy. Trying not to sound too eager, he replied, "I love you enough to sacrifice all I have for you. You know that; but it's not for me to tell Harry I'm taking the afternoon off. If you claim his secretary for the afternoon, he has only either to refuse you or to agree. You can say you need me to drive the car, carry your parcels and that sort of thing."

"What if he says no?"

Rick combed her raven locks with his fingers, searching for an uncompromising answer. After a few seconds, he answered, "If half the business is yours, half of me is yours; so you've a right to my services at least one afternoon now and then."

She seized him, kissed him greedily, and sobbed, "Rick, half of you isn't enough. You're all mine. Mine, honey! Do you hear me? I want you, Rick. I want you now. Love me, Rick! Take me outside! Whip off my panties, and stick it into me! Whip me with your rhythm stick, Rickie."

He raised her to her feet, kissed her gently, and led her to the French windows, which were open. Through them they entered the garden, and hurried in the moonlight to the summer house. Rick would have gone inside, but Bella insisted that he take possession of her outdoors. He was looking about him, trying to decide whether to take her standing up or lying on a blanket stretched out either on the verandah of the summer house or on the lawn, when she exclaimed, "Brilliant idea, Rick! Take off my panties, nothing more, just to be on the safe side. Keep your slacks on, but give some night-air to the most thrilling bird that ever nested in my flue! Then, I'll sit, thighs wide open, on the swing. You'll stand between my legs, with the front of the swing against your knees. Your rod won't need to move at all. You'll be able to do me by rocking the swing so that my pussy moves up and down the length of your Rickie dickie."

As excited as a child on Christmas morning or an Archimedes who has just discovered a new mathematical principle, Bella danced around her lover, chortling gaily. With both hands she raised her skirts so that Rick could see the white of her thighs above her stocking-tops. He seized her, and, during a long, lascivious kiss, he whipped off her panties, as she had suggested. He whipped them off with such abandon that they tore, and he dropped them over the side of the verandah. She clung to him, whispering, "You're going to love me, darling; and tomorrow we're going shopping together...shopping and loving!"

Great as was her sexual excitement and her impatience to be penetrated by Rick's phallus, she could not avoid the peremptory tone in her entreating voice. She loved him and wanted him, but her love did not blind her to the fact he was her lover, but he was also her employee, paid to help Harry with his office chores and to assuage her erotic thirst whenever and wheresoever she chose. Rick occasionally forgot, briefly, that he had to perform on command rather than when, where and how he would have liked; but her words out there on the verandah of the gazebo reminded him that he was potentially on duty twenty-four hours a day; so he went to work on her.

He brought his lips down on hers again. Tonguing the inner side of her lips, he held her tight with his left arm around her waist. He bent her so far back that she was almost lying across his forearm, with her parted legs stretched out straight. Her skirt was raised in front, exposing her up to her navel. Rick massaged the mouth of her vagina with the fingers of his right hand. His fingers were close together, forming a solid phalanx of digits with which he rubbed her hard.

"Oh, I like that, lover boy! I really dig the way you're digging me. Dig into me some more, and then dick me," she giggled. "Harder, darling! Don't be afraid, I like you to rough me up. Hurt me when you love my lady too!"

In her excitement, she had taken a firm grip on the boards of the porch with her stockinged feet, and bent her knees, so that her body formed an aggressive arch. Rick stepped between her thighs, aimed his penis at her sex, and pulled her brusquely towards him. He plowed into her eager flesh, holding her firmly with his left hand at her bottom and his right around her waist. Her head hung backwards, almost touching the floor. In an effort to make herself comfortable, she had her arms stretched out behind her, her hand touching the bare planks whenever the vigor of Rick's movements in and out of her delicious cavity permitted her such a luxury. Her pose rendered active participation in their coupling impossible; she was delighted by the impression of being had, used and dominated. She was wide open, hot for him, vulnerable. She was his thing, and he was taking her. She had said she wanted to be loved on the swinging canvas sofa, and he was defying her. He would pay for his insubordination, but he would be rewarded for the joy he was jabbing into her squelching loins. Bella's excitement rose thrust by fierce thrust. Rick was fully aware of what he was doing to her, and his pride was such that it was with difficulty that he held back his ejaculation of fluid into her entrails until her instant of ecstasy. The sudden cry, as of sharp pain, the tautening of her whole body prior to its helpless jerking against the scorching rock of his sex, released him from the need to grit his teeth. With a deep groan of contentment he let himself go, spewing his spunk into her. She went limp, and he continued convulsively to cream her womb.

The reduction in the size and stiffness of his weapon was surprisingly slight, but he was too fatigued to exploit the situation at once. He withdrew from the coziness of her sperm-filled genitals, and she cried feebly, "No!" He picked her up, carried her a couple of yards, and deposited her on the canvas swing, taking care that her skirt was so bunched up under her arms that he had continued access to those parts of her body which most interested him. He lay down on top of her, and kissed her flaccid mouth.

"You're a wicked, disobedient boy," she gasped, "but that was very nice. We ought to be going in now; but I said how you had to do me, and that's how we're going to have it before we leave this porch."

Rick wanted her again. He wanted her very much, but even she admitted there was an element of danger in their staying out there much longer; so he tried to persuade her to postpone the copulation on which her heart was set until a more convenient occasion. She did not reply.

They stayed there, kissing with slowly increasing passion. She put so much skill into their osculati that he was soon in no condition to refuse her pleas that he pleasure her again. By pushing him lovingly away from her, she indicated that she wished him to get off her recumbent body. He clambered to his feet, and she placed a soft hand under his manhood and scrotum, as though she would weigh them.

"The mixture of our come has dried on it," she said, "like a fine film of icing on a cake. I'm going to mouth it clean, and make it wet with saliva. Then I want it in me the way I said; but I'm going to kneel, and you're going to ram it up my tail."

His penis was happy in her mouth. He thrilled to the way she licked the dried sperm from his foreskin, and that she knew her performance was a good one was obvious from the fact that she took him out of her mouth, threw back her beautiful head, and smiled at him. He kneeled beside the couch, and took her gently in his arms. His kiss was tender at first, but savage towards the end. She held him with a strength which was out of proportion to the fineness of her build. Her passion carried him away, so that he wanted to crush her, bear her and hurt her in every possible way. There came a moment when his grip on her was so fierce that she knew a few seconds of fear. She fought to free herself; and he suddenly realized that he was hugging her with dangerous force. He let her go, and she took him in her arms with such care that an onlooker would have thought he was both fragile and precious. She murmured, "I love you, Rick. I love you dearly. I like you to treat me rough. I want often to feel your hands on me; but it must always be with lovingly wild desire. Never frighten me again like you did just now!"

She spoke softly, without anger, but with authority. He hung his head for a moment, feigning contrition; and he fooled her. She kissed him sweating, but with her mouth wide open; and she said, "If I've hurt your feelings, forgive me! Tell me you know I was genuinely frightened, and that you forgive me for being so silly! Hold me, darling!"

He held her in his arms, but held his face far enough from hers for her to see the tears he had forced to his eyes. He let the warm jewels roll down his cheeks until he tasted their bitter-sweetness on his lips. She was his slave at that moment, so convinced was she that this man loved her as no other man had ever loved any other woman. She dried his tears from the warmth of her lips, and she held the whole length of her body close to the whole length of his.

"From this moment on," she promised, "I'm your girl, your submissive girl. I've bullied you long enough, and you've put up with being insulted and humiliated, because your love is too great for this wicked world...and certainly for a domineering cow like me. From now on we shall make love when you say so, and we shall do it where you like and how you like. All I ask is that you love me with your heart half as much as I love you. I do love you, Rick, and I do want and need you. Love me!"

Her "Love me!" was more a plea than a command, but in Rick's mercenary ears it was an invitation to earn himself a gift of some sort; so he kissed her juicily prior to releasing himself from her embrace. She stroked his cheeks with both her hands, smiled at him with the eyes of an infatuated maiden, and turned her back on him. Her knees as far apart as possible, she knelt in the suspended couch, with her arms stretched out along the backrest. Her posterior, covered by her dress, was thrust upwards provocatively. After caressing her bottom through the material, Rick flipped up her dress, and allowed it to fall in folds about her shoulder-blades. He slapped her hard. Her surprise was such that she cried out; but, almost immediately recovering her calm, she begged him to slap her again and again. Each time his hand descended on the smooth flesh of her bum or thighs, she made such encouraging remarks as, "Yes, Rick, punish the bossy bitch! Harder, lover-boy, I deserve it. Don't be afraid to show this hot-assed bitch who's boss around here! I love you, Rick. I love your doing this to me. Smack my bum!"

Obediently, he increased the weight of his blows until the noise of his hand's contact with her body and her groans of ecstatic anguish would probably have been audible to Harry, had he not been indoors and deep in consideration of the details of Sir Ivan's proposition. Upon the command "Smack my bum," he ceased slapping her, and slashed his erect rod into the greasiness of her tunnel of love. "No!" she cried, "My ass, idiot! My ass!"

Nettled, he snapped, "All right, I'm not deaf, and I'm no idiot either. I'm getting him slimed up, so that he'll go into you painlessly."

"Who cares about pain? Forgive me, Rick! You're a good boy. Give it to me good!"

He held the globes of her rear apart with his thumbs, and touched her anus with the tip of his oiled staff, which was as large and hard as it had ever been. He exerted a little pressure with his hips, and his knob entered her. He went an inch deeper, pulled back a similar amount, and then went in to a depth of about two inches. He withdrew an inch again prior to advancing two further inches. Half a dozen maneuvers lodged him firmly within her rectum. She winced several times during the operation, and, especially at the beginning, she suppressed screams of pain by biting her lips until she nearly tasted her own blood. His sodomitic instrument completely swallowed by the throat of her backside, he made two or three sadistically jolting movements with his crotch, to tighten the contact between his body and hers. She uttered a strangled scream which faded into a breathless moan, and he cruelly swayed his hips from left to right and then backwards and forwards, while remaining deep within her. The tears she shed were genuine, but she longed for him to augment her agony. She regretted that he did not have a penis the size of Harry's or Dane's; but she enjoyed his tool, because she loved him. Furthermore, he was unquestionably making the best possible use of the meager means at his disposal. She whispered his name affectionately and he replied, "Yes, darling?" For answer, she merely repeated his name beseechingly.

He began to move in and out of her with long, slow, ruthless movements. His hands left her hips, which they had been gripping so hard that he had hurt her, and, with his arms round the top of her thighs, all his fingers toyed with the lips of her vagina and her alert clitoris. Soon she knew again the sensation of feeling that her entire body was one enormous sex organ being belabored by two male organs. The mercury in her thermometer rose by leaps and bounds. Sweat oozed out of her pores. Delight having driven pain out of her flesh, she sighed with pause. She moved her rump backwards and forwards, heightening the impression that he was possessing her totally. In and out of her he flashed with arrogant ease. Her pipe had stretched to accommodate him, and she was his without the slightest reserve. Cocksure, he bashed away at her defenseless ass without forgetting his duty towards her genitals, which his savage fingers punished relentlessly. Her pleasure in being his thing was contagious. Her flames set fire to Rick, who burned happily, knowing that it was his spark which had started her blazing. The passion with which she enveloped him was the fruit of his own tree. He was strong, he was her master, and he was her creator, who could destroy her at will. She began to tremble convulsively, and he knew the moment was imminent when she would melt in the heat of their fused bodies. He was glad, for his feeling of strength was no more than a sensation. Had she not arrived when she did, he would probably have endured a humiliation similar to that which had accompanied his first copulation with Bella. She disintegrated to the tune of tiny squeals of joy, and she became a pile of hot jelly into which his phallus hurled salvo after salvo of seminal fluid. Feeble but determined, he clung to her, preventing her spent body from collapsing; and she was deceived into thinking he was still her indefatigable swain. Her affection for him was tinged with wonder, admiration and respect. She was convinced that, had circumstances permitted, he would immediately have transferred his penis from her anus to her vagina, upon which he would have bestowed several orgasms before permitting himself the luxury of ejaculating seed. Rick, however, was saved by the bell. Bella stirred, escaped from his grasp, turned to him, and placed her slender, pale arms about his neck.

"You're very nice," she said, "nice to me, nice for me...nice! This has been one of the most thrilling hours in my life. Ask a favor of me...anything! I want to do things for you. I'm going to do a lot for you; but I'd like to know what you really want or need."

Rick did not put forth a wrong foot. He knew exactly how to increase her desire to do things for him. He took her paternally in his arms, and she made herself even smaller than she was. His lips touched hers in a kiss which was mild without being innocent. He stroked her glorious raven-blue hair, and told her that, thanks to her and Harry's kindness, he had, for the first time in his impoverished life, everything essential for utter contentment.

Let it never be said that Rick did not bring more joy into the lives of the gullible than self-respecting and honest men bestow upon their friends and acquaintances! Rick's canny refusal of excess generosity, as a means of obtaining much more, flooded Bella's heart with the sun of paradise. At the very summit of happiness, she placed her innocent hand almost adolescently in that of her boyfriend, and led him back to the drawing-room.

The way Bella looked at things, he who demands little receives much—it's just that Bella didn't know that her dear, pure Rick manipulated her constantly, based on that philosophy! Later the same evening, while Harry was fingering her vagina during love-making between man and wife, she asked, "Sweet Hank, could you spare Rick tomorrow, to take me to town, to do some shopping?"

Without wondering why Bella needed Rick to help her with an agreeable task she had performed alone during the twenty years of their marriage, Harry answered, "Bella, you don't have to ask if I can spare him. He's here to lighten your burden and mine. I can keep him fairly busy most days, so I do; but, if you need him for a day or two now and then, all you have to do is tell me…not ask me."

She snuggled closer to her good husband, her open mouth seeking his, not dutifully, but eagerly and lovingly. She held herself wide open, and she enjoyed their long copulation. And Harry enjoyed it as well, for his cock was like a rocketship in orbit as it probed his wife's hot cunt. As she gyrated and writhed to the rhythm of their fucking, he felt his cock boiling over with delicious come. He held back for a while, so he could pummel her wetness long enough to make her come, and just as Bella groaned and went wild with an orgasm that rocked her ovaries, Harry too felt his eruption near. He quickly pulled his exploding cock from her clenching cunt and brought it to her mouth. She grabbed hold of his huge weapon, took it deeply in her mouth so Harry could jerk himself off into her awaiting orifice. As his come shot from his cock, she held fast to his vibrating prick and sucked the last ounce of his explosion. She swallowed it all, and kissed the tip of Harry's cock before he moved his body back alongside her in the bed. Soon, she fell asleep in his arms and he quietly moved her to her side of the bed while he slipped out of the room.

As much as he loved sex with his wife, his asshole ached for some male attention and thus he slipped off into his lover's room to seek it, as Bella slept soundly. As always, Rick greeted him with open arms and legs, willing to perform whatever sex act pleased Harry, which in this case was to play the "female" role and have his awaiting orifice filled up with Rick's hot cock.

But first, he wanted to kiss Rick's manhood and fondle it. "Take off your pajamas, lad, and let me see that fine weapon." Rick stripped, coyly, moving the pajama pants slowly over his hips, then over his cock, and over his knees until finally stepping out of them. Harry watched with delight. When the bottoms were off, he moved closer to Rick, who was still standing, and bent onto his knees so that his face was level with Rick's cock. He took the penis in his hands, brought it to his mouth, and took it deeply into his throat, swallowing Rick whole, until the younger man's cock had doubled in size. He kissed the head, he licked up and down the shaft, he fondled the balls, he even sucked on the balls, and then he moved the hard rod back and forth in his mouth until he could tell Rick was wildly excited.

Harry stood, momentarily leaving his lover in the lurch with a hard cock and no place to put it. He walked to the bed, leaned over the edge and with both hands spread open his buttocks.

"Treat me as you would treat a lady," he instructed. "Do to me what you would if this hole was a woman's cunt."

Rick wasted no time in going to his older lover, and kissing him deeply, tongue to tongue, before kissing his shoulders, back, then the small of the back, until making his way down to Harry's hungry asshole. Harry was holding himself apart as wide as possible, which helped Rick to get his mouth right inside the crack. Starting at the top, Rick ran his wet tongue down the crease until it found its way to Harry's opening. Rick pushed his tongue tip inward, and then ran his tongue around the rim, over and over again, until Harry felt numbed with pleasure. Then he tongue-fucked the tight quarters until the opening gradually loosened up and became juicy and wet.

Harry was groaning by now and his cock, which was limp when he entered the room, was hard as a rock. "What do you do if a woman begs you to fuck her?" Harry asked. "I'm begging you to fuck me, now, please fuck me."

"I'll give you anything you want," Rick whispered, pulling himself up so that his cock was level with Harry's wide open asshole. He rubbed his hard prick on the top of Harry's hand. "Is this what you want, lover? Is this what you want shoved up your sweet hole?"

"Yes," Harry said, panting and breathing heavy. "Please, give it all to me now."

"First, we need more lubrication than what my mouth provided," Rick said.

"No," Harry demanded. "Just fuck me. Make me feel all of you, nice and natural."

With that, Rick brought the head of his cock to Harry's opening and Harry could feel the red-hot poker pressing into his intimate anatomy. "Sodomize me," he begged, "bugger me dry."

Rick did not try to ease his cock into the older man's hole; he plunged in, his initial pathway oiled only by the wetness he had earlier provided with his probing mouth. Harry flinched in slight pain, but pressed his butt out for more and cried, "Give it to me deep."

Rick was wild with unbridled passion, having free rein to fuck to his heart's content, so he buggered Harry without mercy, pulling his cock all the way up to the top of Harry's opening, then plunging it back into the depths, until he could feel his own explosion bubbling close to the surface. He grabbed hold of Harry's hips, pulled them toward him, and pressed his prick in to the hilt, just as the first moment of ejaculation began to spurt out. Harry felt himself suddenly filled with Rick's seed, and felt the intense swelling of his frontal equipment, and quickly decided that he no longer wished to play the passive role.

"Now, take yourself out of me and come here and suck my hard cock until I come in your mouth," Harry instructed. With that, he hopped onto the bed, lay down on his back and waved his hard flagpole in the air until Rick joined him, got between his legs and eagerly licked his master's manhood.

He toyed with the swelling sacs and massaged the base of the prick while sucking hard on the head of the cock, until Harry began to gyrate madly and thrash his cock in and out of Rick's mouth so fast that he could barely keep up the sucking. But it didn't matter because the orgasm was on automatic pilot and Harry's jism was about to erupt.

Harry grabbed hold of Rick's head, and pressed his mouth down on his hot cock. "Suck it up, and lick every trace of come," he called out, and the juice of pleasure gushed from his faucet. Rick swallowed the come, and licked the residue from the head of Harry's cock. Harry patted the younger man's head affectionately and rose to leave, as they'd been together for nearly an hour.

As he kissed his employee goodnight, Harry said, "Rickie, I'd like you to drive Bella to London tomorrow. She has some shopping to do. She's a grand lass, but a little bit head-in-the-clouds; and, if you don't watch her, she'll let you pay for drinks, lunch, and what have you; so I want you to put this in your pocket. If you spend more, you must let me know."

Harry laughed, and added, "I shall get it back from Bella one way or another."

Harry returned to his wife. Rick took from the pocket of his blue silk pajama jacket the cash Harry had deposited there. Five pounds! He had received five pounds with which to settle bills which he was sure Bella would insist were her responsibility. Wondering whether his boss would inform their shared female of the advance payment of the special London allowance, Rick drifted into sleep, determined that, if he had to pay for drinks and lunch the following day, it would be draft Guinness and chicken salad at the Salisbury, Saint Martin's Lane. Thus he would show a cash profit of fifty to sixty shillings on the day, without counting the present he was sure Bella planned to give him.

As though he had read the thoughts which had filled Rick's mind at the moment of sinking into sleep, Harry returned to his secretary's bedroom at dawn to say, "Rick...er...Bella...doesn't need to know about my financial contribution to today's trip. She's a fine girl...intelligent, understanding, broad-minded...one of the best; but no female sees these things as we men do. Let her think you're offering her the Savoy grill. She'll be flattered, and it'll prevent any misunderstandings."

Harry was delighted to hear his protégé answer, "We'll play this thing your way, Hank. But, grateful as I am to you for what you gave me last night, I'd be happy to treat Bella and you to a day in London...drinks, lunch, a theater, dinner and dancing..."

No less a sucker than Bella, Harry (the shrewd property-dealer) tousled Rick's yellow curls, and said:

"Sure, we'll have a weekend in town, really livin' it up; but neither Bella nor I would tolerate you standing the expenses of such a ball. We pay you what we can afford to pay you, but, gee, Rickie-boy, if we gave you what you're really worth to us, you'd be able to hire the Dorchester for a long weekend of wine, song and dance. Anyway, as long as things are as they are, I don't want your expenditure to exceed your income. So, when we go out and paint London-town bright red, uncle Harry will sign the checks, and put it all down to tax-deductible expenses."

Rick pulled Harry down to the bed. He pressed his lips against the older man's passionately and then skillfully slipped his tongue in Harry's mouth, slashing against Harry's own tongue in a delicious, exciting way. After a long kiss, Harry breathlessly issued the command, "Soixante-neuf!" Though Rick's knowledge of foreign languages was sketchy, he understood the sort of French which means "sixty-nine." He quickly untied the pajama knots at both his own and his master's waists. They both shucked off their night attire and, lying head to foot, each took the other's penis in his mouth. They sucked, licked and nibbled until Harry felt that the young man's crisis was imminent. With the help of Harry's hand, Rick's phallus emptied itself into Harry's hungry mouth; even through his orgasmic emission, and after he had come, Rick did not forget "the cock that feeds him." He continued to mouth his employer's sex-organ until it hurled its creamy contents down his throat.

"Swallow it, boy!" Harry commanded; and Rick obeyed, squeezing the wealthy financier's penis until it contained not a drop more. The whole lot slid down the whore's throat. Harry patted the boy's butt condescendingly, and returned to the bed he shared with Bella.

No one, observing them at breakfast, would have suspected that Bella and Harry were living a double life—enjoying normal sexual relations as between man and wife, while each of them betrayed the other with Rick. The latter played, to perfection, the role of the servile, grateful, poor little poorboy. All the servants thought Mr. Rick Haylett was such a nice young man. To them, he was a real gentleman, with the common touch. They never guessed that his "touch" cost money and that "common" applied most appropriately to so cheap a swindler as Rick.

Bella took the wheel of the Mercedes-Benz, and drove like wild to Piccadilly Circus, slowing down on stopping only whenever necessary. She parked on Glasshouse Street, and stepped out, resplendent in a low-cut, almost transparent dress of tangerine silk.

All eyes were on her as she and Rick entered the Regent Palace Hotel, where she booked a single room for herself for one night.

After an hour of loving in Room 78, they went out shopping for cosmetics and lingerie for Bella, cigars for Harry and certain cheese and spices which the cook had asked for. Then Bella took Rick walking along Regent Street.

"Oh, I say, Bella, isn't that lightweight suit dynamite!"

She smiled and expressed agreement.

Ten yards further on, "By jove, look at that olive-green jacket! I shall certainly buy that, when I can whip the jolly old lolly together!"

"It's very nice," said Bella, smiling.

"Bella, don't you think those are simply the loveliest crocodile shoes ever?"

"Do you like crocodile shoes, darling?"

"Divine!"

"Would you like them?"

He had no intention of buying himself a pair of shoes priced seven pounds, nor was he inclined to dissuade Bella from paying a similar amount for them. He assured her that he planned to return for them when he had the necessary spare cash; and she had not the common sense to tell him that, having earned twenty pounds per week during the previous two months, without needing to spend more than a couple of pounds per week, he most certainly had the money to buy himself a pair of shoes costing seven pounds. Instead, she entered the shop, followed by Rick, who was somewhat downcast, since he was sure she would not buy him the shoes and the coffee-colored lightweight suit; Rick was the sort of gold digger who would rather receive one suit worth twenty pounds than two pairs of shoes costing seven pounds per pair. In fact, he had to content himself with one pair of shoes, lunch at the Martinez restaurant in Swallow Street and an afternoon of copulation in Bella's room at the Regent Palace. Needless to say, Bella paid for lunch and for the hotel room. She also paid for a visit to the Royal Court Theater. They had supper at the Hungarian restaurant in Regent Street, and danced to the music of Rudi Rohm and his Orchestra, all at Bella's expense; and, after midnight, they set off for Ladbury, although Bella would have liked to spend the night at the hotel. Rick was unwilling to risk arousing Harry's suspicions by absenting himself from the house, in Bella's company, for the whole night; but he was equally reluctant to anger Bella by refusing to halt the car a few miles before Ladbury. They went into a copse, where she retained him so long that Harry was in the breakfast room, waiting for them anxiously, when they entered the house after dawn. Bella greeted Harry confidently, without a trace of shame; but her swain avoided his boss's eyes.

During breakfast Harry and Bella were as gay as a pair of lovers reunited after a long absence; and Rick was as jealous of Bella's interest in Harry as in the latter's loving attention to his wife's chatter about London, the restaurants they had visited and the play they had seen. He begged permission to go up to his room, to sleep for a few hours. Harry was entitled to answer that a man who can keep his employer's wife out all night can also report punctually for duty the following morning. What he, in fact, said was, "Seven or eight hours of sleep would do neither of you any harm. Shall I ask Lena to take lunch up to you? She could take it up to our room, Bella, and Rick could join you there. I must go over to see Sir Ivan, and I shan't be back for lunch."

Bella kissed Harry on the mouth, softly and lingeringly. "After this delicious breakfast, I shan't have
lunch," she said, "but I hope you'll be home for dinner, darling."

He fondled her almost obscenely, as though Rick
were miles away, and Bella's cooing and sighing suggested she too was indifferent to her lover's presence.
Eventually she whispered something in her husband's
ear, and he took her up to their room. Rick waited
more than an hour for Harry's return; and then, very
much in need of sleep, he went up to his own room,
where Bella joined him shortly before noon. He tried
to dissuade her from staying; but she knew that,
when Harry said he would be away from home until
dinner, he did not intend to steal into the house during the morning or afternoon in order to catch her in
the arms of a lover. She insisted on staying with Rick.
They made love twice, and slept in each other's arms
until Lena entered to warn Mrs. Partham that it was
time to dress for dinner.

During dinner, and afterwards, Bella and Rick
told Harry about the play they had seen the previous
evening. Jealous of Bella's admiration of certain
members of the play's cast, Rick whined about the
cruel blow fate had played him in preventing his
training for his true vocation, the theater. Harry, no
less than Bella, was genuinely grieved to think that so
handsome, charming and intelligent a boy should
have been denied greatness as an actor merely
because his parents lacked the wherewithal to send
him to the Royal Academy of Dramatic Art. Neither
of them suspected that he had never bought a the-
ater-ticket in his life, contenting himself with seeing
the plays his paying friends and clients chose to treat
him to.

That night, in their cozy connubial bed, while Rick

108

ate out his heart at the thought of their being happy together, they discussed the possibility of sending him, tardily perhaps, to some school of histrionics; but they reached no definite decision, there being so many arguments against encouraging a man twenty-five years old to start training for a career on which he ought already to have been launched at the age of twenty. The truth, however, is that neither of them was willing to take any step which might have resulted in their dear boy's leaving them. They were not only a mother and father, who were reluctant to send their only son out into the cruel world, they were also a sensual man and woman, each of whom hoped to win Rick for himself or herself, while being content to share him with each other, provided others could be kept at a distance.

V.

Rick continued to talk much of his frustrated theatrical ambitions. He hinted, on several occasions, at his intention to join the Ladbury Amateur Dramatic Society; but neither Harry nor Bella showed for this project such enthusiasm as would have given him the courage to take a step which would have resulted in his having thenceforth less time to spare for them. What he expected of them was that they present him with at least the local thespians on a silver platter. He lacked the self-respect which might have led him to inform his employers that he had decided to devote some of his leisure time to the amateur stage. He wanted to be applauded, the center of admiring attention, and he wanted to be on more intimate terms with the well-to-do members of the drama circle whom he occasionally met at cocktail parties; but he was not going to risk impairing the generosity of Harry and Bella by not doing anything of which they did not appear heartily to approve. For the time being he contented himself with adopting an effusive attitude to Ladbury's smart set whenever he came into contact with them.

The day came when Rick suddenly discovered that the theater had never been his true vocation, surprising in view of the fact that his whole life was an act which he put on to impress people with more money than perspicacity.

Since Harry and Bella accepted no invitations which excluded their protégé, Rick was present at a reception given by Gordon and Mairhi Purtley for their son Rowan, who had just had a short story accepted for publication in a quarterly revue called *Writers of Promise*. Rowan's parents and friends attached more importance to the lad's modest success than it warranted—a fact which embarrassed the young writer considerably—so much that he was glad to escape from their provincial enthusiasm into discussion of the latest literary trends with a fellow man of letters, Rick Haylett by name.

Bella was flabbergasted to hear her permanent guest say to Rowan, "As a writer, Rowan, old boy, I'd like to congratulate you on your success." She would have liked to hear the remainder of that particular conversation, but at that moment Eva Dalheim and Lee Alchard descended upon her. They simply had to talk to her about Eva's exhibition at the Karstein Gallery in Oxford Street.

Going home in Harry's Jaguar, Rick did not allow Bella the time to broach the subject of his literary talents. The sleek black automobile had not left the drive of the Purtley's home, when Rick exclaimed, "What a stroke of luck...meeting Rone tonight."

"Rowan, darling! Rowan! Not Rone!"

Bella had drunk a little too much. Her sharpness towards Rick shocked Harry, who sought to ease the boy's pain by asking, "What sort of luck, Rick?"

Rick and Bella were sharing the back seat of the
Jaguar. Harry's fatherly question caused Bella to recognize that she had been somewhat severe with Rick.
Eager to console him and to obtain his pardon, she
squeezed his sex through his pants. He responded by
stroking her right thigh under her skirts; and she
echoed Harry, "Yes, Rick, tell us about Rowan!"

"Well, I mean…talking to him, you know, about
writing and all that…well, I mean to say, you know it
sort of gives me the urge to get back to my own writing."

Neither of them had hitherto suspected that their
Rick was a young man with literary aspirations; but
their love for him was such that they both pretended
to take this revelation in their stride. Bella said,
"There's a brand new portable typewriter in my den,
darling. It's yours, if you want it; and Harry and I will
give you all the help we can, won't we, Partham?"

"Sure thing, Rick! If the Purtley boy can get stuff
published, I'm damned sure no sane publisher's going
to refuse anything an intelligent, sensitive fellow like
you writes. You know what, Bella? Rick ought to
take time off work for a month or two, settle down in
my study, and hammer away at that typewriter you're
gonna give him. You just get to work, Rick, and I
promise that, when I need to go into the office, I'll
raise so little commotion that you won't be disturbed
one bit."

"Why your office?" asked Bella. "Wouldn't Rick
find more peace in my den? I'll just move out, and
hand it over to him entirely."

"Your den's too feminine…all pink and silk and
perfumed! A man needs to work in a manly atmosphere, a room impregnated with the smoke of good
cigars."

Rick enjoyed their battling for possession of him.

The higher bidder would get him; but he would still accept whatever the loser was willing discreetly to give him.

What actually happened is that Rick, unwilling to offend one by declaring the other the winner, asked that one of the spare bedrooms be converted into a study for him. Within forty-eight hours Rick had his own retreat on the first floor. Harry bought him a new bureau. Bella countered with a filing cabinet. Together they purchased a glass-fronted bookcase, which they stocked with dictionaries, books of reference, the latest novels and anthologies of poetry. They presented him with the key to his sanctum during a champagne toast, with which they rounded off a rather special dinner to celebrate Rick's resumption of his literary activities. Harry announced: "Rick, this key has a significance. It means that, when you're in the throes of creation, you can lock your door, and open it to nobody, under any circumstances at all."

"That's right, darling Rick, if you're hard at work, and you want anything, anything at all—food, drink or what-have-you—you just ring the bell, and I'll be up there like a shot from a gun."

What Harry had in mind was that he would sneak into Rick's study, unobserved by Bella to whom Rick would then deny access on the grounds that the muse had him in its spell. Bella, however, saw this thing otherwise. She anticipated being frequently summoned to the young author's presence for passionate sessions of fornication, while Harry knocked vainly on the door of one whose creative fever militated against his allowing anyone to enter his workroom.

Rick was happy to allow both of them to dream. He would so arrange matters that each of them spent a certain amount of time in his study, without the other knowing. He would no longer have to perform even the light office tasks he had hitherto been required to accomplish for Harry; and he would be free not only to enjoy the bodies of both of his employers, but also to delight them alternately, so that there would be no bounds to their gratitude.

He raised his glass of sparkling wine, and said, "I'd like to drink to the health and happiness of the two best friends any man ever had...to you, Bella, and to you Harry! God bless you both!" There were tears in Harry's eyes, no less than in Bella's, as they both approached him. Bella kissed him full on the mouth, parting her lips, and sucking his tongue as though Harry were in Lisbon or Adelaide. Harry was in no hurry. He let Bella enjoy her couple of minutes in their guest's arms, and then he took the boy in a fatherly embrace. The kiss he planted on Rick's mouth was no more paternal than Bella's had been sororal. He dug his tongue deep into the younger man's mouth, and held him close, kneading the firm flesh of his boyish buttocks. Bella separated them and flowed into the arms of her husband. He kissed her so savagely that Rick turned greenishly pale with jealousy. They all drank another glass of champagne, after which Harry smoked a cigar, while Rick and Bella danced like a couple of teenagers to popular records. After another bottle of champagne, Bella's need of Rick was so urgent that she begged Harry to take her to bed. Both Harry and Bella kissed Rick again passionately prior to allowing him to retire bitterly to his lonely bed.

The Parthams devoted their night to such satisfactory love-making, punctuated by the odd hour of sleep, that they came down to breakfast the following morning as radiant, gay and affectionate as lovers who had just spent their first wickedly delightful night together. Although neither of them knew the other was amorously involved with Rick, each of them felt erotically so much at ease in his presence that they kissed and cuddled without reserve throughout the meal. Bella once or twice expressed regret at the fact that they were not a foursome, and she kissed Rick two or three times, ostensibly for reasons of compassion, but Harry noticed, without jealousy, that she put her entire body into the consolatory kisses she bestowed upon their young guest. Rick was dressed in a sports shirt and tight pants, but his friends were both in night attire. Bella's nightgown was of the sheerest black nylon, while her wrap was of vermilion material scarcely more substantial or opaque than the nylon. Against Rick's body she was practically naked; and he rejoiced in the way she snuggled closer than close to him. Her treating her husband in the same way, however, shocked and angered her swain, who thought himself entitled to distribute his favors wheresoever money was plentiful without surrendering the right to others' fidelity towards him. Not suspecting for a moment that his conduct might rouse his young employee's envy, Harry unfastened the bow at Bella's waist, allowed her dressing-gown to fall from her shoulders, kissed the valley between her scarcely concealed breasts, and stroked her thighs in such a manner that the skirt of her nightdress was raised until her legs were entirely exposed. Her hands wandered inside the jacket of his pajamas, and caressed his powerful chest. She sighed as his hand went under her dress and up to her belly. Rick was livid, but they were both too excited to notice. Rick found himself lost in a fantasy, where he, Bella and Harry shared a threesome of flesh. He was fawned over by both his male and female lover, and then showered with expensive gifts after the fact. He was suddenly jolted from the daydream by Bella's high-pitched voice. She was calling out her husband's name.

Whether her cry of "Harry!" meant "Harry, that's enough," or "Harry, more!" Rick did not know; but Harry put on her exclamation such an interpretation that he patted her bottom, and went upstairs to dress. Bella lost no time in throwing herself into Rick's arms. He smelled of after-shave lotions, pomade and deodorant. She reeked of sex, and his loins ached for her. Her mouth was languorous on his. She begged him to love her; but he argued, "He might come back."

"He's gone up to dress," she insisted.

"But the servants?"

"They can all go to hell!"

She released him from her embrace, but he was not yet out of the woods. She threw herself into a cane sofa, ripped her nightie from top to bottom, opened her legs wide, and thrust almost the whole of her right hand into her sex. Her left hand trembled transparently as she stretched it out to him in febrile entreaty. He hurled himself onto her and into her. With more fury than love he shook an orgasm out of her prior to splashing her innards with his sperm. It was not a brilliant copulation, but Bella was pleased with him. She clung to him, her heart and flesh heavy with love.

"Go for a walk in the park!" she counselled. "Then, do some work in your study, when you come back; but summon your slave to your presence when you think you've earned me. Kiss me, darling. I love you, love you, love you. Brute!"

She ran from him, but, before disappearing from his sight, she opened her wrap, parted her thighs, bent her legs at the knees, and indicated her loins with both her hands. Having performed a brief and obscene belly-dance she danced her way up to the bathroom.

The Parthams' Jamaican maid entered the break-fast-room; and, for the first time, Rick noticed that she was young, lithe and graceful. He had never made love to a West Indian girl, because he had never met one who was willing and able to buy his favors; but that morning Bella had left him in such a state of frustration that only fear of antagonizing Bella and Harry prevented his stroking Nadia's tits as she swayed past him.

While Nadia cleared the table, Rick helped him-self to a liberal glass of Asback Uralt, which he drank in two or three gulps during the few minutes he spent stripping Nadia with his eyes. She smiled at him as she wiggled away to the kitchen; and he decided that his first best-selling novel, which he intended to start writing that morning, should be about a handsome, blond young man, intelligent, cultured, artistic and devastatingly charming, who seduces the brown-skinned maid of his wealthy friends, believing her to be an impecunious nobody, whereas she is no less that the university-educated daughter of the incredi-bly wealthy king of Jamaica.

He went up to his study, warmed by the wine and by his thought of Nadia's brown nudity. Knowing nothing about carbon copies and detail of that sort, Rick rolled a single sheet of thick, glazed paper into his new pale blue typewriter and laboriously tapped out the title of his epoch-making masterpiece: "Brown-skinned Princess." An hour later he under-lined the title, and added, "A novel by Basil de Vere."

When Bella entered Rick's study, at eleven o'clock, the fruits of two hours of creative activity glowed blackly against the creamy pallor of the most

118

expensive paper the local stationer had been able to obtain for her: the title of a novel, the name of the writer and three lines of childish monosyllables interspersed with words of two or three syllables grotesquely misused. It has been said, not once but frequently, that the only people incapable of writing novels are morons and men (or women) of genius. The wise man in question did not actually know Rick, but he knew thousands of Basil de Veres. Bella too had had dealings, of one sort or another, with many Basil de Veres; but, to her, Rick was not so much a dilettante as a new breed of literary genius. Much as she longed to feel his eager young front against the softness of her body, she felt herself dutybound to glance appraisingly at the opening passages of the novel and, although she was no fool, she was genuinely impressed by the illiterate weakness of what Rick had written. Françoise Mallet-Joris, though talented, could not write anything as puerile as Rick's initial essay at the composition of a first sentence of a novel; nor had she ever produced a literary gem which was more highly appreciated than was Rick's debut as an author. Without so much as a trace of hypocrisy, Bella was enraptured by what her lover had written. She read it aloud:

"He was an awfully nice boy. She was nice too, only she was black. But he did not really care about her being black. He sort of fell in love with her at first sight, and she fell in love with him at first sight, so they were both in love with each other from the beginning, and it was spring...."

Bella was rendered speechless by the poetic truth of what her gigolo had written. She had recognized his greatness from the outset, but she had been tempted to allow a born writer to fritter away his creative genius acting in plays written by lesser men.

How grateful she was to her wise Harry, whose lack of enthusiasm for the theatrical project had resulted in their discovering their darling's true vocation!

"Angel!" she gushed, "you've more than justified our faith in you. Up to now, it's wonderful. Let me kiss you!"

Thrilled by her obvious approval of his literary achievement, he obeyed her humble command. He let her kiss him.

"Hold me tight, darling!" she muttered through clenched teeth. "Keep me here with you. Lock the door."

Since he made no move to do as he was told, Bella locked the door herself. He protested, but she replied, "Rick darling, prove your love me by taking the occasional risk. Harry's gone over to see Mendel and Ida about Eva's exhibition, so he won't be back for at least an hour; and, even if he did come back, there's no reason why he should look for me here. If your door's locked, it means you're working; and, darling, like he said, when you're in a frantically creative mood, you open to no one. We'll wait till he's gone downstairs again, and then I'll slip out through the kitchen, come in through the French window of the lounge, and pretend I've been in the park."

Rick said unhappily, "He'll catch us one of these days."

She resisted the temptation to say she was convinced Harry already knew about their relationship. Instead she countered with, "Then what? Harry's no village simpleton. Neither he nor I expect the other to be saintly. He might chase you off the estate; but he wouldn't lock me in my room like the princess in an old-fashioned romance. He's too busy with all sorts of things to keep his eye on me day in day out; so you and I would still have lewd afternoons, evenings and nights in London."

Bella really believed that Rick's one worry was that any imprudence on their part would lead to their being parted. That he was more interested in her money and Harry's than in her body and her affection did not occur to her. Convinced that Rick loved her and desired her as much as she him, she repeated her plea that he love her; and he noted in her voice and gestures the sort of urgency which militated against his attaching the usual importance to prudence. If she thought the risks were worth taking, he had better not appear too cowardly. He put his arms around her, and the suppleness of her impatient body against his chased caution from his mind.

Her mouth was open and alive against his, her tongue delved into his mouth, and her quivering crotch clung to the bulge of his loins. He bent her backwards, and held her tight, putting into his kiss more brutality than tenderness. She remembered a previous occasion when his roughness had frightened her, but she smiled voluptuously. His ferocity no longer terrified her. It excited her. Suddenly he broke from her, and spat out the command, "Get stripped!"

Humbly she hastened to do her imperious lover's bidding. She made a show of it, taking her time with the removal of each item of her finery. Under her pastel-green linen dress she wore a slip of white nylon and matching panties whose brevity was mitigated by the fact that, together with a very short, frilly skirt, they formed one garment. Her firm breasts neither required nor enjoyed the benefit of a bra.

Rick started getting undressed at the moment when Bella lowered her panty-skirt, but his eyes did not leave her body for so much as the fraction of a second. He had seen her bare so many times that he had lost count; but every time she peeled for him he was astounded at the slim, youthful beauty of her figure. She helped him with the removal of his trousers and underpants, and she kissed that part of him which interested her the most.

His right hand found her. His fingers entered her. Her clitoris vibrated at his touch, and she moaned.

A vagina was penetrated by a phallus.

Bella's back was in happy contact with the white lamb's-wool carpet which Harry had insisted Rick must have in his study. Her sex was full of manhood, and her thighs were full of her concubine's haunches. Behind his rump her ankles were insistently knotted, and he slid easily in and out of her sex. His movements were devoid of all gentleness. He had drunk too much too early in the day, and she had begged him to use her. Feeling that, after a night and a post-breakfast copulation with Harry, she needed, not love, but bestiality, he bashed in and out of her with but two thoughts in his mind...to enjoy himself and to make her feel she was being used. Usually Rick sought to impress his generous, moneyed friends and acquaintances; but, even when he briefly forgot that he was a pro, luck would save him. He went at Bella's genitals as though she were either a whore or a penniless nymphomaniac, and she loved it. He was too drunk with wine and literary success to give a "tinker's damn," but he "did" Bella the way she liked to be "done." He tupped her with a "couldn't care less" nonchalance, and she felt that she was being loved. The very casualness of his possession of her delighted her, because it vouchsafed her the sensation of being dominated by a man with no thought in mind but his own pleasure and (secondarily) hers. If she had ever entertained vaguely and fleetingly the suspicion that

Rick was a prostitute, the way he took her that morning in his study banished such ideas from her head. He went into her with a fury which suggested that it was he who was paying her for the brief use of her whorish loins. From Harry she had gotten enough during the night and since breakfast; but her response to Rick's invasion of her secret flesh was that of a hot woman too long deprived of phallus. She rose to him, and she swayed away from him with harsh movements which were dictated by his. Her timing was instinctively perfect, so that each got the best of the other. It was a deep copulation, fierce and sweaty.

"I want to see you going full-depth into me," she gasped.

To oblige her, he stretched his arms full-length, so that his pale chest broke contact with her bosom. His body formed a steely curve. Her legs released his posterior, and fell to the carpet. He lay between her wide-open thighs, the only contact between his body and hers being his penis and her vagina. Riding deep into her, and making long movements of withdrawal, he watched his glistening pole bury itself totally in her sensitive meat. Raising her head from the rug, she too devoured with her eyes the point of contact between her loins and his. She was so excited, so hot, wet and open that he slid in and out of her with puissant ease. Her entire body was an open wound into which his hot knife jabbed callously.

His orgasm was paralysis, dynamite, jelly and then inertia. He left Bella in mid-air, but that was no tragedy, since her consolation lay in the knowledge that he loved her with all his pure, tender heart. She felt him grow small within her, and she held him lovingly close to her vibrant flesh.

Rick dozed for half an hour on top of his mistress.

When he again showed signs of life, she kissed him, whispered her thanks, and added, "You know, darling, this was the first time an artist loved me in his study."

Flattered by the "artist," he sought to hide his embarrassment by retorting, "...and I thought you'd been loved by every sort of man in every sort of place."

She reached for his pocket of Chesterfields, lit two, and handed him one. They both drew deeply on their respective cylinders of tobacco-filled paper.

"I'm going to surprise you, Rick," she answered, "but I think I'm less wicked than you imagine I am. It's my own fault, of course, because, since I fell in love with you—almost at first sight—I've behaved like a tramp. But...can you believe this?...you're the first lover I've asked Harry either to entertain or to help. Until you, I had fun here and there; but I didn't have lovers...regular lovers, and I always made a clear distinction between my home life and my adventures with Tom, Dick, and Henri. I'm pretty sure Harry knows I'm not faithful to him all the time, just as I know he doesn't spit on a juicy quim when it's offered to him; but, apart from our participation in a few wild sex-parties organized by one and another of our mutual friends, neither of us has flaunted our infidelity before the other...that is, until you came along. Now, I don't know Harry's wise to what's going on between you and me, but I respect his intelligence too much to assume he thinks I'm just a big sister to you. As I see it, his attitude is that, as long as he doesn't actually catch me with my legs wide open, and you on top of me, the relationship between you and me is none of his business. What he requires of us is that we don't push our conduct under his nose; and I'm sure that, if he thought you were in me, here or anywhere else, he'd keep out of the way; not so much to avoid embarrassing us as to spare himself the necessity of admitting that he knows his wife is betraying him with his best friend."

Rick stroked her bottom, and wondered aloud, "Well...if you've...sort of...never brought men here before...why did you...I mean...er...I mean...why did you invite me to come and stay with you?"

She kissed him softly before replying. "Why? I don't really know why. You see, darling, apart from Harry, you're the first man I ever loved...really loved. You understand? Yes, my love, you're puzzled. You're thinking of Paris...and Dane."

He did not see the connection, but she mistook his dullness for a sign that he was indeed unable to reconcile her conduct in Dane's studio with her insistence that she had fallen in love with him almost the moment she met him. She hastened to explain.

"Those twenty-four hours with you and Dane," she said, "are as much of a mystery to me as they are to you; because, leaving out of account a few drunken parties, when Harry and I joined with friends in sexual orgies, I've only once before experienced anything vaguely resembling our three-cornered session of love at Montparnasse and in your hotel room; and that was more than twenty years ago. Give me a drink, and I'll tell you all about, if you're interested."

He mixed her a gin and dry vermouth, which she drank in one gulp. He gave her the same again, and she sipped the second glass during the pauses in her narrative.

"I was about eighteen," she began, "when I first met David Malcuzein and his nephew Anton. David's about twenty years older than I and Anton was about my age or perhaps a year younger. David wanted Daddy to provide the capital for the exploitation of his revolutionary anti-freeze system for internal combustion engines. It was the end of July when David called in to see Daddy. He'd been to collect Anton from public school for the summer holidays, and he was killing two birds with one stone. They didn't stay long; but long enough for Anton and I to find each other rather cute. I forgot him within a couple of days, mainly, I suppose, because I had a lover—my first—who worked in Manchester, and used to take me into the woods and corn fields when he came home about once a month. His name was Les. He came home the weekend after my first encounter with Anton, and, although there was no sentiment whatsoever in the relationship between Les and me, I enjoyed the things he and I did together in the undergrowth far too much to waste any time thinking about the shy Polish boy. But, a fortnight later, Daddy told me David Malcuzein was coming again, to discuss details of his anti-freeze project. He said David would be coming to spend the whole day at our house on the thirtieth of August, and that he'd be spending the night, so that they could devote the entire day to examining the matter together. He also said that Anton would be coming along too, because David regarded him as his successor in the business.

"Well, darling, I don't know whether in was Daddy or David who got his dates mixed up; but Daddy thought David and Anton would arrive on the morning of the thirtieth, spend the whole day outlining their plan to him, stay the night, and leave the next day…early or late, according to the progress made. David understood he was to arrive on the twenty-ninth, so that he, Anton and Daddy could get to work the next day at the crack of dawn. Anyway David and Anton arrived quite early on the evening of the twenty-ninth. I wasn't expecting them, so I'd given the staff the evening off, and Daddy was in town until the following morning. They understood my predicament, and were quite willing to motor to London and come back the next morning; but, thinking Daddy was at fault, I insisted on their staying for the sort of cold meal I was then capable of preparing. I think you'll agree, darling, that I'm now more of a cook than I was then."

He kissed her, and sang, "You cook like an angel cooks."

"And you kiss like an obscene devil kisses," she muttered, "and I'm going on with my tale before you have chance to put your evil schemes into operation, or would you rather I didn't unveil my wicked past?"

Rick assured Bella that her erotic experiences intrigued him, so she continued. "We dined together, and drank a couple of bottles of Rosé d'Anjou. During the meal Anton's eyes scarcely left me, but he said nothing, except to answer briefly my questions and David's. David and I, however, got on like a house on fire. He owes most of his success, I'd say, to his gift of the gab. He oozes personality and cocksureness; and, young as I then was, I was an experienced hostess. Since the age of fourteen I'd been allowed, in fact required, to stay up late whenever Daddy received guests for dinner. You see, Mummy left us when I was fourteen, so Daddy and I were more than father and daughter; we were pals. Daddy's confidence in me had given me an aplomb rare in a girl of eighteen years, so that I felt myself closer to David than to his rather nice nephew. Anton was handsome, faultlessly groomed, frightfully polite and a shocking bore—although I was not then prepared to admit the last bit. In fact, I thought him rather sweet, and, although the cat seemed to have run away with his tongue, the way he looked at me flattered and thrilled me. He was so innocent, and I was so sullied after four or five sessions of love in a haystack, that I wanted to rub a little of my dirt off on him. But there was nothing doing. I couldn't even get him to say anything more to me than his one-word replies to my banal questions.

"After the meal we drank coffee, and I opened a bottle of Slivovitz David had brought for Daddy. Ever drunk Slivovitz, Rickie?"

Rick thought for a moment before asking, "Is that the Yugoslavian stuff...like vodka, but with a plummy taste?"

She threw her arms about his neck, kissed him playfully, and cried, "top marks for my beloved man of the world! Powerful stuff, eh, Rickie-boy? Well, it certainly got me going, especially after the vin rosé. We were drinking our second or third generous glass of plum brandy, when Anton excused himself for a few minutes. As soon as he was out of the room, his uncle got to work, putting in a good word for him. He told me Anton had insisted on accompanying him for no other reason than that he'd wanted to see me again, that the boy was in love with me and all that sort of junk. He said he'd been observing me, and he was sure I fancied the boy as much as he fancied me. I admitted that Anton's shyness and gentle good looks attracted me, and David told me I'd have to do the chasing. He made it clear to me that Anton's timidity was pathological. The boy was so lacking in self-confidence that it was tragic. He had all that was needed to please the girls, plus the normal young man's desires, but his only hope of getting himself a sweetheart was that some forward lassie would bluntly ask him to take her walking in the moonlight. Frankly, Rick, I wasn't on the lookout for a boyfriend, but I'd have enjoyed a slap and a tickle with handsome Anton. What I wasn't prepared to do, however, was to cheapen myself by doing the asking, and I told David so. I refilled his glass and mine, and we both drank Slivovitz in silence for a while. Anton was away longer than one would think anyone needs to answer the call of nature, which gave David time to make a strange suggestion. He asked if I'd be prepared to flirt with him in order to arouse Anton's hunting instincts. What he had in mind was that he should warm me up, and then hope his nephew would find me so seductive that he'd acquire the courage to court me."

Rick interrupted, "Sounds like a film I saw some time ago…a historical film with Mel Ferrer."

"José, darling! José Ferrer in the role of Cyrano de Bergerac…Edmond Rostand!"

"Oh, yes! Now I remember…Josie Ferrer!"

Bella knew that any attempt to encourage Rick to pay anyone the compliment of pronouncing his or her name correctly was tantamount to trying to knock down a brick wall with a human head, so she sidestepped the question of José Ferrer's South American origin, and continued. "Well, darling, I was having none of this Cyrano lark; but I expressed agreement all the same. You see, Rickie, I rather liked Anton, but I'd had enough to drink, and that made the excitement of David count for more than his nephew's boyish niceness. I agreed to flirt with David, because I wanted to flirt with him; but I let him think, or I hoped he thought, I was doing it for Anton. Anyway, when Anton came back a few minutes later, he found his uncle and me in a passionate clinch and, boy, you can take my word for it that it was passionate and then some. I'd necked with a few boys in my time, and with a couple of older men too; and I had my special boy-friend, whom I'd allowed to do much more than kiss me; but I'd never felt as filthy during and after a kiss as I did then with David Malcuzein. That first kiss was so deep into me that after it I didn't give a damn. I felt as any girl would if a young man had caught her actually being done by his uncle. The worst seemed already to have happened. I no longer had a reputation, so to hell with caution and pretense!"

"David kissed me again, his hands all over me without actually disarranging my clothing; and, remembering why he and I were supposed to be smooching, he made a present of me to Anton. Without so much as a shadow of shame, I let Anton kiss me. I went to him with my mouth open and greedy. His kiss was not without a certain thrill, but he added nothing to the situation. When David took me back I was no warmer than I had been when he'd handed me over. He soon changed that. On a broad sofa I was a rose between two thorns...or, to be more precise, between two horns. David kissed me again, and his hands stroked my stockinged thighs inside my skirts. I kept my legs together, but not so tightly as to strangle hope; and I really enjoyed David's tongue between my lips, the menace of his teeth and the power in his right hand on the bare flesh between my stocking-tops and the lace of my panties. He felt himself obliged to surrender me to Anton's arms, and playing the part I'd accepted, I let Anton hold me and mouth my lips until it was uncle's turn again. David was stretched back as far as possible from Anton, and he received me on top of him, between his parted thighs. As I lowered myself onto him, his hands floated behind me, raising my skirts and dropping them onto the small of my back as my soft front snuggled against the iron of his short, stocky body. He kissed me, and his hands grabbed my silk-covered buttocks, holding my crotch hard against his living, swollen man. One of his hands went under my ass, and his fingers were only the thickness of silk from the real Bella. His tongue dug into me, and my girl wept into my knickers. I must have cut a very undignified figure in Anton's eyes, my almost naked rump jutting upwards and outwards; but I think I didn't disgust him, because he didn't turn me down when his dutiful uncle threw me into his arms. By then I was wide open. If Anton had had the courage to take me, he could have had me, and I do mean *had* me. David had done what he'd promised to do. He'd gotten me all heated up; he hadn't lied when he'd described his nephew as a sexual disaster. Don't imagine the boy was too tender. He was young and strong, and he hugged me like a bear squeezes an imprudent keeper. The trouble was that it was all wild enthusiasm, with not so much as a vague suggestion of adult fire. He lacked erotic subtlety and imagination.

"Back to David. I don't know now it happened. I went into his arms, my legs were thrown over the back of the sofa, so that my skirts fell onto my belly, exposing the full length of my legs as well as the silken triangle of my panties. David knelt on the rug at the side of the sofa. His mouth and mine were a lewd kiss, and his hands were full of my clothed breasts, which he squashed and massaged most thrillingly. After a while, his lips left mine, and he kissed my thighs until, crazed, I opened my thighs to admit his head; and then I closed them again, holding against me his muzzle and his hungry teeth which sank into my quim through the veil of my panties. I was in a sweat and a frenzy. I writhed, groaned and muttered obscenities. His fingers tore at the buttons of my dress; I was suddenly impelled to jerk myself free of him, and seized Anton with every ounce of strength in my quivering body. He could have saved me from David; but he just accepted what I offered him, making no attempt to take anything more. I'd rejected David at the very moment when I'd otherwise have given in without a struggle; and Anton could have killed two birds with one spear. He could have had me for himself, and he could have saved me from his lascivious uncle; but he let me down, and I was furious. A lovely, hot girl offers her melting body to a boy, and he spits on her drooling vagina. If I'd the strength, I'd have thumped him into a coma; but I was trembling from head to foot. I was drunk with both alcohol and passion. In desperation I'd begged the boy who supposedly loved me to prove that he was worthy of my girlish affection, and he'd behaved like a spineless damsel; so I no longer cared whether he sank or swam.

"It was David's turn, and he set my tits free as he tongued my gums. Between his lips my nipples swelled and hardened, and I sighed, and rubbed myself against him. I held him close to me, and my frantic loins jerked themselves against the vibrant hill of his imprisoned penis. I cried out, 'Stop it! Let me be!' and he poured Slivovitz between my chattering teeth. I was thirsty, and my throat was parched. I swallowed liquor as though it were water; and he hurled me into the arms of his tame companion, who could even then have rescued me, had he but peeled off my panties, which were scorching my sex. He contented himself with kissing me, and David tore me from his arms. I broke away from David's grasp, tried to grasp a glass of liquor, and sent it hurtling to the carpet. David seized the bottle, and poured into my mouth just enough to satisfy my craving. Gratefully, I clung to him, and glued my mouth to his. I helped him to take my dress off. I'd drunk more than enough; but, make no mistake about this! I knew what was going on. It was not a case of a helplessly inebriated wench being taken advantage of by a boy. I really helped him to take off my dress, my under-skirt and my garter belt. My bosom was bare, and I was proud of the glint in David's eyes as he looked at me. All I was wearing were my silk stockings, sagging down below my knees, and a pair of what we called in those days 'French knickers.' We kissed again and his hands were pure delight from my knees to my face, back and front. He kneaded my breasts, he nib-bled on my nipples. He caressed my bottom, and he rubbed my cunt through its covering of silk. He got me hotter and hotter, and then he gave me to Anton again. The lad had nothing to do but whip off my breeches and stab me; but he kissed me at great length. We were still kissing when I felt David's hands at my bum, fondling me languorously. His fin-gers went to the waistband of my pants, and he pulled them down, down, down. Together with my stockings they left me, and I was utterly naked, with a clothed man against my front and another against my back."

Bella halted briefly, kissed Rick hard, and pushed him away from her. She grabbed him again, and kissed him at length and in depth.

"Shall I go on?" she asked; and he hoarsely answered, "Yes!"

"Am I exciting you?" she asked; but, without giv-ing him a chance to confirm or deny her suspicion, she continued. "Anton's mouth and mine broke con-tact, David took charge of me, and told his nephew to get undressed. I didn't like that. I'd agreed to let David flirt with me in order to encourage Anton to make a pass at me; but this stripping business was not part of the plan. I'd let David take my clothes off,

because I wanted him to see me and touch me naked.
I didn't like the idea of one man warming me up and
stripping me so that a spineless boy could spill his
cream in my womb; but, while the younger hurried
out of his clothes, Cyrano did to me such things as no
words of mine could possibly describe. What I mean
is, it wasn't what he did, but the way he did it. He
kissed me all over, fondled me with hands which
passed through all the degrees of tenderness and brutality in a few seconds, and twisted me into every
shape imaginable. During that long embrace and
those kisses I didn't actually put into words my pleas
that he deny me to his nephew and that he take me
himself; but my sighs and groans and the way I
writhed in his arms, rubbing my nakedness against
him, must have left him in no doubt that I wanted
him urgently. When he handed me over to his naked
companion, I revolted briefly, and clung to him,
devouring his lips with my crazed mouth; but he
acted as though I were a whore whom he'd bought
for his nephew's pleasure. It was as though I were
entertaining a client under the supervision of a
whoremaster, instead of taking part in a nice little
love-session. I felt inclined to issue an
ultimatum—either David send Anton to bed or the
party was over. But David took a firm, humiliating
grip on my body, and gave me to Anton. I hadn't the
will to defy him, so I decided to make the best of a
bad job.

"I looked at Anton and wondered what I was
beefing about. Dressed too carefully and almost
effeminately, he'd looked weak and a bit juvenile, but
he stripped athletically. He wasn't heavily muscled,
but there was a subtle air of young power about his
tall, slender, bronzed body; and his penis had a
healthy, threatening springiness about it. In fact, it

was a promising weapon, longer and more robust
that I'd expected on so young, so timid, so inexperienced and so finely built a man; and there was no
doubting its eagerness. It flowed and throbbed as
though it would burst. I compared it with the one
penis my loins had already tasted—a highly satisfying
one—and it seemed that I was in for a good time. A
good time, but a painful one. Even after the first
time, my lover had occasionally hurt me with the
impatience of his entry into my tunnel, and Anton's
tool was larger, so much so that I wondered whether
such a thing could penetrate me without drawing
blood. It certainly needed no caressing to give it the
size and erection necessary for an invasion. I touched
it, and it was like a living thing between my fingers
which trembled as much from excitement as from
fear. I put a hand under it, and it jerked upwards, like
a cylinder of hot metal with a spring behind it.
Hoping to render its bite less painful than its bark
was frightening, I went down on my knees, and
moistened it with my saliva. I licked it from balls to
knob, and then slid it deep into my mouth. It was a
delicious sensation, this gigantic lollipop burning
inside my mouth. His knob almost choked me. The
trembling of his body told me the thrill was as great
for him as for me. I was just going to transfer his cock
from my throat to my vagina, when I felt David's
nakedness behind me. He'd stripped while I was
sucking Anton. He told me to go on gamahuching
Anton, and I obeyed, while he stuck his head in the
triangle formed by my open thighs and the rug I was
kneeling on. I felt his mouth on my sex. His teeth, his
tongue, his lips went into me, and it was heavenly. He
held my haunches with both hands. He licked me and
sucked me. He did me with his tongue. Oh, Rick, I'd
never dreamed it could be like that. His mouth had

me, and he was eating me up. Darling, he ate me until I went out of my mind. With his fingers, he kept my cunt folds spread wide apart, so that he would have total access to my sex. He licked up and down the tingling sexflesh and poked his hot tongue deeply into my burning gash. Then he licked from my asshole to the top of my cunt, until his tongue found my clitoris. I was on fire with desire, a burning pussy just melting into his mouth. I was so deliriously happy that I almost forgot Anton, whose horn I went on sucking absentmindedly. Suddenly Anton cried out, and my mouth was full of muck. I spewed everything out over the boy's deflated phallus and quivering thighs. I was disgusted and disappointed; and Anton was so weakened by his orgasm that he went sprawling backward onto the couch when I feebly pushed him from me. Kiss me, Rick! Kiss me hard!"

Rick lost no time in carrying out his lady's instructions. His arms were strong about her, and their tongues fused greedily. She held her knees apart with her hands, silently begging him to lance the abscess of her lust. "Lick me, the way David did," she begged, and Rick obliged, quickly bringing his mouth to the rescue of her swelling sexflesh. He spread the cunt lips apart, as she'd described, and he licked the length of her cunt—starting at her sweet asshole and traveling to the bud of desire that twitched for his attention.

"Oh Rick, you're eating me just as I want it," she moaned. "It's so perfect; your mouth, your tongue, the way you eat me—it's all so perfect."

Rick's tongue dove into the depth of her pussy, and he plunged in and out of her hole while beginning to rub her hardened clit bud with his thumb. She moaned wildly as he proceeded to plunge and rub her private parts, until her thighs began to quiver uncontrollably. She grabbed hold of Rick's blond head and pressed it into her pussy.

"Suck my clit, now, baby," she pleaded. "Suck mama's clit while you finger fuck her pussy."

Rick obliged again, and within moments, he could feel her cunt muscles tighten around his fingers, and felt her entire cunt swell, as the first orgasmic wave rose in her belly and sent her jism drizzling down through her cunt. She pulled his face so tight between her legs that he could barely breathe. He responded by sucking harder, more intently, until every last drop of come had been drained from her. As he motioned to clean her come-stickied cunt, she momentarily flinched—the powerful orgasm had made her cunt and clit ever-so-sensitive. But Rick pressed on and licked her clean. She then pulled him toward her in such a way that she could take his excited cock into her mouth and return the favor of oral love. She sucked him until he moaned for mercy, crying out for the deeper pleasure of her cunt. She lay back, spread herself open wide and invited him to fuck her.

"It's all yours, my lover," she cooed. "Fill me up with your cock; pour your spunk into the deepest recesses of my womb!" He lifted himself over her, aimed his cock toward her awaiting cunt and cut into her with vigor. They copulated fiercely for about fifteen minutes before Rick bombarded the depths of her sensitive vagina with his sperm. Spent, he professionally behaved in such a way as to deceive her into thinking she still interested him as a woman. Her heart and sweetly replete flesh were full of the tenderest and most grateful love for him, so that her passionless mouth adored his nakedness lazily. They glided into the brief, light sleep of lovers whose bodies are as one.

Bella roused Rick with a kiss. She fingered his

limp penis, which stirred, and he kissed her softly. Her body was fresh against his. His hands were butterflies which brushed her skin from her face to her feet. She rested her tired tongue on his moist lips, his face in her hands; and he went into her calmly, possessed her smoothly, and brought her to a scarcely perceptible orgasm which eased a whispered, "Bless you lover!" from her lips at the moment when his gentle dew oozed into her.

She lit two cigarettes simultaneously, and placed one between his lips. They floated upon clouds of aromatic smoke. Her mouth found his, and they exchanged exhalations of tobacco-tainted breath. She invited him to draw on her cigarette, and she puffed at his, feeling that she and he belonged each to the other. She was his Juliet, his Cleopatra, his mistress and his slave. He gave her strength, and yet, nestling against him, she felt small. She had seduced him, but she was an innocent girl struck dumb with the enormity of what she had allowed him to do to her. Proud of this handsome young man's adoration of her, she enjoyed the ineffable luxury of identifying herself with any and every female child whose pure love has betrayed her into allowing the object of her affections to sully her. Wide awake, she dreamed as they silently smoked their cigarettes.

Bella was the first to speak. Simply and sincerely, her voice thick with emotion and erotic fullness, she announced, "I love you, Rick."

He held her to him, and kissed the top of her head. She stayed in his arms like that for several minutes, until he asked, "What happened after you pushed Anton back onto the sofa?"

She smiled brightly, but wearily, and teased, "So my naughty tupper likes his naughty Bella to perform verbal stripteases! Do you like to visualize me kneeling there, bare and expectant, with my oozing cunt in the mouth of a man I'm meeting only for the second time in my young life? After the way I let you and Dane muck about with me in Paris nothing ought to surprise you about me, and I guess you don't have to have a sixth sense to know what happened next. I don't know whether David made me go on sucking Anton in the hope that what did happen would happen; and I've often wondered since then whether my desire for David didn't cause me subconsciously to wish that circumstances would brush his nephew out of the way. Anyway, whether or not it was planned, the boy had shot his bolt; he could do no more than look on helplessly as his uncle rode into me. David's penis didn't look anything like as promising as Anton's. In fact it was no longer, but much thinner, pale and cold-looking. It seemed to have no life in at all, and, instead of being crowned with a glowing bulb, it tapered away pathetically. Looking at it, I thought it was soft, and that it still had to stiffen and extend. I took it in my hands, and was surprised at its icy hardness. I wouldn't have kissed it for all the bullion in Fort Knox. In fact, if I hadn't been dying for some harsh loving, I'd have waited until Anton's lovely penis got back into fighting shape. I looked from one body to the other. Even with the wind knocked out of him, Anton was handsome, appetizing; but his uncle was anything but the answer to a maiden's prayer. His thin, veinless phallus didn't seem part of the rest of him. Short and stocky, with a windbeaten face that seemed to have been deeply chiselled out of granite, he looked more like a hairy ape than an eighteen-year-old girl's lover. From the base of his throat to the band of his hands and to his toes he was covered with black hair, tinged with red here and there. You talk about fine feathers making fine birds. Well, David proved the point, darling. That he went to a good tailor was obvious. His suit, shirt, tie, shoes and so on had the expensive look about them; he had dress sense, taste and a way of carrying clothes. Dressed, he didn't bear much resemblance to a gentleman, but he was a polished, self-confident man of the world. Naked, he looked like the sort of a man one sees, stripped to the waist, working in the vineyards of southern Italy, like the uncouth morons who pose as inarticulate wild men in third-rate travelling circuses. Even his arms, which seemed to be of normal proportions inside the sleeves of his jacket, hung down below his knees, and his hands were suddenly enormous. His shoulders broad and bulging with muscles, his chest revoltingly inflated, and his waist slim above powerful haunches and short, sturdy legs! Just the opposite of my beautiful Rick!"

Rick was flattered, and he knew what was required of him. He bestowed a cool kiss on her fresh mouth, and cradled her in his arms as she went on. "Anton had let me make a fool of him, but David was made of sterner stuff. He knew the sight of the boy and the taste of his loins had excited me, and that the gnawing at my quim had increased the thrill within my flesh; but he probably guessed that his own appearance somewhat reduced my enthusiasm, so he gave me no time for second thoughts. His arms were strong about me, and his kiss put paid to any ideas about resistance that I might have been entertaining. I clung to him, and hugged his groin with mine. He lowered me to the rug, on my back, and opened my thighs, as though I were a book he was going to read. He took a firm grip on each of my feet with one of his hands, and bent my legs at the knees, so that my heels were pressed against my buttocks. Kneeling, with his knees on either side of my ass, he touched the entry of my girlhood with his man. He leaned over me, raised my shoulders from the rug, and drew my bosom to his chest. At the same time his thin spear pierced my secret flesh. He went full length with one deep thrust, and it was heavenly. He packed himself tight into me and against me, and he whipped me into a frenzy. What strength in those loins. Between his front and mine was a revolting cushion of hair; but, instead of putting me off, it added to the excitement because it rubbed deliciously against my clit bud and heightened my desire. It was beauty and the beast. I was so young, so freshly pretty, so soft and so perfumed; and I was allowing myself to be debauched by an animal who was the uncle of the boy I'd hoped was going to be my playmate.

"It was savage, Rick. That man knew all the tricks, and he didn't leave out one of them. He changed his rhythm every four or five strokes; and he taught me the meaning of tenderness as well as the agony a girl can experience at the hands of a sadist. One thing is certain—David didn't make love to me. He possessed me, he used me, did me, exploited my body, took me, had me. He mastered me, and he fucked me. There seemed to be no limit to his strength and his endurance. He made me come time after time; and I was in heaven, Rick. It was delightful. It was disgusting. Yes, I admit that. There was nothing noble or beautiful about what David did to me. He was out for his own, proud manly pleasure; and he was determined that I should be so satisfied that I'd come back for more. Skillfully he put me through the erotic mill; and I thought he was the Sex God almighty. I don't know how many times I reached the top before he bombarded me with a flood of sperm, but I recall that, when he exploded, the helpless jerking of his

141

rod in and out of me roused me from a sort of dream, the luxurious sleep of one who's absorbed as much pleasure as she can stand. Every orgasm he'd given me had ripped sighs of gratitude from my throat; but his own explosion proved to me that he was a weak mortal like myself, and my heart swelled with love for him.

"Rick, my darling, there's no greater joy than a girl's when the abundant milk of her several comings is topped off with the thick cream of her lover's ecstasy. His stuff gushed into me without appearing to waken him. After his moment of supreme joy he went into me with renewed vigor, while Anton slept in an untidy heap on the settee. His every jag seemed to be timed, measured and weighed for maximum effect, and my tenderest parts sang hymns of praise as the tensions in my guts rose. I got hotter and hotter. My arms held his torso so tight that I ached in all my muscles, and I used all the strength in my legs and my belly to make him feel welcome within me. My nether parts ebbed and flowed with rhythmic force as his delvings into the grease of my twat increased in effortless aggression. I was his. I couldn't have been easier, warmer, messier, more open. Metaphorically, I was on my knees, begging him to filth me, to enslave me, to degrade me and to hurt me. If I could have died, with his hairy crotch against my Venus-mound, his plunger right there, like a hot poker up my chuff, I'd have used my last breath to thank Heaven for little boys who grow up into shaggy gorillas. Christ, he drove me hard. After I'd had God knows how many sighing, groaning apexes of obscenities, he stiffened, crashed against my sore lady, filled me full to overflowing of intoxicating liquor, and swooned.

"I know neither how long we dozed nor how it happened that I awoke to find him lying, as one crucified, about two yards away from me. I crawled to him on my belly, and offered myself to him. He pushed me lazily away, and turned his back on me. Furious, I turned him over, and hurled my tongue into his mouth. He shook his head, rubbed his eyes with his fists, coughed deeply, and fought for breath. I rose, squatted my hot cunt over his face and begged him to indulge me with his tongue, once again. But he pushed me off and laughed again. His breathing was like that of someone on the verge of asphyxiation. Impatient, angry and embarrassed, he turned his back on me. After a few minutes his breathing became more normal, and he turned to me, nodded his head in Anton's direction, begged me not to forget Tony..."

"Who you had forgot," added Rick, with his customary respect for the language of Aldous Huxley and Charles Morgan.

Bella's hands wandered over her lover's body. They fondled his sex, and rose to his face, which they cradled while she bestowed upon his lifeless mouth a kiss which paradoxically combined the heat of flames and the freshness of spring water.

"I'd almost forgotten Anton, it's true; but I joined him on the sofa, and I kissed new life into him. I grabbed hold of his lovely cock and kissed the round head as his whole shaft rose to greet my mouth. Then I took him inside my mouth and sucked the delicious male morsel while toying with his balls through his generous scrotum sac. He groaned with renewed pleasure as my head moved up and down, and my hand helped move his stiff prick in and out of my mouth.

"I maneuvered my body into a 'sixty-nine' position with his, and not-so-subtly placed my burning crotch onto his mouth, hoping he'd know what to do.

If he was put off by the scent and abundance of his uncle's creamy come, which still lingered in my cunt, he didn't show it. He commenced licking my hot slash and drinking out the remains of his relative's spunk. I pushed my pussy down hard, mashing my cunt lips into his mouth, as I generously sucked his engorged cock. Soon, I moved myself slightly, so as to deposit my erected clitoris in his mouth. Slowly, he got the hint, and began to lap away at my swollen love bud. He was somewhat haphazard in his licking, so I pressed my clit onto his tongue until I was in a position that proved delicious for my excited slash. My hips began gyrating and I was humping his mouth, because I felt myself on the edge of a climax. I sucked him harder, while rubbing my clit against his tongue more aggressively, until I felt the come well up in my belly and then explode into his mouth. He just kept lapping away, not quite sure that I'd come. I could feel his own passion coming close to a climax.

"I switched positions, bringing my pussy level with his prick, and lowered myself onto his steel rod of sexual pleasure. It sailed in smoothly, and filled me in a delicious way. I moved up and down on his pole until I could tell by his pumping and panting that he was about to give me a second helping of his spunk. I slammed down on him to greet his increasingly intense upward thrusts and when he suddenly grabbed hold of my titties and began to bite and suck them in a wild and wanton—though inexperienced—way, I knew his rocket was about to blast off.

'Give it to me, Anton, baby,' I cooed 'That's right, shoot it into my hole. It's all open and ready for you.'

"He grabbed hold of my titties and sucked fiercely as he moaned, groaned and gyrated like an animal in heat. His sperm shot up and into me and his face crinkled up in a wild-looking grimace as he spluttered the last drop of jism into my receptacle. I could feel my cunt fill up with his warm come.

"I must say, ultimately, he loved me with a refreshing, unschooled directness which procured me moments of joy; and then David took me over. We went up to my room, and, throughout the night, I passed from one to the other. The next day I stayed in bed until lunch time, and the remarks Daddy made suggested he knew why. But he didn't allow his suspicions to influence his decision with regard to the business at hand. He closed a deal with David, whom I consequently met regularly during the ensuing couple of years. I never met Anton again, but that was no tragedy. I preferred David's loving, although I didn't like him, to Anton's, although he was rather sweet. It was David who introduced me to Harry. Although I've never told the details, he knows David and I often slept together when I was in my late and tempestuous teens. What Harry doesn't know is that David shared me for a night with his nephew. Harry's never met Anton, so I've never thought of telling him about that night. In fact, I've always kept it to myself until today; but—I don't know why—I just wanted you to know about it. I'd like you to know all about me, no secrets! Do you think I'm a slut?"

She posed the question as would a girl who had just lost the flower of her virginity, and who wanted her lover to know she did not grant indiscriminately such favors as she had bestowed upon him. Rick forgot for a moment that she was a woman of considerable erotic experience. He put his arms around her, and whispered, "You're the last girl I'd call a slut, but I think it's time you put your clothes on and went downstairs."

She kissed him girlishly, and whispered, "I'm making a nuisance of myself?"

He slapped her bottom playfully, and answered, "You could never do that, but I wouldn't like Harry to catch us like this."

Making herself as small as possible against his naked front, Bella said, "If he caught us on the job and made a fuss, I'd tell him to go and fuck himself."

She reluctantly dressed and left him to continue his novel, of which he had written three more sentences when Harry burst in on him with a bottle of pre-lunch Tío Pepe.

An hour after Harry's interruption in Rick's study Bella tapped on the door, to announce that lunch was ready; but her men were too busy to do more than grunt, "All right! We'll be down in two ticks."

When they eventually joined her for lunch, Rick was almost as reluctant to meet her gaze as was Harry, who averted his eyes like a guilty boy. However, a few glasses of Guinness gave them both new confidence, with the pride of a woman who knows herself loved and desired by two men.

Rick passed the afternoon in his study, alone, while Harry and Bella wandered off into the sun-drenched woods together.

VI.

Rick's career as a novelist was as short-lived as had been the period of his theatrical ambitions. Like a spoiled boy who destructively throws down his most precious toy the moment he sees that Johnnie next door has something he does not possess, so Haylett forsook his typewriter on the day of Eva Dalheim's exhibition at the Karstein Gallery in Oxford Street. It was a brilliant occasion. Success was no novelty to Eva, whose canvases sold so easily and for such high figures that the exhibition was a superfluous gesture, a little luxury she could well afford, the whim of a retiring artist who likes now and then to emerge from prosperous obscurity and bathe briefly in the lime-light. Even if Eva relied on the purchase of her work by friends, she would sell all a painter of average pro-ductivity can offer for sale; but she was a prolific artist whose work was extremely varied in character. She could not satisfy the demand for her paintings. Exhibitions were, consequently, the last of her requirements; but friends coaxed her, and she agreed to exhibit, so that they could make a social event of the pompous opening of the exhibition. Speeches were delivered, cocktails were drunk, hats and frocks were paraded, and friends who met regularly greeted each other with such an effusion as to suggest they were surprised to meet each other at Eva's exhibition after such a devastatingly long separation.

In such a strange atmosphere, Rick trembled with excitement. He rubbed shoulders with opera divas, actors and actresses, journalists, novelists, playwrights, cocottes dripping with vulgar diamonds, bankers, industrialists and their tastefully, expensively clad wives and daughters. Never before had he been in the presence of so many prospective victims, or, shall we say, clients. They were so numerous that he did not know where to begin. Bella and Harry introduced him to so many people in rapid succession that he had no time to register the relative financial importance of those whose acquaintance he made. He had already met some of those present at parties, but finally he was unable to distinguish between total strangers and those he had previously met. He was comparable with the famished beggar who, erroneously invited to the Lord Mayor of London's inauguration dinner, finds himself expected to eat, at one sitting, food representing a sum of money which would have kept him alive for a month. If Rick had been allowed to meet all the money-bags at Eva's exhibition one by one over a period of years, his troubles would have been over and he'd never have to go out looking for "work." Such were his thoughts; but, for every ten fish that slipped through his net, a fat one got caught, and there was little chance that he would ever find himself without a victim. Much, however, wants more and, despite his success, he felt himself deprived as long as there existed one fool who failed to enrich him.

Both Bella and Harry went out of their respective ways to introduce Rick to as many people as possible; and they tried to ensure that he was not left to his own devices more than was absolutely necessary. It was, however, inevitable that Bella or Harry would be pulled in one direction or another. The result was that Rick was frequently required to paddle his own canoe. To be alone in a crowd is disagreeable; but a positive person solves the problem either by adapting himself to prevailing conditions or by going elsewhere. Rick stayed where he was, but he did not resign himself to being temporarily either to right or left of the center of the stage. That it was Eva Dalheim's day did not enter his head. Every day was his, as was every hour of every day. He was at a total loss to understand why everyone spoke so much of Eva and her work. What could she do that he could not have done, had his parents but taken the trouble to encourage him to cultivate his innate gift for drawing?

Bella had not previously had cognizance of her lover's penchant for painting; but, if his talents in that field exceeded his genius for literature, she saw little point in his continuing to devote to the writing of novels time which he could more profitably spend perfecting his technique as an artist. It did not occur to her to scold him for having allowed her and Harry to entertain such high hopes of his literary propensities; and Harry was no more severe than she was. As a businessman he might reasonably have protested at the waste involved in equipping as a painter a man he and Bella had so recently provided with all that was necessary for the pursuance of a career as a novelist. Instead, he joined his wife in begging Eva to take a

149

pupil for whom her creative work left her no time. Eva eventually agreed to break a rule of long standing, and she undertook to develop Rick's natural gift for painting. In her early, struggling days she had welcomed paying pupils and she had never lost the readiness to help and encourage young artists, but it was a long time since she had been in a position to welcome pupils. The will to create had her so much in its power that the positive desire to associate with others painters (tyros or otherwise) had faded. She was, however, reluctant to refuse a favor begged of her by such dear friends as Bella and Harry; nor did she find it easy to disappoint so charming and handsome a young fellow as Rick Haylett, whom she had met several times at the home of the Parthams and at other people's dinners and receptions.

Before approaching Eva, Bella and Harry insisted on Rick's showing them examples of his drawing skill; and they were astonished at the boy's hitherto hidden talent. He sketched for them a tall ship, a race car and a scantily clad woman, and neither experienced the slightest difficulty in recognizing his drawings as being of respectively a tall ship, a race car and an almost naked girl. Eva was less impressed than were her love-blinded friends. In fact, she was not in the least inclined to regard Rick as having talent. For that reason she thought she ran little risk in agreeing to devote a little of her leisure time to instructing and encouraging him. She knew of his short-lived theatrical and literary ambitions, and she firmly believed his interest in painting would soon be replaced by a passion for some other type of activity. In the meantime she would have rendered her good friends, the Parthams, a service at no great sacrifice to herself. She underestimated, however, Rick's crafty charm. Whenever she had met him (previous to the occasion when Bella and Harry took him to her studio as a prospective pupil) there had been so many other people present that she and he had taken little notice of each other. Rick had made the initial mistake of supposing that the retiring, auburn-haired middle-European woman was an impecunious artist whose passport to homes of the wealthy commuters of Ladbury was her neglected talent. He had imagined she was, like himself, a lame dog which the upper crust of Ladbury had adopted for reasons of sympathy. It was only during the reception on the occasion of the opening of her exhibition that he had learned that she was, in fact, a woman whose income far exceeded her modest needs. That piece of knowledge rendered her suddenly interesting to him. His first claim to have been a promising draftsman as a schoolboy was inspired by jealousy at the amount of attention being paid to her while he felt himself neglected, but the favorable reaction of his benefactors to his boasting about the impact his childhood drawings had made on his art teacher, his parents and friends awoke him to an appreciation of the benefits he might derive from closer contact with Eva. Not only was she a woman of average beauty, with a sturdy, but by no means unfeminine figure, but she lived alone, was quite independent and much wealthier than he had previously supposed. Consequently, whereas Eva anticipated his paying her a few brief visits prior to transferring his attention to the ballet or rock 'n' roll, he planned, from the outset, to concentrate upon her so much loving attention that some of her excessive revenues would fall into his hands.

Neither Bella nor Harry suspected that their darling was interested in either Eva's bank account or her body. Thrilled as they were at Eva's willingness to help Rick to find himself as a painter, they rejoiced in her insistence that she would be able to spare him only a couple of hours per week for tutoring, because that meant he would be with them most of the time, practicing here and there on their estate what Eva taught him during his weekly visit to her studio. However, within a fortnight of Rick's becoming Eva's pupil, she was almost as eager for him to visit her daily as he was. The stumbling-block, from Rick's point of view, was his duty towards Bella and Harry, whom he hesitated to inform of his desire to spend more time with Eva than initially arranged.

Rick's technique with Eva was that which he had used successfully with most of his other victims—a combination of flattery and appeals to sympathy. Eva had had her share of suffering, having fled from Germany with her parents in 1934, when she was only fourteen years of age. They were obliged to leave a considerable fortune behind them, and they knew years of poverty in Great Britain. Eva herself was denied formal training as a painter, and was, to a great extent, self-taught, although her talent was recognized, when she was about twenty years old, by an important mentor, who helped her by employing her in his gallery, where she came into contact with artists who encouraged and advised her. She was, consequently, moved to tears by Rick's accounts of how all his artistic aspirations had been smothered by his parents' inability to finance his training. He humbly admitted that, lacking guidance, he had not previously been quite sure which of the arts was his true vocation.

"One thing's certain though," he told her, as they drank tea after his first tutoring session. "I've never doubted that the artist's life is the life for me. I loathed working in an office where all that matters is money. I know money's one of the things you can't do without; but I despise it myself, and I've always made a point of using the little I could get hold of to help my less fortunate friends and my parents. They just wouldn't get by without the occasional five pounds I can spare them by going without things myself."

Pouring him another cup of tea, Eva said, "Although it's very sad that such poverty still exists in a society which has never had it so good, there is great consolation to be derived from the fact that, in this age when young people are all tarred with self-centered material aims, there are still young men who speak so lovingly of their parents as you do. It makes me hope you will be a successful painter some day, so that you can help your parents and also enjoy for yourself some of the good things of life. I shall do all I can to help you; but I've never before had time to teach, so I may be of less use to you than an inferior painter might be. That sounds conceited, but what I mean is that there are people who are good teachers of painting without being good painters. You see what I mean?"

He smiled sweetly, and answered, "Perfectly, but I'm sure I shall learn a lot from you. I think the mere fact that you're a kind person, who's willing to help a stranger, even though I know your work takes up all your time...well, what I sort of mean is that I think you'll help me because you're willing to. In fact, you really helped me even before you knew I was interested in painting."

The expression on her face implied that she was puzzled. "Yes," he went on, "I know it sounds silly, but I've always been too busy trying to make ends meet to have time to go into smart art galleries and that; but when the Parthams took me to the opening of your exhibition, and I saw all those lovely pictures...well, I don't mind telling you, because you're the understanding kind, but tears came to my eyes. I've never in my life seen anything as lovely as all your pictures. Just looking at them, I knew that the person who had painted them must be nice. And, of course, I already knew you were ever so sweet, but I'd never dreamed anybody could be as good as you are to me."

Tears not far from her eyes, she tapped the back of his right hand very lightly, and said, "You make me sound like a saint, and you make me ashamed that I wasn't keener to take you as a pupil. You did notice that I wasn't really enthusiastic?"

"Well, yes, and I quite understood. In fact, I didn't want Bella and Harry to insist, but of course, I'm glad they did. This'll sort of sound sillyish, but I already feel that we've been friends for longer than I've even known you. I've told you things about my childhood, my parents and my life that I've never told anybody else. You sort of inspire confidence, and it does good for a lonely man to have somebody he can sort of open his heart to now and then."

Her voice trembled slightly with emotion as she exclaimed. "But, my dear, surely you're not lonely with Bella and Harry!"

He hastened to correct himself, while delivering another blow to his hostess' weak spot.

"Oh, they're absolutely smashing people, wonderful friends and all that sort of thing. But, well, they sort of have each other, you know, and I always feel I'm a bit in the way. They're very good to me, of course, and they do all they can to make me feel at home; but, well, you see, although they're jolly good friends to me, they really sort of regard me more as a son, if you know what I mean, than as a friend, whereas with you I feel I can talk. I can't say as between equals, because I shall never be fit to polish your shoes, but, well, let's say I can talk to you as to somebody of my own generation."

Eva laughed so heartily that it was several seconds before she could beg Rick's pardon.

"Don't think I was laughing at you," she begged, "but how old do you think Bella is?"

Cunningly he answered, "Late thirties?"

She laughed again, but with more restraint.

"And my age?" she asked.

He looked at her, pretending to search for the truth, but the way he looked at her caused her to hover briefly between anger and pride. He seemed to be searching for her age in her eyes, her breasts, belly, thighs, knees, shins and feet. His gaze peeled from her every expensive garment she was wearing, and she felt naked. He brought her down in the meadow of womanly vanity by expressing the opinion that she was about thirty years of age. She laughed joyously this time, accused him of being a "wicked flatterer," and informed him, "I'm going to quote no figures, but I doubt whether there's a difference of two years between Bella's age and mine, and I wouldn't like to hazard a guess which of us in the older."

Rick's laughter was forced.

"You know your own age better than I do," he said, "and I think you've known Bella a lot longer than I have, but I'm sure there's a bigger difference than you think, because Bella makes no secret of the fact that she's much older than I am, and I'd say you were about my age."

Embarrassed, but flattered, Eva rose, turned her back on him and exclaimed, "If I knew you better, I'd give you a big kiss for that lovely but dishonest compliment."

He, too, rose, saying, "I'm sorry if I've put my

clumsy foot in it; but I was only going on appearances."

She walked around her chair, and faced him again, with a bright smile on her face.

"You're really begging for that kiss, aren't you?" she teased.

He thought she was going to give it to him, but she made no move, so he answered, "I certainly wouldn't take offense merely because we don't know each other very well."

She changed the subject by inviting him to have a further cup of tea, which he refused since he feared Bella and Harry would be wondering what kept him away so long. He hoped she would suggest he come again before the prearranged weekly lesson, but she disappointed him.

During the following week he devoted a lot of time to sketching in his study, where he received regular visits from Bella and Harry, who never went there together. Rick took care to mention Eva as rarely as possible, lest attention be thus drawn to his interest in her. He entertained hopes of becoming her lover and the recipient of her largess, but it was too early to forecast to what extent his hopes would be fulfilled; and, even supposing Eva adopted him, he had no intention of allowing her to replace Bella and Harry. Rather, he saw her as a second string to his fiddle and a raft to which to cling in the event of his relationship with the Parthams being hit by heavy seas. He thought himself astute enough to share himself between Eva, Bella and Harry without any one of them knowing he was unfaithful. While seeking the means to get Eva into his grasp he continued to use all his charms on the other two. He gave Harry and Bella some ecstatic hours, and if his copulations with Harry were unmitigated labor, he found his recompense in the arms of Bella, whose love for him seemed to grow daily as did the passion with which she gave herself to him. She was his slave, with whom he did what suited him. He was not always available when she wanted him, but, when he indicated that he was eager to use her body for his pleasure, she would hasten to him, however great the risk of their being surprised by Harry. In fact, had Rick not insisted on caution, her imprudence would have betrayed them many times. It sometimes seemed to Rick that she wanted Harry to know his guest was cuckolding him; and that was a reason for Rick's determination to ingratiate himself with Eva, whose door he hoped would be open to him the day when Harry expelled him.

Rick's second visit to Eva lasted longer than his first. As on the previous occasion, they worked for a couple of hours, and then drank tea and talked. He painted a depressing picture of his childhood, his youth, his loveless marriage and the resultant coldness of his parents towards him. She interrupted him to exclaim, "And you still send your parents money, despite their hostility towards you! The more I learn about you, the more I understand Bella's and Harry's devotion to you. Thank God for people like them. If there weren't such people, a boy like you would go through life sacrificing yourself with never a hope of genuine friendship. I've often thought I had it rough, but, compared with your life, mine's been a bed of roses."

Her reaction was even more favorable than he had foreseen, so he consolidated his position with, "Oh, that's just your nobility and generosity speaking. You've conquered difficulties, because you're strong. I get kicked around, because I'm weak."

"Not weak, but much too good," Eva interrupted.

"Bless you! Anyway, estranged parents and ever-absent wife taken into account, I still count myself among the lucky ones of the world. Imagine an ignorant, common bloke like me having tea with an angel!"

Her laughter was contralto and gay.

"Angel?" she said. "You don't know me. You should discuss me with Bella, Harry and the gang."

He knew not to what she made allusion; but the truth is that Bella, Harry and "the gang" held Eva in the highest possible esteem. They accepted that she was not quite like them. She was less gregarious than most of her friends. When she desired company, she was welcome at more firesides than enough; but she did not suffer fools gladly, and she would allow no one to disturb her when she was either working or resting between bursts of creative activity. Consequently, her friends stayed away, unless invited, and usually, when she felt the need for company, she scarcely dared to impose herself on the friends she had neglected for so long. The result was that, underestimating her popularity, she knew periods of loneliness, when people she liked would have been delighted either to receive her or to call upon her. What was certain was that she was less than honest when she hinted to Rick that her friends were in a position to disenchant him concerning her. She was an artist whose friends were mostly wealthy members of the bourgeoisie, but she conformed less to the popular conception of an artist than did the majority of her friends. She worked hard, paid her bills promptly, took a pride in her appearance and in her orderly home, slept alone approximately three hundred and sixty nights per year and voted positively anti-communist and anti-Vatican. Eva was all right!

"Go on!" Rick retorted. "The gang disapproved

so strongly that they all flocked to the opening of your exhibition, and I know what Bella and Hank think about you. They love you, and it doesn't surprise me."

"It doesn't surprise you? Why? Am I so easy to love?"

"I don't reckon they could call you 'easy to love,' but you're lovable, and that's certain."

She poured tea. Her hand trembled so that she had to take a firm grip of herself to avoid filling his saucer. He did not miss a trick. He was on the ball and triumphant.

He stayed so long that Bella rang to ask where he was.

"Yes, Bella, he's still here. I've made him perspire today. No point in dodging the issue! I hope Rick won't mind my saying so..."

She winked at Rick, who winked back, making a right-eye monocle of the thumb and index finger of his right hand.

"...but he's starting late, and he's as rusty as an old bike. I can't really spare the time, but, if we're to make anything at all of this boy of yours—all right, liebling...this boy of ours—he'll have to come for at least two hours a day, and he'll have to work hard the rest of the time. I know, you love him...and I should tell him you love him? Rick! Come you here, and talk with Bella!"

Rick assured Bella he was about to leave, but, like the professor just said, he would have to work hard to make the grade. It was obvious to Eva, from the expression on Rick's face, that Bella's reaction to this unforeseen development was unfavorable.

"I know, darling," he stammered, "but that's the sort of friends you have. Giving me two hours a week was a sacrifice, but she's willing to make time to give me more tutoring, even though it means neglecting her own work; and it's really for you and Harry she's doing it, because she thinks you're a wonderful couple—and she's not the only one either. Pardon, darling? Well, yes, I think her opinion is that there's something there, but it's been left dormant so long that the only thing to do is either forget the whole thing or work like a galley-slave for a couple of years. Anyway, darling, I'm leaving now. Be home in twenty minutes, and we can discuss the matter. You know that if training to be an artist takes more time than you can miss me, I shall be quite happy working in Harry's office."

Not for the first time he made tears glisten in Eva's eyes. Bravely though he made his offer to renounce his birthright, he was too sincere to exclude wholly from his voice the bitterness of his disappointment. Eva knew how alien to his nature was the sort of work he would have to do for Harry—figures, legal documents, contracts, percentages, big deals and so forth. She was determined that he should not be condemned to such an existence. Surely Bella and Harry would encourage him to persevere in his artistic pursuits. If they did not, then she would ensure that he was fed, house and clothed until such time as his admittedly limited talents could be made to sustain him. A year or two of concentrated study would probably render him employable as a commercial artist, and she had friends who, as a gesture of their affection for her, would willingly have engaged her protégé. She decided against saying anything of her project until she was sure of Bella's and Harry's plans for the boy. She was too fond of the Parthams to have wished to compete with them for the privilege of helping a charming and worthy young man to achieve his ambition.

As Rick left, looking very dejected (as only a gift-ed actor can, when he has all the reasons in the world for smiling triumphantly), Eva ran her fingers through his blond curls, and whispered, "Cheer up! Between us we shall see this thing through." She was filled with admiration at the courage required to bestow upon her the sweet smile with which he took leave of her.

He almost danced from Eva's cottage to his home. The look in Eva's eyes and her words at their parting left him in no doubt that he was making excellent progress with her. Unlike Bella, she was not the sort of woman who either wants to dominate a man or is willing to do the courting; but she could not disguise her sympathy for him, and he doubted whether she would realize, when he made a serious attempt to seduce her, that sympathy is not synonymous with love. On the contrary, he believed she already con-fused her pity for him with a love which would per-mit her to admit him to her bed. She was not the kind of woman to indulge in loveless liaisons of a sexual nature, but she was no prude, and she allowed no religious principles to govern her conduct. What counted for her was self-respect and other people's respect for her. Bella had fornicated with Rick and Dane without even entertaining the ridiculous idea that one or the other of them had the slightest affec-tion for her. In that she differed from Eva, who would not give herself to a man hoping his carnal desire for her would develop into love, as Bella believed to be the case with herself and Rick. The latter, therefore, knew he had to convince Eva that he loved her exclusively. She must not know he was Bella's kept man, although he feared she already sus-pected as much. If necessary, he would confess to Eva that he had been her friend's lover, and he would endear himself to her by claiming to have ceased copulating with Bella the day he had realized that it was his artistic mentor he loved. As for Bella, she would never know the man she had bought was another woman's plaything. She too must be convinced she was the sole object of his affections and her possessiveness would be made to pay Rick high dividends.

Drinking dry sherry together after dinner, Bella, Harry and Rick discussed the latter's future. Neither husband nor wife could admit, in the other's presence, that their reluctance to release their darling for daily visits to Eva's studio sprang from the fear that he would consequently have less time for carnal activities with them. Bella was too sure of Rick's love for her to suspect that he would betray her with Eva, whom she believed to be incapable of stealing a friend's man. Harry, however, neither doubted the possibility of the attractive painter's falling under the spell of her devastatingly seductive pupil nor allowed such an eventuality to concern him. He was not in love with Rick. He liked Rick, but, more importantly, he liked fucking Rick—and he didn't give a hoot how many other *clean* people (male or female) also derived pleasure from intimacy with him. All Harry worried about was that circumstances already made it difficult for him to boff the lad as much as he would have liked, and daily afternoons with Eva would render Rick not to mention Rick's delicious bottom and mouth even less accessible to him than hitherto.

At a certain moment Bella posed her left hand lovingly on Harry's right hand, and her right on Rick's left, and cooed, "The fact that we three form a happy little family doesn't mean that any one of us need neglect his or hear outside interests, but I'm sure Harry agrees with me, Rick, when I say that we're a little too fond of you. It's as though you were Harry's or my younger brother, we both feel lonely when you're away. You don't mind my saying that, do you, sweetest Harry?"

Harry kissed her lips with genuine tenderness, and answered, "Of course not. You wouldn't be here, Rick my boy, if you didn't fill a need in our lives. Bella's young enough to call you her brother, although the way you two make my temperature rise when you kiss doesn't make me think of you as brother and sister. Now it's my turn to hope neither of you thinks I'm casting aspersions."

Rick's pallor and the nervous twitching of his lips left Harry in no doubt about the nature of the relationship between his wife and their guest, but he had to raise his metaphoric hat to his civilized Bella for the cool innocence of her smiling reply, "You've hit the nail on the head Harry. If Rick's honest—and that's his most lovable quality—he'll admit that I excite him as much as he excites me."

What does a professional do when wealthy amateurs give him the choice between suicide and the firing-squad? To admit he lusted after his hostess would anger any normal host, who would probably be equally annoyed by his honored guest's announcing that the lady of the house left him cold. Though Rick looked at least five years younger than he was, commercially speaking he had a mature head on his shoulders. He came back with, "There's no doubt about the fact that the best couple I know are the most attractive woman I've ever met and the most virile of men. If you didn't form such a perfect marriage—more like lovers than a staid man and wife—I don't think I'd have stayed here a week."

Harry laughed, bathed Rick in a gaze warm with admiration, and cried, "Damn you, you scoundrel!

We're gonna drink to an actor-novelist-painter who talks like a poet. Bella, to Rick!"

Bella and Harry drank. The latter announced, "Rick my boy, if Bella agrees—and only if she agrees—you go all out for this painting business. Eva wouldn't encourage you unless she saw a lot of talent in you, and there are too many wretches in this world who are flops because their true gifts are left to atrophy. What d'you say, Mrs. Partham?"

Mrs. Partham sought in the eyes of her gigolo a promise that, if she allowed him to spend his afternoons innocently with Eva, he would devote most of his remaining time to wickedness with her. She mistook the smile of gratitude Rick was bestowing on Harry for his acceptance of her condition; and she answered, "All that matters to me is our boy's happiness and the fruition of his aspirations. So, Rick, my darling, if Harry can spare you from his office, I'm all for letting Eva draw out of you the latent genius. Let's you and me drink to that wonderful man sitting opposite you! You'll never again meet the likes of my Harry."

Rick rose, raised his glass, and said, "You can say that again, Mrs. Partham. Let's drink to the health, prosperity and happiness of a great guy!"

Bella and Rick drank. The former deposited her glass on the table, and threw herself ecstatically into her husband's arms, exclaiming, "Rick, never feel you're in the way here, but believe me, if you were elsewhere at this moment, I'd bunch up my skirts, and beg this man to make passionate love to me, here and now—and to hell with the servants!"

Nadia came in that moment. Having heard Bella's last remark she smiled dazzlingly, and drawled, "…and to hell with you too, Mrs. Partham!"

Harry laughed merrily, and hurled Bella into Nadia's arms.

"Beg Nadia's pardon, you drunken whore, and tell her you didn't mean that!" he commanded, slapping Bella's backside playfully.

Bella kissed Nadia warmly on the mouth, and murmured, "Nadia knows I don't wish the servants were in hell, least of all her, don't you, darling?"

Holding her mistress in her arms, the girl replied, "Of course I do, Mrs. Partham. Why, if I thought you meant that, I wouldn't have wasted my breath on cursing you. I'd just have walked straight out of this house forever."

Harry asked Nadia, "Did you hear the remainder of what Mrs. Partham said?"

She smiled, and answered, "No, Mr. Partham, but I figure she's a wicked woman, making Mr. Haylett feel lonely by necking with you that way."

In mock anger, Bella exclaimed, "Well, I like that! First she tells me to go to hell, and then she scolds me for being wifely to my own dear husband. Nadia, you're just jealous, because Harry doesn't neck with you—or does he?"

Nadia, Bella and Harry laughed, but Rick was shocked at such familiarity with the chocolate-skinned maid. He was even more astounded by the attentive ear his friends gave to the girl's riposte:

"I like Mr. Partham. He's a gentleman towards us servants, and he's my idea of a handsome white man; but I wouldn't like him to try to make love to me."

"Harry, you'd better leave us before this girl deflates your ego completely."

"It's too late. I already feel as imposing as a dwarf; but, seriously, Nadia, what I think you're driving at intrigues me. Do you favor the idiotic white man's color bar, but then in reverse?"

"No, no, Mr. Partham! Please don't think that! Like most West Indians, I'm neither ashamed nor proud of my color. Neither you nor I made ourselves, and I certainly don't think I'm better than you. If I did, I wouldn't work for you. In fact, two summers ago, back home, I had a very nice friend—an English girl who was over there for the whole summer vacation, at the university. She's now on the legal staff of the United Nations in Geneva. She was staying at the hotel where I worked, and she was very nice to me. We talked a lot about books, movies, political and social problems. One day, about a month after she arrived, she told me she'd have to cut her holiday short, because funds were running low; and she was so sad that I invited her to save the money she was spending on the hotel and restaurants by coming to stay with my two brothers and me. She accepted, and was able to stay on until the very end of her vacation. My brothers occupied one bedroom, and Merle and I mine. Mike is a year older than I am, Bruce was then only fourteen; so, when Merle and Mike began getting along together very well, he used to come into our room at nights, and make love to Merle alongside me. It wasn't a satisfactory arrangement, but there was no place else for either them or me to go."

Bella interrupted to ask why Nadia did not join Bruce in his bedroom; but Nadia insisted that, among her people, only those in the direst circumstances would tolerate an adult or adolescent girl sharing a bedroom with a pubescent brother.

"You're puzzled," she added. "I can see that, by the fact that I shied away from sleeping with my lovely little brother, but allowed my older brother to make love to my friend, night after night, and almost throughout most nights, just beside me. Well, you see, the way we look at these things is that you may not embarrass or precociously arouse an innocent boy; but that what assenting adults or near adults do

166

is their own business. Mike wanted Merle, and I love him too much to deny him something which is of great importance to a healthy, normal boy of nineteen. Merle was not only willing, but she was eager. He would never have dared to take the initiative with so fine a European lady, if she hadn't given him a lot of encouragement. I too was old enough to know what I was doing, and neither Merle nor Mike tried to put pressure on me. In fact, it was more or less I who put into their heads the idea of doing it in my bed instead of wandering about looking for secluded spots here and there on the outskirts of Bridgetown. Well, what I really wanted to say is this...lying there, watching them, hearing them and smelling them in the act of coition, I was excited and proud of the pleasure my handsome and beloved brother gave my friend. I was glad it had been made possible for them to derive so much pleasure from sweating and groaning by my side. I'd done them both a favor by letting them do it in comfort and in complete safety, and I myself got an unforeseen thrill from witnessing their copulations; but, as I watched his black penis disappearing in the milky whiteness of her belly, there was, to me, something incongruous and unwholesome about it. I hope and believe I have no anti-European prejudices. Would I have come over here, if I had? Would I have shared my bed with an English girl, without accepting a penny from her, except that we let her pay her own share of food bills?"

Harry assured her that they were convinced she had no silly notions concerning the superiority of any one race over any other; and she was emboldened to continue, "What I mean is that I don't condemn my brother for making love to Merle, nor do I disapprove of her opening her pink body to a brown boy's genitals. I've nothing against black-

and-white marriages or against colored boys and girls going to bed with white girls and boys, but the thought of having a white man inside me doesn't excite me. I'd go to a movie, a theater, concert or ball game with a nice white man. I'd dance with him, and sit down to a meal with him. I'd go swimming with him; and I'm not like some white people who wouldn't tolerate the slightest physical contact with a person of a different color. I'd let a white doctor strip me, and turn me inside-out, if he were as good or better than a brown-skinned one. What I don't desire is that any man should ever put a pale phallus between my dark thighs, and lie down on me with his soft, white chest crushing my sepia breasts."

Rick asked sarcastically, "Did you mind Bella kissing you?"

Nadia's frown furrowed her brow for no more than a fraction of a second, after which she flashed a bright smile from Harry's face to Bella's, and declared, "I liked it, because it was a warm, friendly kiss, which I'm sure Mrs. Partham wouldn't have preferred depositing on my sex; and, on my birthday or his, or at Christmas or New Year, I wouldn't object to Mr. Partham kissing my lips, to wish me a Merry Christmas, a Happy New Year or many happy returns; but, if ever I allow a white man's tongue to enter my mouth or his hands to wander over my naked belly, it'll be out of curiosity. Mike enjoyed Merle, and she was crazy with joy, and she kissed me a hundred times, to thank me for making it possible. Well, if they liked it, perhaps I too would be carried to the summit of ecstasy by intimacy with a white man; so I might try it some day, so that I shall know either that I haven't been missing much or that it's worth having more of; and, if I find I like white penis, I shall have some whenever I feel like it and can find a nice white man, like Mr. Partham, to give it to me."

After a pause of several seconds, Nadia asked, "And now, would you like me to serve the dessert?"

Bella answered affirmatively. Harry rose, and stopped the girl as she was about to leave. He took both her hands in his, and said with utter sincerity, "It's strange, Nadia, how a man can think for months that a certain girl is just a good, keen, willing, polite worker; and suddenly as a result of a joke, he discovers that she's a damned sight too intelligent to wash dishes and wait at table. I don't agree with all you said about the incongruity of a white and brown body sweating together in the excitement of making love, because I've been intimate with colored girls who seemed to enjoy me as much as I them, but your whole attitude does you credit. I'm not trying to flatter you into letting me be your European erotic guinea-pig, but I want you to know I'm proud to have you under my roof. And, from now on, either you call me Harry or I shall call you Miss Dalhousie. Another thing, if you aspire to higher things than being a maid, Bella and I will help you to realize your dreams. You could study, and go to Geneva, and work with Merle."

Nadia's voice was husky with emotion as she thanked Harry. She promised to meditate on his kind offer, but assured him that, in the meantime, she would like to continue addressing him and his wife as Mr. and Mrs. Partham. Her parting words were, "You've probably noticed I never address as 'sir' or 'madam' anyone whose surname I know. You've never insisted, but I'd have looked elsewhere before calling you 'sir' or 'madam.' Mr. and Mrs. Partham is the happy medium. It doesn't mean you're necessarily superior to me, but it does acknowledge that you pay me decently and treat me well in return for my services and my respect."

"Remarkable girl!" exclaimed Bella after Nadia had left for the kitchen, and Rick hypocritically agreed.

VII.

The weeks during which Rick had visited Eva daily
had borne at least two kinds of fruit. Firstly, Eva had
succeeded in making something of his meager talents. Eager to run before he had learned to walk,
Rick wanted to paint. But, being equally keen to
curry favor with her, he did not insist; and bowed to
her will, which was that he master the art of sketching before tackling colors. The second harvest of
their association was that the stage had been reached
at which she could not disguise her joy at seeing him
arrive and her regret at the necessity of his returning
every evening to the home of his "foster-parents."
Not for an instant did she entertain the idea of his
not going home in the evenings. She had not the
slightest intention of suggesting he spend the night in
her cottage; but, without facing the reality of the
alternative, she wished Bella would not insist on his
spending every evening with her and Harry.

Over-generous with her praise of his work, she
had convinced Rick that he was on the way to

becoming a second Rembrandt, with the result that he came along one afternoon unshaven, and asked her, "Do you think I'd look silly with a beard?"

"Oh, no!" she enthused. "I'd like you with a golden beard."

"Don't you like me without a beard?"

"Like is a mild word."

He scrutinized her face, for a few seconds, until she blushed, and averted her eyes. He took his chin in his fingers, and raised her face again.

"Do you really mean what I think you just said?" he asked, and she answered, "You don't need to ask me that."

His arms went reverently about her waist. He held her close to him, and kissed her tenderly, chastely. Her hands rose to his fair head, as she drank his warm breath gratefully. After this first kiss, she whispered, "The trouble with nice, respectful boys is that it takes them a long time to reach the stage an impetuous woman's long been hoping they'd get to."

"I've wanted to do that from the moment we met, but you awe me a bit."

She kissed him, and this time she parted her lips enough to encourage him to take labial possession of her mouth. They held each other close, the front of their respective bodies in dangerously close contact. He lowered her to a divan, where he joined her, saying, "You're looking lovely today."

"And I don't usually look lovely?"

"So lovely that I can hardly wait for the moment when you tell me I've made enough progress with my studies to be allowed to sketch you."

She chuckled, and assured him that the painting or even the drawing of portraits is one of the most difficult and advanced aspects of their art. He parried with, "Oh, I'm not suggesting I could draw a true likeness of the loveliest face I've ever been privileged to kiss, but I'd like to sketch your...your figure."

"Without clothes?"

"Would you let me?"

"Is it because you want to sketch me in the nude or because you want to see me like that?"

He contemplated the situation for a few seconds, and decided that the answer which best suited his purpose was the one which might shock her slightly, but which would certainly flatter her.

"Both," he answered, "but most of all because I'd like to see the body of the girl I love."

"You do really love me?" she asked, her words vibrant with emotion. "It is really love, and not just desire?"

"I've always loved you. Even before we met I dreamed of meeting some day a woman as soft, tender, honest and good as you...a woman who lives for something higher than money, liquor, clothes and proximity."

"I think you mean promiscuity, darling, because I love proximity...your proximity to me."

"What I mean...what I loathe is all this running from one bed to another...all this loveless love-making. That's one of the things I love you for. You live at home, like I've always wanted to. You've got a nice home, with all the comforts, and you're happy here, with your work, your radio, your records and the kitchen where you take pride in cooking the delicious things you offer me every time I come here. You're a great artist, but you're domesticated; and that's the only sort of woman a simple, home-living, one-woman man like me could possibly love. So I fell in love with you at first sight. Desire came later, and, even now, if that's the way you want it, I shall be happy to go on worshipping you with my lust pushed firmly into the background."

"My love for you would be of a strange sort, if I asked you to deny your true nature; but, darling, loving me, desiring me, and wanting to see me with no clothes on, why didn't you undress me weeks ago?"

"Because I respect you. You're the sort of girl a man behaves decently with. There are woman enough to whom stripping is just like saying, 'Hello,' but it does a man good to be with a girl like you, who he can respect, admire and treat like a lady."

Their lips met in a long, ardent kiss.

"I like to think I'm a lady in your eyes, my knight in shining armor," she murmured, "but I'm still a woman. I'm no less feminine than you're masculine, and, in the arms of a man who's dear to me, my desires are the same as yours when the only girl you love is close at hand."

"Darling!"

There was a sob in his voice. He bent his head to her clothed bosom and nuzzled her breasts. This filled her heart with compassion for the man who, a victim of destiny, was incapable of resisting the temptation to become intimate with the woman he loved. That his anticipatory shame was great did not surprise her, for she knew that the man she adored was too sensitive for this cruel world of flesh and blood. She nursed him as though he were a baby. She kissed him, and rendered his commission of the inevitable crime lighter on his delicate conscience by taking the blame upon herself. She began to unbutton her dress, and she whispered, "Undress me, darling! I want to be loved by the man I love. Take off my clothes, and make me happy and proud by admiring me in my undraped naturalness. Prove your devotion to me by treating me with the tenderness a saintly lover owes to his gentle mistress. My mouth longs for your kiss, my sweet darling. My body yearns for your respectful hands and for the warmth of your sacred touch. Look, darling! I've bared my breasts. The die is cast. I love you, darling. I love you trustingly, as a virgin loves, and my one regret is that I'm not as pure of body as you are of heart and of soul. Yes, darling, that's right! Oh, my sweet one, your mouth is on the hard nipples of my breasts. You're my unblemished young lover, vainly seeking the milk of my love. Bless you, darling! You love me, and I'm your loving slave. Take off all my clothes. All my clothes. Enjoy me, and place me eternally in your debt. Your hands are blessing my bare thighs above my stockings. My thighs know no shame, because it's to the hands of love that they're opening. To stop now, Rick, my Rick, would be cruel. There's no going back, darling, and I'm a woman who won't go to heaven unless you're there too, with your fingers plucking at the lace of my saucy panties. But leave my panties, for now, sweetheart! Take my dress off, and my unfastened bra. Ah, you obey me as though I were a princess and you my slave. A prince, a saintly prince deigns to unfrock his handmaiden. Kiss me, darling, with all the cruel tenderness of your gently fierce mouth! Kiss me, Rick! I need your lips on mine. I need your tongue."

The haute couture dress of a love-crazed woman lighted on the back of a chair, and her brassiere fell to the carpet. The rose-colored nipples of her ample breasts glistened with the drying saliva of one that she adored.

He silenced her temporarily by crushing his mouth against hers. He slipped his hot, wet tongue between those lips and searched her mouth with a soul kiss.

Her entire body closed in about him, so that he was powerless, as in the grip of an octopus; but, after a minute or two she voluntarily released him, begging him to repeat his sermon of true love.

"My heart and my whole life are yours," he gasped, "my love and desire are as one sentiment with your love and lust for me. I love you. I love you dearly, and I'm taking off your pink slip with the maddening black lace bodice. Now you're wearing only your garter belt, your nylons and your cute little panties, and you're even more enticing than I'd thought you would be."

"Do I entice you, Rick? Am I irresistible? Don't resist me, darling! I don't want to be resisted. I want to be...I want to be...Oh, darling, make me yours! That's it. Make me yours. Lay claim to me. Put a notice on me. Sold! Belongs to the Rick Haylett collection. Are you going to collect me, Rick? You're naughty...peeling off my stockings like that...as carefully as if my nylons and I belonged to you. Do I belong to you, Rick? Drop that stupid slip on the floor, darling! Do you know how to unfasten my garter belt? Did Bella teach you all about garters? Do you love me more than you love Bella? Oh! That was a lovely kiss, darling. It means you love me, and me alone. Rick, cradle me for a minute! I'm naked except for my panties, and I feel so wicked that I'm afraid. That's the way, Daddy. You're cradling me like I was a little girl. Tell me you'll still love me, afterwards. Will you still respect me, and will you do what you're doing now every day? Every single day? Except when I'm sick, of course. Rick, give me a baby! Then I won't be ill for several months, and you'll be able to take my clothes off every day, except Sundays, when I never see you. Rick, why never on a Sunday? Will you sometimes make love to me on Sundays?"

He peeled off her panties, saying, "I promise you I'll sometimes make love to you on Sundays. I love you always, but, whenever I can get away, I'll come and make such love to you on Sundays that the people will come from far and near to watch us copulating."

She held her naked body along the entire length of his clothed front. Her arms were a warm, soft garland of sweet-smelling roses about his neck, and her mouth was an audaciously opening bud against his lips. After a minute of tenderness, she whispered, "I'd like to lie here lazily, watching your lovely young body emerging from the smart clothes you're wearing. If you'd rather I undressed you, I will, because you're the master. I want it that way. I want you to make me do things. I want you to make me let you do things to me. I'd like you to debauch me; and, on the day of reckoning, when you're being led away to hell for seducing me, I shall give you a final, undeniable proof of my love. I shall confess that all the guilt is mine, and I shall insist that we go either to Hades or to paradise together. Whatever happens and wheresoever we go, will you do what you're doing now? Will you denude me and look at me with that wicked glint in your dreamy eyes? Will you go on desiring me, and converting your lust into obscenely lyrical gestures? Lyrical, darling!"

As she raved sentimentally and erotically, he slipped out of his suede jacket, corduroy pants, shirt, shoes and socks. Then, clad in brief underpants of white nylon, he approached her in such a manner that his loins were within inches of her face. Knowing what was required of her, she lowered the nylon triangle, allowing his phallus to spring forth like a shining, arrogant fighting cock. It was more than a year since she had seen or felt a man's genitals. Her eyes

shone as though his were either the first or the most
exciting she had ever seen. She reached for it, drew it
to her lips, and kissed it, without even thinking of
putting it in her mouth.

"Mine!" she claimed proudly, indicating that she
wanted her nakedness to make contact with his bare
body. He lay beside her on the divan, and appraised
her. She was fleshier than Bella, not so finely boned.
The breasts had a heavy downward swing, but proud
tips, hardened and swollen by the wickedness of the
situation, pointed upwards. The waist would have
been slender, if the belly had just a little less of a
curve to it. The hips were sturdy, while the immod-
estly parted thighs would have gained aesthetically
by losing a few inches of their sexually exciting thickness. Her knees were smooth and subtly dimpled,
and she had beautifully generous calves, slim ankles
and feet of a rare prettiness. Indeed her feet, hands,
arms and shoulders were pretty enough to cause one
to forget the merest tendency to plumpness about the
breasts, belly, haunches and thighs.

His fingers went to the hairs of her mound of
Venus. Whereas the hair of her head was of a rich
copper color, that of her loins and armpits was much
paler, more blond than auburn.

He found the orifice of her sex. For a woman who
had already demonstrated her warmth and sexual
eagerness she was remarkably dry, so much so that
her lips seemed reluctant to part. Sensing his deception, she whispered, "Let me!" and the fingers of her
right hand went in search of her vaginal juices, which
started to flow immediately. She smiled again, and
her soft, deep voice uttered the timid prayer, "Touch
me now, darling!"

Two of the fingers of his right hand went into the
wetness of her. He touched her keen clitoris, and she

moaned, "Darling!" Her already invitingly parted thighs jerked involuntarily open to their full extent, and her hands gripped her hips, as she thrust her head spasmodically deeper into the cushions of the divan. Her mouth was wide open, her suddenly pale lips apparently petrified. Her loins twitched up and down against his fingers, and the button of her vagina quivered and expanded. His mouth went to hers, and life returned to her lips. She was aflame with a desire which was fed by love, and she was a stranger to shame. All she said, was, "Rick! My darling, beloved heart, I do love you." Her body, however, indecently begged him to possess it.

Pride and joy brought a strong glow to his whole being. Feeling strong, he held her left knee up with his right hand, and, lying on his left side, he touched the mouth of her loins with the throbbing helmet of his sex.

"Rick!" she sobbed, and he slid into her. There was incredible power in the movement by which she tightened the contact between her nether parts and those of her lover. She seemed to suck him into her, and grip him with muscular movements of her love-sleeve. She flowed to him and away from him, possessing him without denying him the chance of taking her. The grip of her arms on his torso combined ferocity and tenderness. It was as though her embrace were there to protect him from some anonymous, hostile force. He drove deep into her, and glided smoothly out again. He teased her briefly, and she was too desirous of his happiness to steal the initiative from him, much as her throat yearned for further contact with the rock of him. She waited until she sensed the beginning of his fresh lunge into her, and then she went forward, open-thighed and moist-holed, to welcome him back into the happy depth of her womanhood. He took her easily at first, with long, slow, profound probings; but soon excitement mounted within both of them. Indeed they were fused utterly, so that her sexual temperature was his, while his delight was part and parcel of her ecstasy. She loved him so sincerely that she identified herself with him. She gave herself, but there was nothing negative or pathetic about her surrender. She made him feel that it was he who gave himself to her, and that, if he found pleasure in her, her gratitude for what he was giving her was boundless. Her every movement, gesture and sigh blessed him and thanked him for the fact that every second of their copulation was a thousand brilliant orgasms in her entrails. He was aware of her joy in him and of her pride in the consummation of their love. He knew that, if he failed her, she would love him, while, if he satisfied her physically, she would worship him. He did not fail her. She was with him, strongly with him, loving him with every ounce of her religiously wanton strength. The full length of her soft tunnel knew intimately every hairsbreadth of his staff of masculinity, and her groans were a hymn of praise to the perfect man.

She uttered a hoarse cry, called his name almost as though she reproached him for something she could scarcely believe so nice a boy would do to her, and then a series of little shrieks broke from her ecstatically trembling lips. Each squeal was accompanied by a frenzied twitching of her crotch against his cock. She went limp, soft and painfully lovable in her vulnerability. Rick knew he could safely give her sperm at that moment. She was probably too far away to appreciate his gift, but she was not too spent by the completeness of her own orgasm to welcome his continuing to work at her loins. His ejaculation of seminal fluid into her was not so much exciting as a sweet relief. It flowed from him, bringing him the sort of ease one knows when a painful abscess has been lanced. She registered his explosion by swaying her loins gently to and fro, as though she wished to help him to get rid of the last drops of jism. She smiled tiredly, and enfolded him lovingly to her.

They slept right through the afternoon, so that he received no tutoring that day. Their second loving lasted longer than the first had. She had several orgasms without fading even briefly from the scene. In fact, each time she reached the summit her energy seemed to increase, as did also the wantonness of her surrender. She appeared to open wider as their copulation continued, so that he finally had the feeling that his whole body was within her. After his orgasm the power of his movements diminished for a few moments, during which she rocked him gently into a new zest for activity and then they climbed together to the highest point of excitement. He hurled a third helping of cream into her receptive passage, and she broke down into a trembling contentment in which her flaccid mouth loved him into somnolence.

Her kisses roused him from sleep more than an hour later. She washed his cock and loins with a soapy cloth and he dressed hurriedly while she freshened her own nether parts. He was late, and he was dressed before she was, but she begged him to wait a moment, because, in order to spend another twenty minutes with him, she wanted to escort him to within a hundred yards of the Partham villa.

Before allowing him to go in for dinner she extracted from him a further assurance that his heart loved her. She also made him promise to arrive as early as possible the following afternoon.

Rick went in to dinner, and Eva sauntered home through the woods, seeing her beautiful, naked lover in the shadow of every tree. For the first time she slept on the divan that night, for no other reason than that it was there that she and Rick had loved each other. She slept in his arms, and awoke feeling refreshed and rejuvenated. She looked at herself in the full-length mirror of her dressing table, and she found herself much more beautiful than she had been twenty-four hours previously. Her heart overflowed with love for her own body, because she believed Rick loved it, and she was grateful to her flesh for delighting him so.

She decided to bathe and start dressing earlier than usual, in order to have time to make herself more beautiful than she had ever previously been; and, throughout the morning, as she did her household chores, she turned over in her mind which of her clothes he would derive the greatest satisfaction from removing from her body.

Not for a moment did she suspect that he had spent half the night in Harry's arms nor that he was devoting his morning to undressing and loving Bella, who, for her part, was happily ignorant of the fact that Rick's by no means brilliant performance was the result of his having poured out too much of his passion on Harry and Eva.

The question Rick asked himself unceasingly was, "How long can I keep up this lucrative deception?"

VIII.

Bella was pouring Harry his after-breakfast cup of coffee, with which he was enjoying the first cigarette of the day, when the telephone rang. Harry answered it.

"Hello, Mendel! So early in the day? Yes, I know, but, even for Karl, eight o'clock is an unheard-of hour for making business phone calls. Well, when he mentioned it to me a couple of weeks ago, I wasn't particularly keen; but, if he's willing to take sixty percent of the risk, I don't mind sharing the remainder with you. I agree there's not much risk involved, if Karl thinks it's a good proposition. It beats me why, after all these years, he still imagines himself so indebted to us that he insists on offering us a slice of every promising transaction that comes his way...Oh, no! If he weren't keen on it, he wouldn't go in for sixty, and he doesn't need your twenty or mine...Yes, old chap, today suits me as well as tomorrow. I was planning to go to town one day this week anyway, to take my new gun back to Ziegler's. The action's not

183

all it should be…Good idea! I can sit in the back with Ida, and make love to her all the way…Ha-ha! Just you tell her that I'd still be asking for more long after she'd begged for a respite!…No! No need to pick me up, unless you specially want to see Bella or Rick. I've got to go to the hut, to get the gun, so I'll walk through the park, and meet you somewhere along the back road. Keep an eye out for me. In about half an hour? Bye!"

He hung up, and said to Bella and Rick, "Traubmann wants to see Mendel and me about the Boltinov scheme either today or tomorrow. We shall probably stay and see Harold's play at the Duchess, so don't expect me back before the wee small hours o' the morning! We're going in Mendel's car, and Ida's going with us. She wants to spend the afternoon with René. I'm going up to change. If you want anything from town, let me know when I come down!"

He had not been out of the room half a minute when Bella threw herself into Rick's arms, exclaiming in a whisper, "A whole day and half a night to ourselves, for lots and lots of what the doctor said Bella can't get too much of…Rick, dick, Ricka-dick-dick!"

She tugged open her olive-green bathrobe, under which she glowed nakedly and aromatically after the hot bath from which she had emerged but twenty minutes previously. He gestured nervously in the direction of the door, the stairs and the conjugal bedroom, but Bella was in no mood for prudence. During the three weeks since Rick and Eva had become lovers, the embryonic artist and his mentor had spent so much time together that Bella had been reduced to contenting herself with brief, stolen moments of fornication. The fact that Harry was going to London for at least fifteen hours meant that she would be able to savor Rick in comfort and with-

out keeping one eye on the clock. The thought inebriated her. It was not the moment for caution. She
reminded her kept man that her husband had gone
up to put on a dark lounge suit, and that he would
not be back for at least ten minutes.

"Ten minutes!" she repeated. "Ten minutes for an
appetizer! Finger me, darling! Give me a feeble fore-
taste of the fireworks we're going to let off from the
time Harry goes till three or four in the morning!"

Her bare front would have made a normal man
throw prudence to the winds. Even Rick was affected
by the pale beauty of her flat belly and firm little
breasts; but he would have mastered his urge to
touch her, if he had not been afraid of offending the
gander whose eggs were bullion. He fondled her
slender thighs and humid sex. He kept one eye on
the door until Bella's mouth found his and sighed
him an open-legged kiss of groaning fervors. Way out
on a peninsula of passion neither Bella nor Rick
noticed Harry's return to the door of the breakfast-
room. Suddenly recalling he had left a cigarette burning and an undrunk cup of coffee, the master of the
house had retraced his steps. Seeing his guest's hand
in milady's vagina, he withdrew discreetly.

Ten minutes later Harry returned to the breakfast
room, where he found his wife sipping a cup of coffee
while their protégé lazily smoked a thin, sweet cigar.

Spring had arrived early. Harry's stroll through the
park was an idyll. What he had witnessed on his premature interruption in the breakfast room did not
trouble him. He had more or less known for some
time that the relationship between Bella and Rick
was other than that which binds a young working-
class man and his wealthy protectress; but he had
chosen to avoid drawing attention to his awareness of
the situation. He had mistresses and he amused him-

self with Rick, and he was too intelligent a man to claim for himself privileges which he would deny to his wife.

He halted for a few moments, thrilled for the thousandth time by the sight of a red squirrel scurrying up the trunk of a pine tree. He resumed his ambulation, wondering in what way he could exploit his conviction that Bella was Rick's paramour.

Walking briskly along what he called "the back road," his new gun under his right arm, Harry was singing "I just met a girl named Maria" from Leonard Bernstein's "West Side Story." He was thinking of Ida in the back of Mendel's Armstrong and of lunch at the Cheshire Cheese on Fleet Street. There was no mistaking Mendel's old, maroon-colored car, which was dearer to him than is the latest Mercedes to the man who insists on being ahead of the Joneses. Mendel slowed down in time, came smoothly to a halt exactly where Harry stood, and opened the front door on the passenger's side. He noticed his friend's surprise at Ida's absence, and explained, "Ida's trying to contact René, to make an appointment for this afternoon. By the time we get back to our place she'll know whether or not he can fit her in today."

In fact, René's schedule was full for that day, but he was prepared to find time for her the next day.

"Would it inconvenience you boys very much to postpone your trip to London until tomorrow?" Ida asked, pressing her slim young body against Harry's solid front, with her arms about his neck.

He kissed her on the mouth and answered, "If Mendel doesn't mind, I'm only too happy to be able to ingratiate myself with you by agreeing to put off our expedition for a day." He spoke with a mock gallantry which made her laugh gaily.

"Why haven't you brought your charming friend with you, Harry?" she asked.

"Because I wanted you all to myself."

"You're mean," she snapped playfully.

Mendel sneered, "I don't understand what any of you see in that guttersnipe."

Harry said, "Steady on, old boy! If Bella heard you talking that way, she'd never speak to you again."

"That's because it takes a civilized woman to appreciate a boy as charming as Rick," added Ida.

Mendel countered with, "I do wish you'd all stop calling him a boy. He's fully adult, and as charming as a hostess at one of those shady clubs which appear overnight in the Leicester Square area. He plays you all for suckers, and it beats me, Harry, how an astute operator like you gets taken in by a cheap, effeminate gigolo who takes the most atrocious liberties with English grammar while simpering with that caricature of a polished accent which always makes me suspect he's taking the mickey out of the very people he's living off."

"You're a bloody snob," Harry responded.

"He's green with envy, because we girls dig Rick," added Ida.

"You're not too big to have your bare bottom slapped for being disrespectful to your brother. Tell Rose to serve us some strong coffee and Grand Marnier, will you darling?"

She rang for the maid.

"Your epithet 'snob' is idiotic, Harry. You know that our father ran a coffee shop in Whitechapel, and that I've never laid claim to being more than a shrewd businessman whose money is his only passport to respectable society. I, too, massacre the English language, and I wish I didn't, but I don't do it in a voice that sounds like a parody of a BBC announcer. I don't mind Haylett having a regional accent, and I don't give a damn for a decent bloke's grammatical errors. What I loathe is any attempt to put on style, to curry favor with people of a higher social and economic class, by pretending to be what one isn't. And what really makes me sick is that real snobs—and lots of our set are snobs, Ida included— that real snobs accept a whore like Haylett, and don't seem to notice that he's common, illiterate and interested only in their generosity."

Harry was not disposed openly to admit that Mendel's judgment of Rick contained a lot of truth, but he was less than sincere when he said, "You talk as though Rick sought contact with moneyed members of the middle classes, and I think it'd be fairer to say they feel drawn to him. I don't deny that he's probably thrilled that the people who like him tend to have money and class; but then, Mendel, you, who admit to having known poverty, ought to realize that there's nothing more natural than that a deprived boy should welcome the chance of mixing with the best people, whenever the occasion presents itself. If there's any guilt involved, then we're the ones you should indict, not him. Bella, some of our friends and I do spoil him, it's true; but we do it voluntarily because it gives us some sort of satisfaction; so why talk as though we're victims of some gigantic confidence trick?"

"But, my dear Harry, you are just that. He's a whore, who has you all paying high prices for his trash. That's what his vaunted charm is—trash! The whole thing is calculated, mercenary and deceitful. He knows whom to charm and whom to ignore."

Stroking her brother's hair with her left hand, Ida asked, "How can you say such a thing, when you only see him in the company of our gang, who are all in more or less the same income bracket?"

"Darling sister, observe his treatment of servants! Harry and Bella know how to treat servants—their own and other people's—because they were both brought up in an atmosphere where servants were an everyday thing. You and I are good employers, even if for no other reason than we don't forget what it's like to earn one's bread and butter by taking orders from others. None of our set is afraid to chatter intimately with domestics, because we're sure of ourselves, and we know that our servants and those of our friends will never take unfair advantage of the fact that we consider them as equals, but Rick plays a double game, a silly game, and he takes you all in with it. To win our sympathy he talks of his poverty and his parents' vain struggle to give him a decent education, which would have brought out his innate qualities; but he also pretends to be one of us. If he's a poor clerk, the son of hard-working members of the proletariat, why doesn't he talk English instead of the insipid undergraduate jargon with which he thinks he convinces us of his upper middle-class antecedents? He always reminds me of one those delicious North Country comics making fun of the bowler-hat-umbrella-and-briefcase fellas. He daren't address servants politely, for fear they'll consequently fail to recognize him as being of noble blood. He despises them, because they belong to his own class or to a class only slightly superior to his own. They're not wealthy and influential, so he turns up his nose at 'em."

Rose brought in coffee, which Ida started serving at once. Handing Harry a cup, she said, "I think you must admit, darling, that Mendel's disposed of your charge of snobbery."

Harry smiled at Mendel, and answered, "Yes, I agree with Ida. In fact, snobbery's the last crime I'd accuse you of normally. As you say, you're neither ashamed nor proud of the fact that your father ran a coffee shop while your mother took in other people's washing. You've made your own way in the world, and you accept your origins without trying either to make capital out of them or to deny them. Rick, it's true, does seem to be a bit inconsistent on the subject of his background; but you must bear in mind, Mendel, that your poor parents were smart. They recognized your flair for business, and they did two things which give you the edge on a boy like Rick—they sweated you through university, and they borrowed the money which gave a brilliant student of economics the capital with which to exploit his genius for his own profit instead of for that of others. Also, humble though they were, they were able to get you introduced to people who could be useful to you while you were of some value to them. You never needed to rely on charity. By the time you were Rick's age, you'd set your parents up in what's become one of the most prosperous catering businesses in the East End, and you were able to talk to me as to an equal. The result is that, with the best will in the world, you can't possibly appraise a boy like Rick. He's less intelligent than you, to begin with, and he's had less opportunity than you have. All he has is charm, and it seems to me that he's perfectly entitled to exploit his sole gift as long as he doesn't resort to fraud."

Mendel poured three glasses of Grand Marnier, and said, "Fraud is precisely what he does resort to. He persuades people he's fond of them, when he doesn't give a damn for anybody but himself. He flatters you all without meaning a word of what he says.

All that interests him is luxury, other people's finance, mixing with the sort of people who give expensive presents without calculating the cost of what they receive in return and getting a fat salary for doing nothing. I'm sorry, Harry. I'm sticking my nose into things that don't concern me, but I know you still pay him as much as you did when, theoretically, he was your secretary. It's none of my business, and, if you'd like me to button up, I won't say another word."

He paused, and all three sipped Grand Marnier. After a few seconds Ida asked, "Mendel, what's wrong with wealthy people trying to help struggling artists? Why shouldn't such an artist accept hospitality which is so spontaneously offered?"

Mendel laughed until he spilled liqueur on the carpet. He placed his left hand affectionately on his sister's right shoulder, exclaiming, "Artist, darling! Harry, did you hear that? Artist!"

"The boy has talent—it falls short of genius—even Eva admits that."

"Thank God somebody's mentioned Eva! If I'd been the first to bring her name into the conversation, Ida would have had an excuse for repeating her charge of jealousy. Well, I'm very fond of Eva. I think of her as a sister, but that wouldn't prevent my going to bed with her, if ever I had the chance. What matters, though, is this: Eva's a perfect example of your beloved scoundrel's sense of values. He never mentioned his talents as a writer until Rowan got a story published in *Writers of Promise*. It was only jealousy of Rowan's success and the fuss we all made of him that made Haylett suddenly recall his forgotten literary ambitions. Damn it, Harry! An artist doesn't forget the particular form of art he's addicted to. I said addicted, and that's the only word for it. Art devours its victims, makes them shrug their shoulders at comfort, wealth, success, esteem, security. Can you imagine Eva ever having done anything other than paint? If Haylett wanted to write, he'd have written in the dismal little apartment he evokes to whip us all into generous gestures, but he decided to become an illiterate man of letters only when he noticed that we were all thrilled at Rowan's success. He reasons the way you do, Ida. A clerk may not scrounge, but an artist may shamelessly sponge on his friends and neighbors."

"Mendel, old sport, I don't regard what you're saying as interference in Bella's affairs or mine, but I don't like to hear you make such charges against a lad who never asked me either to employ him or to find him a job. It was our idea that he should devote himself to his writing, because we hoped, I think, to bathe in the sunshine of his success."

"And you fitted up a study for him, and you went on keeping him and paying him wages, and you went on showering him with presents and getting him invited to all the dinners and receptions you and Bella were asked to; and where's your great writer now?"

Ida poured more coffee, and Mendel refilled the liqueur glasses.

Handing Mendel his cup, she remonstrated, "Sweetheart, you say yourself that his mastery of English isn't perfect. If you'd occasionally listen to Rick, instead of finding an excuse to wander over to the other side of the room the moment he approaches, you'd know that he only turned to writing, in his teens, because he thought writing required less technique than painting, and, in a way, that's true. All sorts of people write novels—actresses, politicians, army officers, farmers—because there's probably at least one good book in every one of us, while painting requires special study. Rick was able to devote time to such study only when Bella and Harry agreed to persuade Eva to take him as a pupil."

"All right, darling! So you're in love with a confidence man! Well, here's a question for you, and for you too, Harry! He met Eva at least ten times before there was any talk of his having nourished hopes of developing his inherent gifts for painting. He knew Bella and you, Harry, cherished him as your own son. He knew Eva was a painter, and he knew we're all such a big, happy family that Eva wouldn't have been offended at your suggesting she give him lessons. Eventually, you did ask, and she accepted. Now, then, here's the sixty-four-thousand-dollar question: Why did it take him so long to disclose his ambitions as a painter? Well, come on! The ball's on your side of the court. Smash it back to me! Remember how he tried to steal Rowan's thunder by astonishing even Bella and you, Harry, by his announcement of his own literary aspirations? He knew Eva much better than he knew Rowan; so, if he found it so easy to place himself on a jolly, old boy sort of writer-to-writer relationship with Rowan, what prevented his being drawn to Eva, a true mistress of the art which he has since claimed is the great love of his pathetic life? What held him back for so long, and what eventually spurred him into action?"

Harry struck a match with which to light the cheroot which Ida held between her lips. He lighted her cheroot, and pensively allowed the match to burn out against his fingers. The blackened match fell to the carpet, and Harry flicked his slightly burned fingertips. He picked up the charred match, and paused a further half-minute before answering, "I think you've got me there, old chap. What does Ida think about it?"

Ida shrugged her shoulders and raised her hands to convey the fact that she was at a loss for words. Mendel chortled, and answered himself, "I admit I didn't like your golden boy from the moment I made his acquaintance. Being myself a chap of humble origin, I have, perhaps, a sharper nose than the rest of you for a working-class fake. I'm telling you I saw through him at once. It's no secret to anybody in our set that I'm very fond of Eva, and that she and I always seem to be together, however large may be the party we're attending. Consequently, I've often been able to observe his attitude towards her. Ida won't mind my saying this—and I know Bella wouldn't, if she were here—but Eva was usually as beautiful and attractive as any woman present, and, to a normal man, more attractive than any of the males. Yet his indifference to her would have been downright rude, but for the fact that she's so humble that she never expects anyone to take an interest in her. He would walk past her without a glance or he would politely say 'Hello!' as he moved on to some man or woman in whom one would have expected a would-be painter to show scant interest as long as there was a painter in the room. Suddenly all that's changed. The latter-day D. H. Lawrence becomes a student of painting. He sports a margarine-colored beard, and he's Eva's most devoted admirer. Why the change?"

Mendel gave his sister and their guest time to reply, but neither was able to do. He sipped the cognac, and then continued. "Until Eva's exhibition at the Barstein Gallery he thought she was a flop, an artistic hanger-on, our pet, impoverished painter. Since she herself was living on charity, there was little chance that she'd be in a position to contribute to his financial well-being, so, handsome and seductive or not, she didn't count. But I noticed the look on his face, when, during the first afternoon of the exhibition, we heard that this or that picture had been sold for so many pounds. It was obvious that, because we, Eva's friends, had encouraged her to exhibit, Haylett had supposed it was a bit of harmless flattery we offered her. There wasn't the slightest chance that this mock exhibition would result in any sales, but we were all willing to contribute to the futile expenses involved, as a gesture of friendship to our pathetic little painter-friend. When the truth dawned on him, and he noticed that Eva's paintings were going to total strangers for astronomical figures, he woke up to her commercial value. Her true worth is evident to anyone with an ounce of feeling for painting. I doubt whether you've taken him into one house where there wasn't at least one Dalheim; but they meant nothing to him. He thought we hang her pictures as a gesture of sympathy and when he realized that she is, in fact, a highly successful artist, and, consequently, a woman of considerable means, he did some quick thinking. He suddenly noticed what other men see the moment they meet her: that she's pretty of face, trimly built and subtly voluptuous. I'm not sure about this, but I think he wouldn't have been deflected from his course by her being physically repulsive. It may be that he's always managed to find clients who combine a worthwhile balance in the bank with beauty, gaiety and all the other things that make for attractiveness, but the case of Eva leaves me in no doubt that all the sweetness, intelligence, talent and beauty in the world mean little to him until he discovers they're allied to wealth. I'm sorry if I seem to tearing apart someone you and Bella are obviously very fond of, but it wasn't I who first mentioned Rick Haylett, and, when I hear his name, my blood begins to boil."

"Because he's the lover of the woman you desire more than any other in the world," Ida taunted.

"Cheap gossip!" snapped Harry, although Ida's revelation was but the confirmation of a probability he had long accepted.

Both Mendel and Ida stared at him incredulously. It was Mendel who asked, "Did you know?"

"Well, I suppose I did, more or less; and yet I didn't really. Are you sure?"

Mendel knew he had committed one of the gravest of faults; assuming his friend was as well informed as he of the relationship between Eva and Rick, he had spoken with complete frankness. Ida had also believed that Harry knew his protégé and Eva were lovers, and when it became clear this was not the case her regret was obvious. She pretended she needed Rose for something or other, and she left her brother to extricate them both from an embarrassing situation.

"I'm sorry, Harry," he began, "but I assumed it was evident to you that Eva's sudden enthusiasm for the reluctantly accepted role of teacher was due to the sharpness and accuracy of Cupid's dart. Since we've already said too much, I think I'm duty-bound to answer your question. We are as sure as one can be after hearing a dear friend's ecstatic confession that she devotes almost the whole of six afternoons a week to love-making with her sole pupil. She's more intimate with us than with anyone else, and I don't expect she'd speak so frankly to Bella and you, but I rather think she's convinced you both know how things stand."

Pale and pensive, Harry was silent for a few seconds, after which he drank the contents of his glass. Mendel refilled it, Ida's and his own. Mendel and Harry drank their liqueur as though their lives depended on it. Licking his lips appreciatively, Harry looked his friend deep in the eyes; and Mendel, his shame dissipated by his confession and by Harry's obvious realization of his innocence, did not avert his eyes. He knew Harry had something of importance to say to him, and he waited until Harry begged, "Look, old chap, unless it appears clear to you, when you meet Bella, that she knows about Rick and Eva, don't mention this conversation, and if I forget, will you warn Ida not to let Bella know anything about this business! I'll be perfectly frank with you...for the moment I don't know what I'm going to do about it. I don't know how much this thing means to Bella. On the face of it, Rick's sexual conduct is none of her business. She ought not to care, because he's sup- posed to be our protégé, guest and secretary, who's entitled to his free hours and to his privacy. I doubt whether there's another person to whom I'd talk like this, but I wonder whether he doesn't mean more to her than that; and if he and she are lovers, does she love him enough to want to be his unique mistress or is it just a physical love which leaves her indifferent to whom he lies down with in her absence? You know, Mendel, that I'm very fond of Bella. After all these years and after my many infidelities, and in spite of hers, of which I've no evidence, but which I think she'd admit if I ever showed any curiosity about her sexual behavior when we're separated... well, in spite of all that, her contentment is still of great importance to me, and I'm not going to stand idly by while some pretty young whipper-snapper two-times her, plays tricks with her feelings and makes her unhappy. What I have to decide is whether to tell her before she gets too deeply involved with Rick, if it's not already too late, or to hope that either she or Eva will tire of him before either gets to know of his intimacy with the other—always assuming, of course, that Bella is his mistress. What do you think, Mendel?"

Mendel had never doubted that there was a strong bond of deep affection between Bella and Harry, neither of whom needed to stay with the other a day longer than she or he wished; but he was surprised by his friend's almost boyish fear that she should suffer as a result of her adultery with a fellow who was deeply in his debt. If Harry was asking him for counsel, Mendel was tempted to advise him to "Throw the nasty little devil out on his ear!" He was sure Bella's pain would be of short duration. She was not, in Mendel's opinion, the sort of woman who could permanently hold the affections of a man fifteen years her junior. He imagined she was enjoying a romp with Haylett as long as it lasted, with no thought of allowing their relationship to destroy either her or her marriage. Her pride would suffer briefly at the knowledge of Rick's infidelity, and she would miss him physically at first; but Mendel realized that Harry was anything but impotent or sexually cool, so Bella would find some consolation in conjugal copulation, and, when she felt the need to change her erotic diet, she would make one of her sporadic trips to London, Paris, Menton, Madrid or Düsseldorf, where her beauty, astonishingly youthful figure, brilliance and crazy gaiety would soon have her surrounded by admirers from whom she could choose the man who would share her bed for a few nights. What caused Mendel to hesitate before giving his friend brutal advice is that the question "What do you think, Mendel?" could, in the circumstances, have meant so many things. After a few seconds of meditation, he asked:

"Harry, do you want to know whether I think

Bella and Haylett are lovers or do you want to know what I'd do in your shoes?"

"I was really asking for advice, but tell me, is Rick Bella's lover as well as Eva's? It's commonly supposed that the wronged husband or wife is always the last to know the truth."

Harry laughed uneasily, and Mendel joined him sympathetically.

"It's strange," the latter answered, "but you and Bella, Eva, Ida and I are so intimate that one would think we all knew each other inside out; and yet I have to admit to being flabbergasted to learn you've ever doubted for a moment that Bella slept with Haylett in Paris, and that he came here as her lover. Eva thinks he's ceased making love to Bella since he started doing just that with her; but she's a lady in love, so we must pardon her gullibility. Your naïveté, however, falls into another category. We supposed all along that you'd taken Haylett in, knowing he was Bella's boy-friend. It was generally believed that, like a loving father, if you'll excuse the suggestion that you're old enough to be Bella's daddy, that you didn't want to refuse Bella her human plaything. It's probably the first time she's asked you to house, employ and play uncle to one of her lovers; but we thought you did all that with your eyes wide open. Frankly, we didn't foresee this relationship continuing so long and I seem to be the only person in the whole of our gang who hasn't wholly approved all along."

"You take exception to a husband's tolerating his wife's cuckolding him under his own roof?"

"Oh, no, Harry!" replied Mendel anxiously. "I'm so fond of Bella that, if she has fun with Haylett, and you don't mind, I'm only too happy, although, of course, it's none of my business. What I mean is that I think it's a pity Bella doesn't get herself loved by some more worthy man, instead of that damn prostitute. I'm by no means a woman-hater, but what I loathe most about him is his gift and tendency for making people think it's their duty to shower him with generosity of one kind or another. I've never previously met a man who could so coolly and unflinchingly take without giving. However, I'm repeating myself. Let's drop the subject of Haylett!"

"Yes. We shan't see eye-to-eye about him, although I confess that the certainty that he's been playing Bella and Eva off against one another cools my affection for him. The difference is that you seem to think he's wicked, while I can't avoid seeing him more as a weakling who's blinded and flattered by the attentions of two beautiful women of a class so far removed from his. Well, I think I'll be on my way now. May I leave my gun here until tomorrow?"

"Of course! I'll run you home."

"No, thanks, Mendel. It's a lovely day, and I'd like to wander back the way I came. Give me a chance to think this thing out. I think that, if I were sure Bella's his mistress, I'd feel it my duty to put both her and Eva in the picture, and let them decide whether he stays or not; then, the three of them can sort out the question of whether he belongs to both of them or to which one of them. I'd like to say good-bye to Ida before I go."

Mendel went in search of Ida, whom he found in the kitchen.

"It's all right," he assured her, "Harry realizes we said too much in the conviction that he knew all we knew, and he's taking it like a man."

They rejoined Harry in the hall, and Ida invited him to stay to lunch. He told her that, since they were going to town the following day, there were certain tasks he had to perform before midday—telephone calls, letters and so forth.

The kiss she bestowed on Harry's mouth was gentle, but not devoid of a hot-blooded young woman's excitement at physical contact with an older, experienced, handsome, manly male for whom she had a deep affection.

As Harry left the two at the front door of their lovely house, he asked, "About half past nine tomorrow morning?"

"Half past nine? Fine, old boy!"

"Don't forget our date for loving in the back of the car, Harry!" Ida said, half jokingly, as Harry strolled away laughing.

IX.

It was about eleven o'clock when Harry re-entered his house. Having wandered from room to room on the ground floor without finding either Bella or Rick, he ascended quietly to the first floor, and looked in Rick's study, where he found Nadia nonchalantly flicking dust from Rick's neglected typewriter.

"Is Mrs. Partham about, Nadia?" he asked.

"Yes, Mr. Partham, in her room, I think."

"Mr. Haylett?"

The poor girl did not want to betray either her mistress or Mr. Haylett, but she could not resist the urge to smile. Grasping the full meaning of her tacit answer to his question, he, too, smiled, and exclaimed, "You little devil!'

She laughed softly, defending herself with, "I'm not a devil, Mr. Partham. I'm just a good girl, doing my best to answer the master's questions."

He closed the door prior to saying, in a conspiratorial whisper, "If you're a good girl who does her master's bidding, I'll bring you back some pretty lingerie from London tomorrow. Would you like that?"

Unhappy, but neither angry nor afraid, she replied, "Mr. Partham, you remember what I said about not wanting a white man's flesh to come into my black girl's body?"

Genuinely sorry that he had caused a moment of embarrassment, he hastened to assure her that he was not trying to seduce her. Paradoxically, she seemed disappointed.

"You don't find me attractive enough for that sort of proposition, do you, Mr. Partham?"

He placed one of his hands on each of her cheeks, and drew her face to his until their mouths were fused in a kiss of ineffable sweetness. Against the moistness and softness of his lips, hers were warm and firm. Her tongue's tip tickled his gums behind his upper front teeth, and his hands gently exerted pressure on her buttocks so that their respective genitals hugged each other closely. Her hands held his head when he tried to bring their kiss to what she regarded as a premature end, but, a few seconds later, she released him. Her smile was broad and bright.

"If you're willing to earn the undies I spoke about," he said, "and if you'll accept such a gift from a man with a white phallus, I'll go up to your room, when you put them on for the first time, and tell you whether they suit you."

A slight frown furrowed her brow as she stammered, "Mr. Partham, you're going to make me do something I'll be sorry for."

Not sure whether she referred to what would happen when she was putting on the underwear he intended giving her or to the means by which she was to earn the gift, he answered, "My dear Nadia, I'm going to make you do nothing. I've already told you how highly I respect you, so it ought not to be necessary for me to assure you that I'd never make you do anything that'd make you unhappy afterwards. All I want you to do is this…I want you to phone Miss Dalheim at noon, tell her Mr. Haylett won't be able to go to see her today, for his lesson, and ask her to come over for lunch. Say that, at lunch, we shall explain why Rick isn't free. If she accepts, knock on the door of whatever room we're in, when she arrives, and I shall come out. If she doesn't accept, let me know at once. Is it complicated?"

She admitted sadly that it was, but she repeated his instructions in such a way as to leave him in no doubt that all would go as he wished. She added, "Mr. Partham, there isn't going to be any trouble, is there?"

He took both her hands sympathetically in his.

"Not for you," he said reassuringly. "You know nothing of what's going on, and it wasn't you who told me where I'd find Bella and Rick. I just wandered around the house until I found them, which I was doing anyway when I happened to see you in here."

They kissed again warmly, and as they embraced, Harry imagined what it would be like to make love to the bright, attractive black woman. He pictured himself picking out a beautiful pair of panties—white lace, which would look gorgeous against her chocolate skin—and turning his head as she tried them on. But immediately afterward he would take them off, working the panties over her thighs and hips with his teeth, until they were pulled off her pussy, and down her legs. In this fantasy, she wanted him without reservation, she beckoned and begged for the invasion of his white cock into her sweet chocolate cunt. He would first honor the inner limbs of this woman with kisses that would lead to her cunt and he would, with awe, pry open the plump pussy lips with two fingers and gaze into the depths of her dark insides. The cunt would be pinker than the legs and pubic mound and he imagined the sweet smell of Jamaican ginger emanating from her loins. He'd sniff her aroma, and kiss her mount and then work his lips over her cunt lips until his tongue found her cunt-hole. It would be juicy and wet and waiting, and he would easily glide his tongue to the opening and press it in deeply, as his fingers probed and parted the silky opening even more, allowing him to ease his lips inside her cunt while his tongue probed further.

"Oh, Harry," she would cry, using his first name. "I want your white cock. Oh, please, please give me some of that white cock."

His cock would have already risen to the occasion and all he would have to do would be rise on top of her and press his penis home, into her juicy cunt. As he lowered himself onto her, he'd discover her beautiful full and rounded tits, with erected nipples, hard as chocolate chips. He'd devour them, like candy, and chew on the tasty morsels until the nipples became even more erect and inviting. She'd be groaning with pleasure, her cunt beginning to swell with excitement. And his cock would be ready to harpoon her ripened slash.

He would rejoice as she took the initiative, grabbing hold of his hardened spear and placing its swollen purple head at the opening of her tunnel of love. She'd pull him forward, and press her hips upward, until the cock slipped inward, teasingly at first, and then deeper and deeper with each proceeding thrust.

She'd grab hold of his buttocks and hold tight as she rode him, begging for "all of it," and pressing upward to greet it. Seeing her need to be more fully satiated, he would fling her athletic legs above her shoulders, so that her cunt was totally accessible, and he would plunge deeply, his hands grabbing on to her deliciously fleshy thighs as he pummeled her pussy with his raging prick.

In the middle of this, the two would notice they were facing a mirror and they would suddenly catch a glance of the huge white prick moving in and out of the plump brown cunt, and they would realize the sweet taste of forbidden fruit was all theirs.

She'd hold on to his shoulders as her orgasm neared, and he'd rub himself into her and against her, and pinch her ass cheeks, to heighten her pleasure. As her pussy muscles would start to clench and squeeze his cock, his own jism would be getting close to the surface. He'd bend, and kiss her, and thrust his tongue into her mouth as he thrust his cock into her cunt, and suddenly the earth would move and the two bodies would become one in a glorious simultaneous orgasm that would thrill each partner from head to foot. It would be an orgasm that would bond employee and employer, woman and man, black and white in a universal way.

In the end, Harry would unleash the last drop of his white man's sperm into her sweet black hole, and she in turn would wriggle and writhe until the last of her own come juice cleared her channel. Harry would then take her cheeks in hand, kiss her forehead and thank her for giving herself so lovingly and for taking him in so hungrily. They would hug, and then, they would part, knowing that they both had turned one another on to something new.

Harry was nearly in a daze with his sensual fantasy of love with his maid and it was she who broke the embrace and reminded him he had to be off somewhere to take care of some business. So he went along to the bedroom he shared with Bella. The door was closed. He paused for a moment, and then opened the door quite normally, and went in with the casually quizzical air of any man who has returned home unexpectedly and is in search of his wife, whom he merely wishes to apprise of his presence. His arrival could not have been better timed. Bella was standing on the bed. Her body was bent forward at the waist, and her feet were wide apart. His hands on her haunch, his feet close together between hers, and his legs bent at the knees, Rick was flashing mercilessly in and out of her wet vagina. The door had opened so smoothly, Harry's step was so light on the thick carpet, and the fornicators were flying so high on the wings of ecstasy, that he was half undressed before either became aware of his intrusion.

Rick broke the contact between his and Bella's genitals, and whirled round to face his disappointed benefactor and his mistress' irate husband; but Harry did not appear to be contemplating a resort to fisticuffs. In fact, his being jacketless and shirtless suggested that he was going to join the erotic fray.

Bella's surprise was tinged with amusement. Her anger at being abruptly deprived of Rick's copulatory attentions was slight in comparison with her curiosity. She had long known her imprudence would one day lead to her betrayal, and the consequences did not frighten her. Harry knew she had taken lovers here and there, although he had no evidence of her infidelity, any more than she had of his, which she nevertheless did not doubt. He would not divorce her; and, even if he did, her regret at losing a husband to whom she was devoted would have been softened by the fact that she and Rick would be able to live comfortably on what he could earn plus her considerable private income. At the same time, she was thrilled at the prospect of what his stripping seemed to signify. She wondered whether his anger was not so slight that he was going to condone her misconduct by join- ing her and her lover in a three-cornered session of love-making such as she had enjoyed in Paris with Rick and Dane. She could ask for nothing better. It even occurred to her that Harry's catching her and Rick in the act was a blessing rather than the disaster the latter had insisted it would be. From the moment Harry knew Rick was her lover, the need for secrecy and caution would cease to exist. Henceforth she would be able to share herself quite openly between her two beloved men, with the result that she and Rick would spend more time together than hitherto.

Harry was too occupied with the removal of his pants and footwear to bother about explaining his unexpected return. Rick was paralyzed with fear of what the future held in store for him, and conse- quently could summon neither the strength nor the courage to pose any questions. Bella was too excited to care why Harry had not gone to London. She seized Rick, and kissed him passionately. He tried to break from her grasp, but she hissed, "You were lov- ing me. Love me some more!" Rick was at a total loss for words. All he could do was cast apprehensive glances in Harry's direction until Harry calmly sug- gested:

"Just go on as you were when I burst in on you. Go on, Rick! We all know now where we stand. There's no point in trying to pretend things aren't as they really are. You were in Bella. She's begged you to get back inside her, so the decent, polite and lov- ing thing to do is not to oblige her to humble herself by asking you twice. Go on. Do as I tell you. Get stuck up Bella, and prepare yourself for a hard length of rod in your ass!"

Bella's eyes opened wide, and so did her mouth. She gasped, but words would not come. She threw herself into her husband's arms, and found just enough breath to exclaim, "Harry!"

He held her lovingly, and kissed her mouth which incredulous disgust rendered cold and pale. He fondled her until warmth returned to her. She began to respond to the ardor of his embrace, her arms tightening themselves about his powerful shoulders. Her tongue advanced to meet his, and she pressed her belly against his urgent penis. Their kiss was long. At the end of it, she looked into his eyes, and her mouth contorted by sad doubts, she whispered again, "Harry?"

He imperiously beckoned Rick to join them.

"Don't worry, darling!" he consoled her, "I shan't hurt your young lover."

"Harry, you're my lover, forever."

"Of course I am, and you're my hot-assed mistress-wife; but Rick's your lover too; and, like I just said, what I'm going to do to him won't hurt him. In fact, he likes it, and he's used to it, aren't you, lad?"

"Rick! Darling! Tell me! Is it true?"

She turned to Harry, and asked, "But you, darling? How do you know? Why are you...?"

Twisting round to face Rick again, she asked, "Rick, have you done that with...?"

Back to Harry, to whom she said, "Darling, I want to know...everything."

"You already know everything, Bella. Who introduced you to Rick? What sort of a man is Jorge? He's been a ladies' man, and I dare say he still enjoys an hour with a warm woman; but, daring, don't pretend you don't know he's had a succession of boyfriends. Surely you knew when you met Rick that he was Jorge's latest? You don't think Rick could, at that time, afford to stay at one of the most expensive hotels in Paris on an each-man-pays-for-himself basis? Of course you don't; so why not face the truth? Your body doesn't seem to enjoy Rick any less because he also goes with men, so why does your brain not accept the fact?"

Her voice was thinned and hoarsened by the effort she had to make to grasp the full significance of the situation. She said, "I suppose I did know about that side of Rick's life, Harry, but I don't see where you come into it."

Harry commanded Rick to enlighten her, but he paled greenly at the thought of confessing to his mistress that *he* was her *husband's* mistress. He spluttered, "Well, I sort of jolly well don't think...well, I mean to say...really, it's a bit thickish and all that sort of thing, don't you think?"

The lack of coherence in Rick's words told Bella all she needed to know. She felt that her world was crumbling about her, and that, unless she hurried, she would be able to salvage nothing from the debris. Her treasured lover and her beloved husband were not only both homosexuals, or at the least, bisexuals, but it was for the purpose of gratifying this craving for each other that they had so often left her on her own for hours on end. The first time Harry confessed to being unfaithful to her, his mistress was not some other woman, but her own lover for whom she had imagined Harry's feelings were paternal. She scarcely knew what to do next, but she was tempted to take herself off to one of the guest rooms, and sleep for at least twenty-four hours, leaving Harry and Rick to have fun together.

Harry saw things differently. He did not desire Rick in the least. He would have preferred to love his wife until she was convinced that he was a normal man, who had dabbled in homosexuality out of curiosity; but he felt the need to show her Rick for what he was, for what Mendel had finally convinced him he was…a whore whose knife cut both ways…a gold-digger who'd grovel before both men and women, provided crawling on his belly paid high dividends. He was convinced that, if Bella could see Rick giving himself to a man and a woman at the same time, she would be so disgusted that the discovery that her lover also betrayed her with Eva would not have upon her the destructive effect it might otherwise have had. He hoped that, if a separation between Bella and Rick became inevitable, she would feel that she had not lost a lover, but that she had been delivered from a swindler. He wanted it to be Bella who made the decision to send Rick away. He was determined that she should never reproach him with having denied her a few weeks, months or years of sexual pleasure with a dear young lover; nor was he willing to run the risk of Rick's choosing to cast Bella aside in favor of Eva.

"Listen, Rick!" Harry said sternly, "I'm adopting a very tolerant attitude to your relationship with Bella, and it seems to me that her reaction to the situation is as generous as mine. The least you can do in the circumstances is to complete the task you were performing so admirably when I came in here. Bella's already asked you once to give her some more loving, so don't leave the initiative to her any longer! Take her the way you were doing, when I came in! Do you agree, darling?"

She kissed Harry lingeringly. He touched her sex with his fingers, and ascertained that she was still juicy enough for immediate penetration. He lifted her onto the bed, and placed her in the pose she was adopting at the moment of his arrival. Then he roughly jerked Rick into position behind her, and indicated with manual gestures that the young whore was to perform the duty he was paid for.

Although her heart was heavy and her brain was in a turmoil, Bella thrilled to Rick's reinvasion of her love-sleeve. A few lunges into her welcoming oils hardened his penis, whose growth within excited her. Soon he was tupping her as though nothing unusual had happened. Her fine, milky bum moved with exquisite strength to the rhythm dictated by the strong motions of his loins.

Harry's phallus was swollen to its full glory and Rick's back door of love was dry. Harry was intent on going in without lubricating the culprit's canal. It was going to hurt Rick, and that was no more than just. The younger man's movements in and out of Bella's sweet lady were somewhat thrown off beat by Harry's thrusting his tool into the proffered anus; but, after his first three or four probings, Harry was sufficiently master of the situation to permit reconciling his undulations with those of Bella and Rick.

The air was soon heavy with their labored breathing. Bella's sighs were completely abandoned to luxury, Rick's groans, where the joy of his possession of Bella was mingled with the scorching agony of Harry's merciless belaboring of his sodomitical orifice, and the hoarse grunts with which Harry accompanied each sharp forward drive of his sex. During the intense excitement of her approach to an orgasm, Bella eliminated Rick from the game by imagining that it was Harry's penis which was pleasuring her. At the precise moment of her shivering arrival at the summit of pleasure, her sighs formed the name "Harry." With that, Rick's warrant of expulsion was signed.

Bella had enjoyed several orgasms before Harry's

return from the Levines. Consequently she felt slightly enfeebled by this latest outpouring of her jism.
Rick, however, was in too high a state of expectation
to allow her to slip from his grasp. He held her limp-
ness close to him, and jagged away at her ruthlessly,
snatching pleasure from her unwilling loins. Sweat
prickled his temples and trickled down the valley
between his buttocks, moistening Harry's granite col-
umn as it went deep into the aching posterior. By the
time Rick's shattering climax came, Bella had recov-
ered sufficiently to be once again lazily working her
rear to and fro in unison with the lurchings of the two
men behind her. Cream flooded into her, and it was
welcome. It was delicious, like glycerine poured over
a burn.

"Harry!" she whispered, and the order evicting
Rick was sealed.

Bitterly Rick continued to "love" her, his heart
full of hatred for these ungrateful people, who took
all a man had to offer without giving him as much as
a word of thanks in return. His movements no longer
had strength, but he ground himself deep into her,
and then jerked his crotch against the tender mouth
of her sore sex. His cruelty filled her with joy, and she
sought closer, more agonizing contact with his vicious
weapon. Her rear pushed against him, and she cried,
"Yes, hurt me!"

As though her entreaty were addressed to him,
Harry started to batter Rick's behind with bestial
ferocity. Rick cried out, "Bastard! Bastard!" and
took his revenge on Bella, whom he rode with the
fury of a wounded wolf. Bella responded with fervor,
and the three of them rocked in a frenzy of animal
"loving." Rick's sperm oozed into Bella, triggering
off within her a calm, delicious arrival at the portals
of paradise. Harry, weak at the knees after holding

back his ejaculation so long, let himself go, angrily hurling into Rick's backside salvo after salvo of cream. He pressed his ejaculating cock deeply into the younger man's sore canal as he expelled the last of his seed.

They all collapsed onto the bed, Bella and Harry seeking each other, and drifting into a light sleep during which their appeased bodies continued to love each other motionlessly. Feeling left out in the cold, but fearing the results of his withdrawing without permission, Rick dozed at their side, bitterly brooding over the brilliant "career" he had sacrificed in order to bury himself in the Partham mausoleum on the edge of the dreary little township of Ladbury. After all he had done for them and after his months of selfless devotion to their well-being, there they lay, sleeping in each other's arms, like young lovers, while tears of disillusion burned his eyes. The pathetic prostitute cried himself to sleep, wondering when one of them would notice his sobs, and seek to comfort him.

In answer to Nadia's light tap on the door, Bella lazily called, "Come in!"

Although she had had good reason to expect to find her master, his mistress and their guest naked and, perhaps, indulging in sexual fantasies, Nadia was, nevertheless, embarrassed by the spectacle of them all lying on one bed, disheveled and in provocatively abandoned poses. She tried to avert her eyes from the bodies of the wakening men, but the temptation was too great. She looked from one phallus to the other. Both appeared to be ready for further action after a period of strength-giving repose. Nadia found herself wondering which of these bodies would most attract her, in the event of her curiosity concerning the erotic prowess of white European men

215

getting beyond her control. The questioning lasted but a few seconds. Rick's thin, girlish pallor was sickly alongside the bronzed suggestion of power in the chest, arms and thighs of Mr. Partham.

"What it is, dear?" Bella asked.

"It's for Mr. Partham, Mrs. Partham."

Bella laughed softly, and said, "Now you see how silly it is to have refused Mr. Partham's suggestion that you call us by our Christian names. 'It's for Mr. Partham, Mrs. Partham.' Ridiculous! Give him his bathrobe, dear, and take him down gently! He's half asleep."

Harry wrapped himself in the robe Nadia obediently handed him. She picked up a comb from the dressing table, and deftly restored a little order to his iron-gray hair.

Outside the bedroom Harry kissed Nadia with no mean ardor. Her response was so flattering that he took her hand, and placed it on his phallus under the dark green folds of his robe. She caressed it lovingly, allowing her fingers to run from its tips to its root. She weighed his scrotum in the palm of her hand, and murmured, "It feels as healthy as it looked back there in the bedroom."

He smiled, and asked, "So you took a good look at it, did you?"

She nodded her head affirmatively, her face illuminated by a smile of approval.

"Do you think its going into your brown quim would disgust you as much as you once suggested it would?"

She squeezed his organ, replying, "If it happened in the dark, perhaps I wouldn't even think of the color of my belly and your hard, proud penis."

He kissed her hard, and asked, "When?"

"If you don't bring me a present from London, I

might feel like it next Friday or during the following week."

Puzzled, he asked, "Why next Friday?"

"Because I don't want my first white penis either to give me a baby or to be wearing a thin rubber coat, and I calculate I'm just about at the beginning of my fertile period."

He held her close to him, and whispered, "And why, if I don't bring you lingerie from London?"

Her lips touched his, and her tongue went deep into his mouth. She opened his bathrobe, and rubbed her clothed front against his nakedness. After a long, groaning, writhing kiss, she told him that to allow him into her bedroom and to accept gifts from him would be like resorting to prostitution. She admitted that, like any normal girl, she liked receiving presents from admirers; but she insisted that, if she accepted from him anything further than her wages, her brown body would never be his. As she retied the belt of his robe, she added, "I haven't said I shall feel like having your body on mine next week. You've got me excited today, so I think I might want you, but I'm going to try and cool down, so that I can keep your respect by not surrendering to you."

Determined to put no pressure on her, he kissed her gently, and they continued on their way. Descending the stairs, she said earnestly, "I like you very much. You're nice, and you're kind to me. Don't make me do anything which will lower me in your estimation!"

He tenderly touched her face, and then she went into the kitchen, while he entered the lounge. His brief interlude with Nadia had rejuvenated him, refreshed him and warmed his blood.

Eva approached him with a "Hello, Harry! Are you ill or are you going for a bath?"

Into their kiss Harry put all his sexual fire. Eva was surprised, but neither angry nor shocked. She knew him to be a sensualist, and she never ceased to find his gallant attentions towards her flattering. However, he had not kissed her as significantly as that since the occasion, seven or eight years previously, when, after a party at the Levines', a man she had initially hoped would spend the night with her insisted on being driven home by no one other than Bella, with whom he had flirted throughout the evening. The Levines had invited the man in question on Eva's behest, but he had taken little notice of her from the moment he had set eyes on Bella. Eva had driven Harry home, and had been glad to accept his invitation that she sleep in their guest room instead of going home to a lonely cottage where she had planned to spend a night of love. They had drunk a whisky as a nightcap, and Harry had taken her, their glasses and the bottle up to the guest room. He had undressed her and joined her in the bed, where he had robustly but tenderly consoled her for the fact that the man she desired would probably take Bella into his bed. It had been daylight when, upon hearing Bella's car in the drive, Eva and Harry had bidden each other a fond "Good night!"; they then promised they would henceforth behave correctly towards one another. Each had kept the promise, but neither had forgotten their delicious night together, and their friendship had since then deepened with their every meeting.

Their second kiss was on her initiative. After it, she asked anxiously, "Has something happened to Rick? Something terrible?"

He shook his head negatively, and said, "No, dear. Nothing's happened to him. You're very fond of him, aren't you?"

218

"It may sound like something out of a romance novel, Harry, but Rick and I are deeply in love with one another."

He placed his arm soothingly about her shoulder, and she kissed him again, but briefly and with more gratitude than passion.

"Do you know he and Bella are lovers?"

Tensely she gripped his shoulders, a look of terror in her dark brown eyes.

"Harry!" she cried. "They haven't gone away together?"

"No, but tell me. Did you know they're lovers?"

"I know they were lovers until circumstances opened Rick's eyes and mine."

"You became his mistress, and he told you he'd ceased fornicating with Bella?"

Eva put aside her own fears, and concentrated on the problem which seemed to be exercising Harry.

"You sound so bitter," she said, "but...you've known all along?"

His right hand toyed with the lobe of her left ear, as he answered slowly and pensively, "I didn't want to know, so I didn't know. I knew, in other words, but I was the classic example of the complaisant husband. All I asked was that I be not obliged to admit I knew. This morning, just after breakfast, I saw something which roused my suspicions; but I'd have forgotten that by tomorrow, if circumstances hadn't sent me away from home for the whole day and then brought me back in the middle of the morning. Eva darling, I know you're not like the rest of us, but I'd like to give you the truth."

"I know what you mean, Harry. Tell me the truth, even if it's brutal. You don't have to use the sliver platter technique with me."

He took her in his arms, and whispered, "I don't

feel sorry for myself. As I say, I've known Bella and Rick long enough not to go to pieces now that the truth has been pushed under my nose; and then, as you know, I'm the last man who could righteously reproach his wife with infidelity. What gets my goat is that Rick isn't content with cuckolding his host and his employer, who pays him sixty percent more than he was getting from his previous boss...and for doing what?...for starting writing novels he doesn't intend finishing. No, he goes further. He seduces a woman who's as dear to Bella as she is to me. That's true, darling. We're both very fond of you; and what upsets me is that, sooner or later, both you and Bella are sure to find out that you've been sharing a lover you both thought was yours exclusively."

"But, Harry darling, you're making a tragedy of nothing. Rick ceased all misconduct with Bella from the day he and I became lovers."

Harry suspected that Eva was playing a psychological trick with herself; deep inside she knew, but refused to acknowledge, the truth seeming somewhat jittery, she asked, "Darling, where is Rick now?"

"In our bedroom...Bella's and mine."

"And Bella?"

"With him...both naked, and probably having a go at it, because neither of them knows you're here; and I'm almost sure she hasn't the faintest suspicion you and Rick take off all your clothes every afternoon."

"Harry! I thought you both knew. I thought Rick and Bella had...dried up...faded out, and that she didn't care. He told me I was the only one. Harry, you do believe that? I'm no angel, but you do believe?"

In tears, she threw herself into Harry's arms, and he cradled her. Her mouth sought his, and he was prepared to deny her nothing. His hands molded her body from her pretty, smooth knees to her tear-moist face. His lips drank the salt water which dropped warmly from her dark eyes, and he answered, "Of course I believe you. I came home, unexpectedly, about mid-morning. They were standing on our bed, she with her back to him, and he rafting her from behind, as though they were a dog and a bitch in heat. It's been going on all the time, darling, before Rick seduced you and since. He's been two-timing you both, and I feel myself duty-bound to see that he's taught a lesson. I'm telling you first; but I warn you that, whatever you decide, I'm going to tell Bella he's been making a fool of her. I'm devoted to both of you, but Bella's my wife, so I feel more responsible for her than for you. I daren't run the risk of her discovering the truth of his intimacy with you when she's too deeply involved with him to come out of this farce unscathed."

"Harry, don't call it a farce! It's a tragedy for me, and I'm sure it will be for Bella too; but I'm surprised at how calmly I can take it. Perhaps I don't yet really believe it; but, once I'm sure he's done this terrible thing to me, I shall hate him as I've never previously hated anybody except Hitler, Mussolini and Franco. Harry, I want to see them. Can you arrange it for me?"

During the long kiss which followed her question she raised no objection to his right hand's running up her thighs inside her skirts. She trembled with excitement as his fingers gripped the flesh above her stocking-tops, but she resisted his attempt to slide her panties down. His mouth left hers, and moved to her right ear, in which he whispered, "If you'll believe what I've told you about Rick only after seeing him and Bella copulating, I'll have to show you nothing less than that. I'm going to take you up to the guest room, where I once before peeled you down to the skin, and I'm going to strip you again."

"Harry!"

"No point in arguing, darling! I'm going to take all your clothes off, and ogle your true beauty. I'm going to touch you everywhere. I'm going to kiss your body from head to foot, and drive you wild with desire. I'm going to spread open your legs, and part the tender flesh of your cunt lips so that I can tantalize your sweet love bud with my tongue and drink the sweet liquid love that pours from your quim. Then you'll have the choice between an intimate session of sweet loving with a man who's very fond of you and an invasion of the room where, if Rick isn't making love to Bella, I shall order him to do so."

She gripped both his wrists and insisted, "Harry, teach him a lesson, if you must! But don't break him! I love him, and I wouldn't be surprised if Bella does too, in her own promiscuous way; so she won't want him to be permanently hurt any more than I do. I just want to be sure. I want to see him inside Bella, so that I shall hate him enough not to suffer agonies at his going out of my life."

His arms tenderly about her, he asked, "What if he doesn't want to break with you? You're a warm, handsome woman, and you have money. If Bella gives him his cards, as I'm sure she will when she knows he's been riding two mares simultaneously, he'll probably want to move into your cottage."

She clung to him. Their mouths met in a savage kiss, throughout which he squeezed her ample breasts through her dress.

"Don't let him touch me, Harry!" she begged. "Keep him away from me! Make me send him away!"

"Come up to the guest room, and let me look at

you, touch you, kiss you and make you. Lie down with me, and I'll protect you from all the Ricks and dicks in the world. Kiss me, Eva!"

She obeyed, and he almost carried her up to the room where they had once pleasured each other in the early hours of the morning.

Like Bella she was younger half-dressed than fully clad; and she dropped years as each of her garments fell. The difference was that stripping rendered Bella slimmer than she appeared with all her clothes on, while Eva glowed, healthily robust as she disrobed. Under her dress she wore a cognac-colored slip, which Harry eased upwards until she was rosily girl-ish in bikini briefs and bra, the flesh above her stock-ing tops bulging ever-so-slightly.

She threw herself into his arms, and sighed, "Admire me, darling. Protect me. Hold me tight, and love me!"

He broke the straps of her bra, tore her panties from her and ripped her stockings off.

"Beast!" she said, the light of love in her eyes.

She opened his robe, and looked at his erect, throbbing penis. Her warm, sad nakedness went to his heart, and she was a defenseless darling in his arms. He wanted to please her. His mouth went all over her, and hers wandered from his mouth to his anus and she seemed bent on devouring his asshole, and filling him up with tongue and fingers, as if she knew he loved having that part of his body invaded. She spread the tight hole open and darted her tongue in and out, as wave after wave of ecstasy shot through Harry's spine at the feel of her hot, wet tongue buried in his butt. After she was satisfied with her tongue-lashing to his back door, she crawled over him, and started working on his front, her mouth going hungrily for the scarlet bulb of his elongated sex. She licked the cock head like a lollipop and then took him whole into her mouth and sucked him deliciously until he groaned, "If you keep that up, I'll be off in your mouth in a minute. Why not put your sweet cunt lips on my mouth and let me stir you with joy as well?"

Eva maneuvered into a "sixty-nine" position and eased her hot cunt onto his awaiting mouth. He was amazed at how wet she was, simply dripping with juices, which he hungrily and adeptly licked out of her burning gash. She groaned as she sucked him and, realizing he was close to coming, his mouth latched onto her clit and began suckling her distended bud so deliciously that it brought her to the peak of joy immediately. Within moments her richly pink, smoothly muscled cunt was contracting violently with pleasure. At that same moment, Harry came in her mouth, as she raptly and diligently continued to work her mouth up and down his cock.

So joyous were these two lovers who had rediscovered one another, that they were ready for more love. Harry's penis never lost its hardness and while her tongue continued to pay homage to his hero, he kept licking the opening of her cunt until the two of them were once again in a tizzy of sexual lust.

At the moment when his phallus would have penetrated her genitals, she said, "Lay me, darling, but lay me where he can see! I want him to know he's not the only man who can make me cry out with joy. Give it to me where I can see Bella getting it from him. Then I shall believe it, and casting him off won't be hard."

From the wardrobe he took a red silk kimono, the touch of which chilled and thrilled her.

"You're so good," she gasped, and they stepped out of the guest room, arm-in-arm. In the corridor they paused, and she tongued his mouth beseechingly.

"The first time," she said, "it was a short night that developed into nothing more than ever-deepening affection; but this time, if Bella agrees, will you come to the cottage, now and then, and spend a night with me?"

Under her gown his hands savored her warm, fleshy beauty. He answered, "Will you come here, at least once a week, and go to bed either with me alone or with Bella and me?"

Radiantly she cried, "Oh, Harry, I'd love to have you adore me with Bella's approval."

They warmed each other with a long, lascivious kiss and cuddle, after which they surreptitiously entered the conjugal bedroom, where the spectacle offered to Eva's eyes was such that it brooked no doubt as to the relationship between her idol and Bella, whose combined bodies epitomized sexual repletion. They both lay on their backs, his left foot touching hers, while her right calf rested on his right shin. The middle finger of his left hand was lifeless in her satiated vagina, and her right hand lay lazily on his deflated penis. They both looked cold, their open mouths giving them the air of dying fishes whose breath is heavy between paralyzed lips.

Eva observed them for a full minute. She pressed the forefinger of her right hand against her lips, pleading with Harry to make no noise; and she placed her left hand on Bella's belly. Bella stirred, groaned voluptuously, and turned towards Rick, her hands floating instinctively to his face, shoulders, chest, waist, buttocks and genitals. Rick began to come to life. Eva stroked Bella's shoulder-blades, the small of her back and the crevice between the globes of her ass. On the bed the lovers emerged from drowsiness, the body of each imagining itself invited to action by the hands of the other. Eva drew Harry into a shadowy corner formed by a wall and the side of the wardrobe. The coming together of Bella's body and Rick's ought to have shocked and pained her; but Harry had warned her. Consequently, instead of agonized astonishment, there was within her the thrill of seeing a man and a woman moving ineluctably towards the frantic fusion of their bodies. She pressed herself against Harry, her silken back against his terry cloth façade, and her mouth sought his greedily. Her lips moistened his, and her tongue quivered. She pushed her veiled bottom against his painfully stiff hero, and his hands pulled open her kimono, baring the ripe fruits of her bosom and the pink curve of her belly. His fingers found her clitoris, and she had to fight herself to quit her groans of sexual frenzy. Her hands seized her lust-inflated breasts, and the back of her crazed head battered his left collarbone.

She uttered the name "Harry!" in a ghost of a whisper, and froze against him as she saw Bella's half awake mouth go down on Rick and swallow his worm. Bella sucked the harlot's manhood until it became hard as a rock. His loins began to move to and fro between her lips, and his hands clawed at the bedclothes.

"Bella!" he bellowed.

Bella responded by sucking his ramrod more vigorously, and jerking her hand up and down the lower part of his hard pole.

She threw herself backwards, with her shoulders against the foot of the bed. Her thighs were wide open, and her knees were raised. Rick shot upwards into a sitting-position, aimed his spear at her cunt, caught sight of Eva and Harry, and spluttered, "Bella!" in such confusion that Bella twisted

herself angrily round until she saw Harry's left hand
on Eva's breast and his right hand buried in her
vagina.

As though she were not quite sure she recognized
her friend, Bella queried, "Eva? Harry?"

Eva threw herself into Bella's arms, and Bella realized just then that Rick must be a triple-crosser—and
that this was his "other woman" coming to see him in
action for herself. The two women hugged one
another, comforted each other and wept together
until, in the passion of the moment, Bella's hands
grabbed hold of Eva's face as her tongue carved a
path into her mouth. The two women tongue kissed
as if it were a natural extension of their relationship,
and both Harry and Rick watched as the tongues
dipped in and pulled out of the female mouths, like
sexy snakes on the loose. Next, Bella began massaging Eva's breasts, kneading the nipples between two
fingers, until it was clear that Eva was quite excited;
she reached for Bella's tits and did the same.

Before anyone really knew what was happening,
the two women maneuvered themselves into a "sixty-
nine" position, with pussy against mouth and mouth
against pussy, and eagerly spreading one another's
hot cunts open so their mouths could have access, the
two began to lick and suck in deliciously charming
ways. Bella was on top, and her fingers pulled mercilessly at Eva's cunt lips, spreading the folds far apart,
yawning open the cunt-hole, as her tongue went to
work darting in and out of the wet slash, and licking
up and down the corridor of love. Meanwhile, she
frantically pushed her own cunt into Eva's loving
mouth and could feel that her friend was sucking
exclusively on her hardened clitoris while finger-
fucking her wet pussy with two juicy fingers. Next,
Bella could feel Eva's finger creeping toward her

anus and soon enough the finger plunged inward, jolting Bella into sexual ecstasy with the sensation of having all her holes filled with fingers, while her clit was being sucked deliciously.

Eva too was growing wild with Bella's delicious cunt-licking, and her gyrating hips and heaving thighs were a signal that an orgasm was near—Bella brought a lone fingertip to Eva's bulging clitoris and gently rubbed the bud, while continuing to tongue-fuck her; in response, Eva sucked harder on Bella's clit. Within no time, the two gyrating cunts were wet, dripping pussies spewing tiny ejaculations onto each woman's face. Knowing that each had clearly come, they finished one another off by plunging tongues deep into still-vibrating cunts and licking out the orgasmic moisture and finished with a soft kiss to the clit or cunt folds.

At that point, both Harry and Rick had again found one another and both women watched in shock as Rick sucked Harry's big cock, deliciously fondling the balls and massaging the loins, as a well-practiced male prostitute would. Bella and Eva clung to one another as their young lover's mouth swallowed their older lover's pole in an obviously enjoyable way—for Harry was grabbing hold of Rick's head and pressing it toward him, softly demanding, "take me whole, you whore, and lick every last drop from the tip of my cock."

Rick complied, and his hands reached around to spread open Harry's ass-cheeks so he could gently finger fuck Harry's bum while sucking his cock. Harry swooned at the feel of the probing finger and, again to the shock of the two women, he knelt on the bed they were sitting on, and instructed Rick to lick his ass, make him wet and then bugger him. Rick complied with an obedience that neither women had quite seen in him, since he was usually the dominant stud in their lovemaking. And they watched as his adept tongue disappeared into the depths of Harry's anus, making Harry groan with great pleasure until he said he was ready for more. "Give me the cock now, lad, stuff it in as you know you love to do."

Rick, realizing this was probably his last chance to get back in Harry's good graces, ramrodded the older man with all his might. He brought his hard cock to Harry's wet opening, pressed the head inside and then rocked himself into the awaiting asshole until he was buried to the balls. Then his movements were basic back and forth, in and out, fucking until Harry next told him to grab hold of his hard sword and rub it as he pummeled his ass. Rick took hold of the familiar cock, its swollen head, the sac of balls, and massaged the whole organ. Then he began to jerk Harry off, timing his jerking hand movements with the rhythm of his cock movements, until Harry was so swept into the pleasure that he was near coming.

"I'm going to come," Harry called out, "but not you. Hold it back, whatever you do."

This made it extremely difficult, because Rick's cock was about to burst, but nevertheless, he followed instructions and he was still hard and ready when Harry's cock exploded all over his hand.

"Show the ladies what's next," Harry commanded. And Rick licked the male jism off his own hand, swallowing every last ounce of the fallen seed. Harry told him to pull himself out and stand at the foot of the bed where both women could see. Rick stood, his hard cock waving in the air, and seemed a bit weak in the knees. Harry got behind him and rubbed his cock against the younger man's butt until it was once again hard. He pushed Rick down so that he was bent over the bed, nuzzled his dick into the orifice and then began to slam into the opening with brute force.

"Don't worry, ladies, I'll give him something to feel good about," Harry said, and with that, he grabbed hold of Rick's throbbing manhood and masturbated him while fucking him mercilessly. Rick cried in pain and pleasure until his organ finally blasted off all over Harry's hand.

Harry again instructed Rick to show the ladies what was next. Obediently, Rick licked his own semen from Harry's hand and then, as Harry rose off him, he bent between the older man's legs and lapped away at his soiled cock until his loins were clean and the evidence of the ass-fucking was swallowed by the male slut who had tricked all three people in the room into believing they were the "only one."

At this time, Harry was not aiming to teach any more lessons. He could see the two ladies, his wife and lover, had grown excited by the sex act between the two males in the room and rather than deprive them of any more sex by wasting it on Rick, he decided it was time to fill their wet pussies with the kind of cock meat that God meant for a woman's hole. They rested only shortly before Harry turned to Rick and said, "Now we must truly satisfy these women so that they do not feel any more abused than they already do by your cheating and lies."

Harry then pointed at Bella and commanded Rick to "take position."

Harry and Rick attacked simultaneously. Bella lay with her rump on the edge of the bed and her feet on the thickly carpeted floor. Lying on her belly, Rick went deep into her from behind, and tupped her frantically. Eva kneeled on the opposite side of the bed, and met Bella's face halfway across the bed. Her mouth and Bella's were joined in a kiss, as Harry, on his knees behind Eva, pulled off her kimono, and thrust his penis into her vagina from behind.

The girls clung to each other as the men rode into them furiously, fucking them wildly from behind.

It was a wild symphony of sighs, groans, grunts, entreaties and sexy obscenities. Eva and Harry sought to avoid contact with Rick, but Bella wanted to feel herself close to her lover, to her husband and to her friend, who was now Harry's mistress. Rick played safe. He knew Bella still desired him, angry though she undoubtedly was; and he was obeying a command which Harry had given him. Eva had not said a word to him, but he did not underestimate his charms. In the unlikely event of the Parthams showing him the door after the four-cornered orgy, he was mistakenly sure Eva would welcome him to her cottage, her bed and her bank balance. His confidence gave him sexual strength, and Bella rejoiced in it. She jagged herself wildly against his savage prong, her eyes bright with the joy of her copulation with the male strumpet. She gave herself without reserve, and she took voraciously all the brutality he had to offer her. He possessed her as though he knew she had to come back for more. He tore into her ferociously, eager to prove that he could do her more effectively than any former lover had done her. He did, indeed, procure her orgasm after orgasm before he capitulated; but, if Bella's immediate joy was great, it was not equal to her determination to rid herself of a lout who had thought he could share his precious self between her and her dear friend. After his explosion she made him go on "loving" her. She rubbed her lubricated snatch up and down his shrunken member, making sure her clit bud was stimulated by the friction of her movements. Finally, she worked herself off against his lifeless member, and continued to flatter him until he hardened again. Eager to acquit himself honorably, he gritted his teeth, and pounded her afresh. She squealed with delight, and quickly reached yet another climax which calmed her.

In the meantime, Harry and Eva really loved each other. Free from all bitterness and egoism, each gave body, heart and soul to the other. They rose together to delirious heights of joy, glided tiredly downwards, and climbed again. His cock plunged deep, deeper, deepest into her ever warmer, wider gash of delight. She rose to greet him expectantly, and swayed away from him when he withdrew. Her vagina lisped joyfully as he moved in and out of her; and the grip of her arms on his shoulders and her legs on his rear tightened with his every probing of her intimate flesh. Her juices flowed copiously and the warmth of her joy opened her sex as a rosebud unfolds under the sun. His vigorous motions within her were easy, and she rejoiced in the honest vigor with which he used her and served her. She reached climax several times, sighing, trembling convulsively and uttering little cries which included his name, words of encouragement, expressions of gratitude and whispered obscenities. When his semen thundered into her, she knew such ecstasy as she had not previously thought existed. Proud of the look of thrilled contentment on his face, she held him close, and buried her tongue in his mouth. His staff softened in the oils of her sexcup, and lost some of its size.

"Sleep, my darling!" she cooed, "Sleep on me, in

me and with me. You've loved me into the sweetest of fatigues. You're wonderful."

Rick too reached another climax, and slipped away into an hour of well-earned repose against the frail and lovely body of his tired lady.

An hour later Eva, but not her companions, was nonplused to discover, upon being awakened by the sound of voices, that Nadia was in the room. On her own intelligent initiative, the girl had brought in a tray of drinks, which she was dispensing to Bella, Harry and Rick when Eva opened her eyes and frantically reached for a pillow with which to hide the salient points of her nudity. Harry laughed at her lovingly, and took the pillow from her.

"It's too late, darling," he said. "Nadia's already seen your bare body, and she's pretty sure I've been doing more than looking at it. Isn't that right, Nadia?"

Her smile enveloping Eva and Harry, Nadia answered, "Since you ask, Mr. Partham, I'd say Miss Dalheim looks like you've been giving her some really good loving. She's been sleeping it off, and she now looks refreshed enough to want me out of the way so's she can have more of the same treatment. You're not offended, Miss Dalheim?"

Eva's embarrassment dissolved in Nadia's sensible acceptance of things as they were. She returned the girl's smile, and said, "Atone for your rude perspicacity by giving me a large gin with a little French vermouth, you shameless hussy!"

Rick smiled weakly and hypocritically at Eva, and admitted that he had no objection to copulating with her prior to swearing eternal fidelity to Bella; but Eva did not even address her answer to him. Instead she said to Bella, "No, thank you, darling! I couldn't bear a man I despise coming into intimate contact with my love-parts. If you want to make a gesture to a woman who's been jilted by the man she thought she loved, you can send Harry to the cottage whenever you and your gigolo want a free run of the house."

Livid, Rick exploded, "Who do you think you are calling a gigolo? Just because you're jealous, because I prefer Bella to you!"

"Rick!" Bella remonstrated. Harry, fed up with the male whore, hurled half a glass of whisky in his face.

"I'm sorry, Bella," he said heavily, "but, although I don't want to come between you and a 'friend' you seem to want to stick to, even though he's humiliated both you and Eva...well, I no longer want any part of Rick, and I don't want him about the house. Meet him in London or elsewhere, if you wish, but get him out of here within forty-eight hours!"

Bella threw her arms around Harry, pouting like a school-girl.

"Harry!" she wheedled, but her husband, rubbing her belly and thighs with his right hand, while his left arm held her, went on: "Until he has time to move out, I'll impose myself on Eva at her cottage, if she'll have me."

"I'll have you, darling, in more ways than one. In fact, I'd like you now."

Harry did not delay in appeasing his new lover. He simply fucked her immediately, as she suggested! As Harry's phallus eased itself into Eva's vagina, Bella took Rick in her arms. He had not taken the trouble to dry Harry's whisky from his face, down which ran large teardrops; the tears were aimed at melting the hearts of Eva and Harry. They would have melted Bella's heart, had it already hardened against him. As it was, they filled her with a great compassion, which grew as he whined, "Why does everybody hate a person because he's poor and a failure?"

"I don't hate you, darling, I love you. Love me tenderly now, and all your pain will flow out of you through your cock, and through my quim I shall absorb it. Love me, darling!"

He obeyed, and half an hour later two pairs of replete fornicators were refreshing themselves again with alcohol, when the telephone rang. Harry answered it lazily.

"Hello, Lee!...oh, fine!...and Laura?...good! Give her a big kiss for me, will you!...Yes, Bella's in the pink, yes, in the pink...Yes, he's here. I'll pass him to you. See you at the Donovans' on Friday!"

He handed the telephone to Rick, who brightened instantly at he thought that Lee Alchard should be asking for him. Rick knew that Lee was the leading light of the Ladbury Amateur Dramatic Society, one of the most important figures in the social life of Ladbury, a member of the board of directors of at least thirty companies and almost sole shareholder in his family's prosperous lingerie factories. Consequently, Rick put on for him his most revolting caricature of a frightfully happy and blasé member of the smartest of smart sets. Making the opening of his mouth so tiny that one could not have passed a pencil between his lips, he gushed, "'Ello Lee! Jolly good of you to call poor old Rickie. Nah, you're kidding me...the lead in your next play, little old me? You're flattering me, right?" Then Rick listened intently to the rest of what Lee said, repeating out loud all the praise and good fortune, so the others could hear.

It turned out that Lee, who Rick had of course met through Bella and Harry, was offering him the lead in his next production—an opportunity that would easily take the conniving moocher-slut out of his presently dreary situation of having been caught with his pants down and hence ordered to a life of exclusivity with Bella.

Lee was calling to tell Rick that the theater's board of directors had voted him the star, and that Lee and Laura wanted Rick to come to dinner Friday. Cast members would join them after the meal for a script reading of the play.

No more tears, no more sadness! He glowed with such joy as any harlot experiences when she or he knows that, as one client goes out by the back door, a bigger one is breaking down the front entrance. Eva and Harry thought they were dismissing him, but it was he who cast them aside in favor of Lee and Laura Alchard. If all that was needed to prevent their new, unanimously voted, leading man from leaving them in the lurch was a well-paid job and some hospitality, then the moneyed members of the Dramatic Society would fall over each other to offer him an extravagantly remunerative sinecure and to invite him to receptions, dinners and, of course, bed—where Rick would give his best performance!

The world was Rick's oyster.

Once again the very people who had tardily realized that he had been scrounging on them for months discovered that he no longer needed them, since they themselves had introduced him to their own successors. Bella was hurt at first, but having discovered his three-timing, she expected as much. Besides, it would be easy for her to find another gigolo to fuck while Harry had his way with Eva!

Rick's new victims seemed likely to be the Alchards, who would bring him into contact with other people of wealth, and, amongst those people, he would find someone who would maintain him when the wicked, ungrateful Alchards ceased to consider him worthy of their extravagant generosity.

It would seem the gods who care for harlots and gigolos never sleep, for the supply of men and women who desire their "services" is endless.

Other Books Available From
MASQUERADE'S
EROTIC LIBRARY

PROFESSIONAL CHARMER

She was the
most desirable,
exciting woman
he had ever
laid hands
on…

$4.95 (CANADA $5.95) • MASQUERADE BOOKS

ANONYMOUS

PASSION IN RIO   54-8 $4.95

For four days and nights during the great Carnival of Rio, when all sexual inhibitions are temporarily cast aside, Rio de Janiero goes mad. For the fanatic Gottfried von Arnheim, the carnival begins with the American tourist, Lorna Destry, helpless in his pillory. For lesbian designer Kay Arnold it begins when the lovely junior designer who accompanies her returns her kiss. For Roger and Lucille Porter, the carnival begins when they learn from celebrating Brazilians how to satisfy each other. The world's most frenzied sexual fiesta!

THE DELICIOUS DAUGHTER   53-X $4.95

When widower Arthur Hadley and his daughter Hester meet the beautiful widow, Eleanor Stanfield, and her daughter Betty, they have no idea they are about to sexually enter another world. Eleanor is a disciplinarian, and Arthur finds himself aroused by the spankings she gives. He asks her to marry him, and on their honeymoon in Mexico he joins her in voyeuristic sessions, watching spankings while they indulge each other sexually. An education in sexual discipline!

THE DISCIPLINE OF ODETTE   47-5 $4.95

In turn-of-the-century France, young maidens were threatened with whippings to teach them to protect their virtue. But Odette's family was harsh, even for that less-enlightened time. Whippings, public humiliation—not even these punishments could keep Odette from Jacques, her lover. She was sure marriage to him would rescue her from her family's "corrections." But, to her horror, she discovered that Jacques, too, had been raised on discipline. She had exchanged her father's harsh hand for the more imaginative corrections of a loving husband.

THE KING OF PLEASURE   45-9 $4.95

Stanton Ames has delved deeper into the sexual arts than ordinary men dream of. In his memoirs, he recounts the sexual education administered by his governess, Fraulein Schneider, a devotee of spanking and sado-eroticism. She taught him the resemblance between a whip and a penis, and how they can be used together to achieve wondrous delights. Throughout his career in the publishing world, he sought beautiful masochists who longed for the ecstasy and pain he could bring them. Strong stuff!

LUST OF THE COSSACKS   41-6 $4.95

The Countess Kalinikoff enjoys watching beautiful peasant girls submit to her perverse lesbian mania for flagellation. She tutors her only male lover in the joys of erotic torture and in return he lures a beautiful ballerina to her estate, where he intends to present her to the countess as a plaything. Painful pleasures!

TURKISH DELIGHTS   40-8 $4.95

During the Allied attack on the Central Powers in Turkey during World War I, the Turks exercised unbelievable sexual sadism against the Greek women guerrillas and English spies who fell into their hands. "With a roar of triumph, Kemil Chokar gripped the girl's whip-streaked breasts and forced her back upon the thick rug on the floor...He went at her like a bull, buffeting her mercilessly, and she groaned...to her own amazement, with ecstasy!"

THE TEARS OF THE INQUISITION   34-3 $4.95

"Even now, in mortal terror, Rosanna's nakedness reminded her of her happily married nights. There was a tickling inside her as her nervous system reminded her that she was ready for sex. But before her was a man for whom she could feel only the most deeply rooted horror—the Inquisitor!"

POOR DARLINGS   33-5 $4.95

Here are the impressions and feelings, the excitement and lust, that young women feel when they submit to desire. Not just with male partners—but with women too. Desperate, gasping, scandalous sex!

THE LUSTFUL TURK   28-9 $4.95

In 1814, Emily Bartow's ship was captured by Tunisian pirates. The innocent young bride, just entering the bloom of womanhood, was picked to be held for ransom—but held in the harem of the Dey of Tunis, where she was sexually broken in by crazed eunuchs, corrupted by lesbian slave girls, and then given to the queen as a sexual toy. Turkish lust unleashed!

THE EDITORS OF PLAYGIRL

PLAYGIRL FANTASIES   13-0 $4.95

Here are the best and hottest female fantasies from the "Readers' Fantasy Forum" of *Playgirl*, the erotic magazine for women. From a passenger who pays her fare in the back seat of a cab, to a sexy surveyor who likes to give construction workers the lay of the land, to a female choreographer who enjoys creating X-rated dances with a variety of perverted partners, these 38 fantasies will drive you wild.

MORE PLAYGIRL FANTASIES   69-6 $4.95

The editors of *Playgirl* bring you more of their favorites from the "Readers' Fantasy Forum." This collection is even hotter than the last, as the readers of *Playgirl* share their most intimate and imaginative fantasy encounters, revealing every steamy detail—daydreams only *Playgirl* readers could pen!

THE MASQUERADE READERS

DOUBLE NOVEL   86-6 $6.95

Two bestselling novels of illicit desire, combined into one spellbinding volume! Paul Little's *The Metamorphosis of Lisette Joyaux* tells the story of an innocent young woman seduced by a group of beautiful and experienced lesbians who initiate her into a new world of pleasure. *The Story of Monique* explores an underground society's clandestine rituals and scandalous encounters that beckon to the ripe and willing Monique.

A MASQUERADE READER   84-X $4.95

Masquerade presents a salacious selection of excerpts from its library of erotica. Infamously strict lessons are learned at the hand of *The English Governess* and *Nina Foxton,* where the notorious Nina proves herself a very harsh taskmistress. Scandalous confessions are to be found in the *Diary of an Angel,* and the harrowing story of a woman whose desires drove her to the ultimate sacrifice in *Thongs* completes this collection. Leaves you hungry for more!

INTIMATE PLEASURES   38-6 $4.95

Indulge your most private penchants with this specially chosen selection of Masquerade Erotica. Try a tempting morsel of the forbidden liaisons in *The Prodigal Virgin* and *Eveline*, or the bizarre public displays of carnality in *The Gilded Lily* and *The Story of Monique*, or the insatiable cravings in *The Misfortunes of Mary* and *Darling/Innocence*. Every forbidden desire is flaunted, every inhibition surrendered, in these six savory samples!

DANGEROUS LESSONS   32-7 $4.95

Throughout history the lessons of the lash and sexual dominance have been taught by the powerful to their victims. Here are the corrupt priests of the Inquisition, raping their victims at the stake...lesbians imprisoning helpless maidens...motorcycle gangs and the female motorists they captured. The ultimate in sexual dominance!

LAVENDER ROSE   30-0 $4.95

A classic collection of lesbian literature: from the writings of Sappho, the queen of the women-lovers of ancient Greece, whose debaucheries on her island have remained infamous for all time, to the turn-of-the-century *Black Book of Lesbianism;* from *Tips to Maidens* to *Crimson Hairs,* a recent lesbian saga, here are the great lesbian writings and revelations. Sappho herself would be turned on!

EASTERN EROTICA

HOUSES OF JOY   51-3 $4.95

A masterpiece of China's splendid erotic literature. This book is based on the *Ching P'ing Mei,* banned many times. Despite its frequent suppression, it has somehow managed to survive.

KAMA HOURI   39-4 $4.95

Ann Pemberton, daughter of the British regimental commander in India, runs away with her servant. Forced to live in a harem, Ann accepts her sexual submission and offers herself to any warrior who wishes to mount her. The natives kindle a fire within her and Ann, sexually ablaze, became a legend as the white sex-bitch of Indian legend!

ROBERT DESMOND

PROFESSIONAL CHARMER   3003-2 $4.95

A dissolute gigolo lives a parasitical life of luxury by providing his sexual services to the rich and bored. Traveling in the most exclusive social circles, this gun-for-hire will gratify the lewdest and most vulgar cravings for nothing more than a fine meal or a shred of stylish clothing. Each and every exploit he must perform is described in lurid detail, in this story of a prostitute's progress!

THE SWEETEST FRUIT   95-5 $4.95

A twisted tale of revenge and seduction! Connie Lashfield is determined to seduce and destroy pious Father Chadcroft to show her former lover, Ben Trawler, that she no longer requires his sexual services. She corrupts the priest into forsaking all that he holds sacred, destroys his peaceful parish, and slyly manipulates him with her smouldering looks and hypnotic sexual aura. But little does she know that he's followed her lecherous lead—and taken a saucy lover of his own!

MASTERING MARY SUE

Her behavior was cruel, absolute, and erotically demanding

$4.95 (CANADA $5.95) • MASQUERADE BOOKS

ANONYMOUS

PETER JASON

WAYWARD   3004-0 $4.95
A mysterious countess hires a bus and tour guide for an unusual vacation. Traveling through Europe's most notorious cities and resorts, the bus picks up the countess' friends, lovers, and acquaintances from every walk of life. The common thread between these strangers is their libertine philosophy and pursuit of unbridled sensual pleasure. Each guest brings unique sexual tastes and talents to the group, climaxing in countless orgies, outrageous acts, and endless deviation!

THE CLASSIC COLLECTION

THE YELLOW ROOM   96-3 $4.95
Two complete erotic masterpieces. The "yellow room" holds the secrets of lust, lechery and the lash. There, bare-bottomed, spread-eagled and open to the world, demure Alice Darvell soon learns to love her lickings from her perverted guardian. Even more exciting is the second torrid tale of hot heiress Rosa Coote and her adventures in punishment and pleasure with her two sexy, sadistic servants, Jane and Jemima. Feverishly erotic!

THE BOUDOIR   85-8 $4.95
Masquerade presents a new edition of the classic Victorian magazine, including several bawdy novellas, ribald stories, and indecent anecdotes to arouse and delight. Six volumes of this original journal of indiscretion are presented here in all their salacious glory. Good old-fashioned smut!

A WEEKEND VISIT   59-9 $4.95
"Dear Jack, Can you come down for a long weekend visit and amuse three lonely females? I am writing at mother's suggestion. Do come!" Fresh from his erotic exploits in *Man with a Maid*, randy Jack is at it again!

TICKLED PINK   58-0 $4.95
From her spyroom, Emily sees her aunt, Lady Lovesport, lash her maid into a frenzy, and then tongue-whip her as Mr. Everard enters the bounteous Lovesport's behind. Emily is joined in her spying by young Harry, who practices the positions he observes. An erotic vacation!

THE ENGLISH GOVERNESS   43-2 $4.95
When Lord Lovell's son was expelled from his prep school for masturbation, his father hired a governess to tutor the motherless boy—giving her strict instructions not to spare the rod to break him of his bad habits. But governess Harriet Marwood was addicted to domination. The whip was her loving instrument. With it, she taught young Richard Lovell to use the rod in ways he had never dreamed possible. The downward path to perversion!

PLEASURES AND FOLLIES   26-2 $4.95
The Erotikon of an English libertine: "I got astride her, rode her roughshod, plied the crop....Ashamed by these excesses provoked by my reading, I compiled a well-seasoned Erotikon and it excited me to such a degree that I...well, pick up my book, gentle reader, and you'll see whether it has a similar effect upon you."

STUDENTS OF PASSION   22-X $4.95
When she arrives at the prestigious Beauchamp Academy, Francine is young, innocent, and eager to learn. But her daily lessons have nothing to do with grammar and spelling. Her teachers and schoolmates enroll her in a course devoted to passion, anatomy, and lust...and she's determine to graduate with honors.

SACRED PASSIONS   21-1 $4.95

Young Augustus comes into the heavenly sanctuary, seeking protection from the enemies of his debt-ridden father. Soon he discovers that the joys of the body far surpass those of the spirit.

THE NUNNERY TALES   20-3 $4.95

Innocent novices are helpless in the hands of corrupt clerics. The Abbess forces her rites of sexual initiation on any maiden who falls into her hands. Father Abelard delivers his penance with smart strokes of the whip on his female penitents' bottoms. After exposure to the Mother Superior and her lustful nuns, sweet Emilie, Louise, and the other novices are sexual novices no longer. Cloistered concubinage!

MAN WITH A MAID   15-7 $4.95

The ultimate epic of sexual domination. In the "Snuggery," a padded, sound-proofed room equipped with wall pulleys, a strap-down table, and a chair with hand and leg shackles, untiring pervert Jack bends beautiful Alice to his will. She not only gives in to his lewd desire, she becomes more lascivious than he. She corrupts her maid and her best friend into lesbianism. Then the three girls lure a voluptuous mother and her demure daughter into the Snuggery for a forcible seduction and orgy. Perhaps the all-time hottest book!

FRUITS OF PASSION   05-X $4.95

A classic study of Victorian sexual obsession. From his initiation into end-less orgiastic delights by the slippery lips of the chambermaid sisters, Rose and Manette, the Count de Leon continues his erotic diary for forty years, ending with his Caribbean voyages with the two most uninhibited Victorian Venuses he has ever known. A life totally dedicated to sex!

ALEXANDER TROCCHI

WHITE THIGHS   3009-1 $4.95

A dark fantasy of sexual obsession from a modern erotic master, Alexander Trocchi. This is the story of young Saul and his sexual fixation on beautiful, tormented Anna of the white thighs. Their scorching, dangerous passion leads to murder and madness every time they submit. Saul must possess her again and again, no matter what or who stands in his way. A powerful and disturbing masterpiece!

SCHOOL FOR SIN   89-0 $4.95

When Peggy Flynn leaves the harsh morality of her Irish country home behind for the bright lights of Dublin, her sensuous nature leads to her seduction by a handsome and mysterious stranger. He recruits her into a training school with an uncommon curriculum. Together with the other students, she embarks on an unusual education in erotic pleasures. No one knows what awaits them at gradu-ation, but each student is sure to be well-schooled in sex!

YOUNG ADAM   63-7 $4.95

Two British barge operators discover a girl drowned in the river Clyde. Her lover, a plumber, is arrested for her murder. But he is innocent. Joe, the barge assistant, knows that. As the plumber is tried and sentenced to hang, this knowledge lends poignancy to Joe's romances with the women along the river whom he will love then...well, read on.

MY LIFE AND LOVES (THE 'LOST' VOLUME)   52-1 $4.95

What happens when you try to fake a sequel to the most scandalous autobi-ography of the 20th century? If the "forger" is one of the most important figures in modern Erotica, you get a masterpiece, and *this is it!*

THONGS   46-7 $4.95

"Spain, perhaps more than any other country in the world, is the land of passion and of death. And in Spain life is cheap, from that glittering tragedy in the bullring to the quick thrust of the stiletto in a narrow street in a Barcelona slum. No, this death would not have called for further comment had it not been for one striking fact. The naked woman had met her end in a way he had never seen before—a way that had enormous sexual significance. My God, she had been..."

THE CARNAL DAYS OF HELEN SEFERIS   35-1 $4.95

Private Investigator Anthony Harvest takes on his greatest challenge. He is determined to find and save Helen Seferis, a beautiful Australian who has been abducted in Algiers. Following clues in Helen's diary, he flies to North Africa and descends into the depths of the white-slave trade. Through exotic slave markets, forbidden harems, and sadistic rites he pursues Helen Seferis, the ultimate sexual prize!

CLASSIC EROTIC BIOGRAPHIES

THE STORY OF MONIQUE   42-4 $4.95

Lovely, innocent Monique found her aunt's friends strange, curious, inviting. There were seven lesbians who came to Aunt Sonia's parties. And a convent nearby where nuns and monks whipped themselves into a frenzy and then fell upon each other in orgiastic madness. Monique became the mistress of *all* their ceremonies; and discovered within herself an endless appetite for sex—the more perverted, the better!

THE MISFORTUNES OF MARY   27-0 $4.95

Mary came from her uncle's parsonage in Ireland to be a writer's assistant in London, in response to an ad run in the *Gazette* by Mrs. Coates. But the lady was a procuress, and the writer was a libertine who paid a hundred pounds for Mary's virginity. As he broke her in, Mrs. Coates sold spectator seats in her secret viewing room to Lord Strongcock and his two randy friends. Then she sold the no-longer-virginal Mary to them. White-hot white slavery!

THE FURTHER ADV. OF MADELEINE   04-1 $4.95

"What mortal pen can describe these driven orgasmic transports," writes Madeleine as she explores Paris' sexual underground. She discovers that the finest clothes may cover the most twisted personalities of all—especially the that of mad monk Grigory Rasputin, whose sexual drives match even Madeleine's. History-making sex!

THE MASQUERADE AMERICAN COLLECTION

DANCE HALL GIRLS   44-0 $4.95

The dance hall studio in Modesto was a ruthless trap for women of all ages. They learned to dance under the tutelage of sexual professionals. So grateful were they for the attention, they opened their hearts and their wallets. Scandalous sexual slavery!

LUSTY LESSONS   31-9 $4.95

David Elston had everything; good breeding, money, a secure job with a promising future, and a beautiful wife—everything except the ability to fulfill the unrelenting demands of his passion. His efforts to satisfy his desires end in failure...until he meets a voluptuous stranger who takes him in hand and leads him to the forbidden land of unattainable pleasure.

WAYWARD

She tossed aside her
single garment and
stood revealed in all
her lusciousness…

$4.95 (CANADA $5.95) · MASQUERADE BOOKS

ANONYMOUS

THE GILDED LILY   25-4 $4.95

Lily Caldron, struggling actress, knows what she wants—pleasure, passion, and new experiences. But more than that, she wants her big break—one that will launch her career in the movies. She looks for it at Hollywood's most private party, where nothing is forbidden and the only rule is sexual excess. There she meets one of Tinseltown's hottest directors, and becomes submerged in a world of secrets and perversions she never imagined.

JOCELYN JOYCE

THE WILD HEART   3007-5 $4.95

A luxurious hotel in Switzerland in the setting for this artful web of sex, desire, and love. A newlywed wife sees sex as a conjugal duty, while her hungry husband tries to awaken her. An opportunistic hotel employee entertains the wealthy guests on the side for money. A swinging couple introduce some new ideas into the marriage of two American guests. A delicious variation on the old Inn-and-out!

PRIVATE LIVES   91-2 $4.95

The wealthy French suburb of Dampierre is the setting for this racy soap opera of non-stop action! The illicit affairs and lecherous habits of Dampierre's most illustrious citizens make for a sizzling tale of French erotic life. The wealthy widow who has a craving for a young busboy, who is sleeping with a rich businessman's wife, whose husband is minding his sex business elsewhere, are just a few of Dampierre's randy residents. An unrestrained look at the more sophisticated side of French life!

DEMON HEAT   79-3 $4.95

An ancient vampire stalks the unsuspecting in the form of a beautiful woman. Unlike the legendary Dracula, this fiend doesn't drink blood; she craves a different kind of potion. When her insatiable appetite has drained every last drop of juice from her victims, she leaves them spent and hungering for more—even if it means being sucked to death!

HAREM SONG   73-4 $4.95

Young Amber flees her cruel uncle and provincial English village in search of a better life, but finds she is no match for the streets of London. Amber becomes a classy call girl and is eventually sold into a lusty Sultan's harem—a vocation for which she possesses more than average talent!

JADE EAST   60-2 $4.95

Laura, passive and passionate, follows her domineering husband Emilio to Hong Kong. He gives her to Wu Li, a Chinese connoisseur of sexual perversions, who passes her on to Madeleine, a flamboyant lesbian. Madeleine's friends make Laura the centerpiece in Hong Kong's underground orgies. As she is being taken by three men while the guests watch, Laura sees Emilio with a beautiful, dark-haired girl: he is about to start another on her downward path. A journey into sexual slavery!

RAWHIDE LUST   55-6 $4.95

Diana Beaumont, the young wife of a U.S. Marshal, is kidnapped as an act of vengeance against her husband. Jack Beaumont sets out on a long journey to get his wife back, but finally catches up with her trail only to learn that she's been sold into Mexico. A story of the Old West, when the only law was made by the gun, and a woman's virtue was often worth no more than the price of a few steers!

THE JAZZ AGE   48-3 $4.95

This is an erotic novel of life in the Roaring Twenties. A Wall Street attorney becomes suspicious of his mistress while his wife has an interlude with a lesbian lover. *The Jazz Age* is a romp of erotic realism in the heyday of the flapper and the speakeasy.

LUSCIDIA WALLACE

THE ICE MAIDEN   3001-6 $4.95

Edward Canton has ruthlessly seized everything he wants in life, with one exception: Rebecca Esterbrook. Frustrated by his inability to seduce her with money, he kidnaps her and whisks her away to his remote island compound, where she learns to shed her inhibitions and accept caresses from both men and women. Fully aroused for the first time in her life, she becomes his writhing, red-hot love slave!

KATY'S AWAKENING   74-2 $4.95

Poor Katy thinks she's been rescued by a kindly young couple after a terrible car wreck. Little does she suspect that she's been ensnared by a ring of swingers whose tastes run to domination and wild sex parties. Katy becomes the newest initiate into this private club, and learns the rules from every player!

ALIZARIN LAKE

THE INSTRUMENTS OF THE PASSION   3010-5 $4.95

All that remains is the diary of a young initiate, detailing the twisted rituals of a mysterious cult institution known only as "Rossiter". Behind these sinister walls, a beautiful young woman performs an unending drama of pain and humiliation. What is the impulse that justifies her, night after night, to consent to this strange ceremony? And to what lengths will her aberrant passion drive her?

CLARA   80-7 $4.95

The mysterious death of a beautiful, aristocratic woman leads her old boyfriend on a harrowing journey of discovery. His search uncovers a woman on a quest for deeper and more unusual sensations, each more shocking than the one before!

TUTORED IN LUST   78-5 $4.95

This tale of the initiation and instruction of a carnal college co-ed and her fellow students unlocks the sex secrets of the classroom. Books take a back seat to secret societies and their bizarre ceremonies, in this story of students with an unquenchable thirst for knowledge!

DIARY OF AN ANGEL   71-8 $4.95

A long-forgotten diary tells the story of angelic Victoria, lured into a secret life of unimaginable depravity. "I am like a fly caught in a spider's web, a helpless and voiceless victim of their every whim." This intelligent and shocking novel is destined to become an underground classic.

BUSINESS AS USUAL   56-4 $4.95

Alain, president of a Parisian import firm, awoke to find his maid beneath his covers while his wife bathed in the next room. On his arrival at work, Alain took the youngest of his three secretaries on his couch in his office, while his other two secretaries listened to her moans on the intercom and pleasured each other A customer arrived to relieve their frustations in a threesome. And this was just the warm-up for the afternoon and evening's sexual entertainment which Alain and the customer had planned. Non-stop sexual business!

FESTIVAL OF VENUS   37-8 $4.95

Brigeen Mooney fled her home in the west of Ireland to avoid being forced into a nunnery. But her refuge in Dublin turned out to be dedicated to a different religion. The young women she met there belonged to the Old Religion, devoted to sex and sacrifices. They were competing to become sexual priestesses on the Isle of Man. The sexual ceremonies of pagan gods!

CHINA BLUE

SECRETS OF THE CITY   03-3 $4.75

Her beautiful daughters, fifteen-year-old Eurasian twins, have been abducted by Thai pirates and sold into white slavery. China Blue, the infamous Madame of Saigon, a black belt enchantress in the martial arts of love, is out for revenge. Her search brings her to Manhattan, where she intends to call upon her secret sexual arts to kill her enemics at the height of ecstasy. A sex war!

MARY LOVE

VICE PARK PLACE   3008-3 $4.95

Rich, lonely divorcée Penelope Luckner drinks alone every night, fending off the advances of sexual suitors that she secretly craves. Alone, she dreams of a lover who can melt her frigid façade. Then she meets Robbie, a much younger man with a virgin's aching appetites, and together they embark on an affair that breaks all their fantasies wide open!

MASTERING MARY SUE   3005-9 $4.95

Mary Sue is a rich nymphomaniac whose husband is determined to pervert her, declare her mentally incompetent, and gain control of her fortune. He brings her to a castle in Europe, where a sadistic psychiatrist and his well-trained manservant amuse themselves with disciples recruited from a local private school. To Mary Sue's delight, they have stumbled on an unimaginably depraved sex cult, where panting men and women suffer beneath cruel instructors and every kind of corruption is practiced!

WANDA   3002-4 $4.95

Wanda just can't help it. Ever since she moved to Greenwich Village, she's been overwhelmed by the desire to be totally, utterly naked! By day, she finds herself inspired by a pornographic novel whose main character's insatiable appetites seem to match her own. At night she parades her quivering, nubile flesh in a non-stop sex show for her neighbors. An electrifying exhibitionist gone wild!

ANGELA   76-9 $4.95

A lonely bartender in a Parisian café thinks he's run every con in the book, until a mysterious woman walks in from of the cold and changes his mind. Angela's game is "look but don't touch," and she drives everyone crazy with desire, dancing and writhing for their viewing pleasure but never allowing a single caress. Soon her sensual spell is cast, and she's the only one who can break it!

HARRIET DAIMLER

THE PLEASURE THIEVES   36-X $4.95

They come in the night, cleaning out the contents of the safe while the orgy rages downstairs. They are the Pleasure Thieves, Harry and Philip, a pair of ex-cellmates and lovers whose sexually preoccupied targets are set up by Carol Stoddard, the publisher of *Femme* magazine. She forms a sexual threesome with them, trying every combination from two-on-ones to daisy chains—because forbidden pleasure are even sweeter when they're stolen!

WANDA
Her skin tingled with delight, and she was hungry for kisses and love
$4.95 (CANADA $5.95) • MASQUERADE BOOKS
ANONYMOUS

LOUISE BELHAVEL

FORBIDDEN DELIGHTS   81-5 $4.95
Clara and Iris make their sexual debut in this Chronicle of the Forbidden.
Sexual taboos are what turn this pair on, as they travel the globe in search of
the next erotic threshold. The effect they have on their fellow world travel-
ers is definitely contagious!

FRAGRANT ABUSES   88-2 $4.95
The sex saga of Clara and Iris continues as the now-experienced girls enjoy
themselves with a new circle of worldly friends whose imaginations definitely match their own. Against an exotic array of locations, Clara and Iris sam-
ple the unique delights of every country and its culture!

DEPRAVED ANGELS   92-0 $4.95
The third and final installment in the incredible adventures of Clara and
Iris. Together with their friends, lovers, and worldly acquaintances, Clara
and Iris explore the frontiers of depravity at home and abroad. Their scandalous sexcapades delight and intrigue everyone, and their natural curiosity
and sweet, sexy personalities guarantee that there will always be new and
exotic thrills for them to experience just over the next horizon!

TITIAN BERESFORD

JUDITH BOSTON   87-4 $4.95
Young Edward would have been lucky to get the stodgy old companion he
thought his parents had hired for him. Instead, an exquisite woman arrives at
his door, and from the top of her tightly-wound bun to the tips of her impos-
sibly high heels, Judith Boston is in complete control. Edward finds his com-
pulsively lewd behavior never goes unpunished by the unflinchingly severe
Judith Boston!

NINA FOXTON   71-8 $4.95
A young aristocrat finds herself bored by the run-of-the-mill amusements
for ladies of good breeding. Instead of taking tea with gentlemen, outrageous Nina invents a device to "milk" them of their most private essences.
No one says "No" to Nina!

SINCERITY JONES

SEDUCTIONS   83-1 $4.95
Twelve short stories of erotic encounters, told with a woman's sensibility.
This original collection includes couplings of every variety, including a
woman who helps fulfill her man's fantasy of making it with another man, a
dangerous liaison in the back of a taxi, a uncommon alliance between a Wall
Street type and a funky, downtown woman, and a walk on the wild side for a
vacationing sexual adventurer. Thoroughly modern women!

PALMIRO VICARION

LUST   82-3 $4.95
A wealthy and powerful man of leisure recounts his rise up the corporate
ladder and his corresponding descent into debauchery. Adventure and political intrigue provide a stimulating backdrop for this tale of a classic
scoundrel with an uncurbed appetite for sexual power!

MARCUS VAN HELLER

ADAM & EVE   93-9 $4.95

A young couple, Adam and Eve, long to escape their dull lives by achieving
stardom—she in the theater, and he in the art scene. They're willing to do
anything to become successful, including trading their luscious bodies for a
big break. Eve soon finds herself acting cozy on the casting couch, while
Adam must join a bizarre sex cult to further his artistic career. Corruption is
the price paid for fame in this electrifying tale of ambition and desire!

KIDNAP   90-4 $4.95

Nick Harding is called in to investigate a mysterious kidnapping case involv-
ing the rich and powerful in London, France and Geneva. Along the way he
has the pleasure of "interrogating" a sensuous exotic dancer named Jeanne
and a beautiful English reporter, as he finds himself further enmeshed in the
sleazy international crime underworld. A sizzling mystery of sexual intrigue
and betrayal!

A Complete Listing Of
MASQUERADE'S
EROTIC LIBRARY

ORDERING IS EASY!

MC/VISA ORDERS CAN BE PLACED BY CALLING OUR TOLL-FREE NUMBER

1-800-458-9640

OR MAIL THE COUPON BELOW TO:
**MASQUERADE BOOKS
801 SECOND AVE.,
NEW YORK, N.Y. 10017**

PF 003-2

QTY	TITLE	NO.	PRICE
	SUBTOTAL		
	POSTAGE and HANDLING		
	TOTAL		

Add $1.00 Postage and Handling for first book and 50¢ for each additional book. Outside the U.S. add $2.00 for first book, $1.00 for each additional book. New York state residents add 8 $\frac{1}{4}$% sales tax.

NAME _____

ADDRESS _____ **APT #** _____

CITY _____ **STATE** _____ **ZIP** _____

TEL (___ **)** _____

PAYMENT: ☐ CHECK ☐ MONEY ORDER ☐ VISA ☐ MC

CARD NO. _____ **EXP. DATE** _____

PLEASE ALLOW **4-6 WEEKS** DELIVERY. NO C.O.D. ORDERS. PLEASE MAKE ALL CHECKS PAYABLE TO MASQUERADE BOOKS. PAYABLE IN U.S. CURRENCY ONLY.